THE BLACK CROW FLIES

BOOK 1 OF THE WHITTAM CHRONICLES

L. B. PERDAN

To my older brother, Joshua, who told me he'd read my book when it was "all done."

Well, I did it. It's all done.

You have no excuse.

(also, thanks for the motivation <3)

ANOCICA
-THE GREAT NORTH-
-THE FROZEN SEA-
-REWONIAN OCEAN-
SERPENT'S GULF
KING'S LAKE
CORIP
-RELION-
SHIMMERING SPRINGS
ICECAP MOUNTAINS
NORTHERN TIMBER
THE WHITE PINES
YAN
SPLIT COVE
-BURGDEN-
FATHING CHANNEL
GINEVA
-FATHING-
PEAKS OF REFUGE
-WHITTAM-
SAPID RUINS
THE SACRED WOODLANDS
IRECROFT
THE HIGH NEST
GEEN RIVER
ASHIRA
BORDERLANDS FOREST
-TRIUM-
HOOK'S BAY
FLOWING WAY
ORAM ISLANDS
-ORAM STRAIGHT-
-DEPTHS OF TRIUM-
-ORIK-
MULTIN
N
W
E
S
-TYPHOON DEEP-
ANOCICA
-THE SOUTHERN ABYSS-

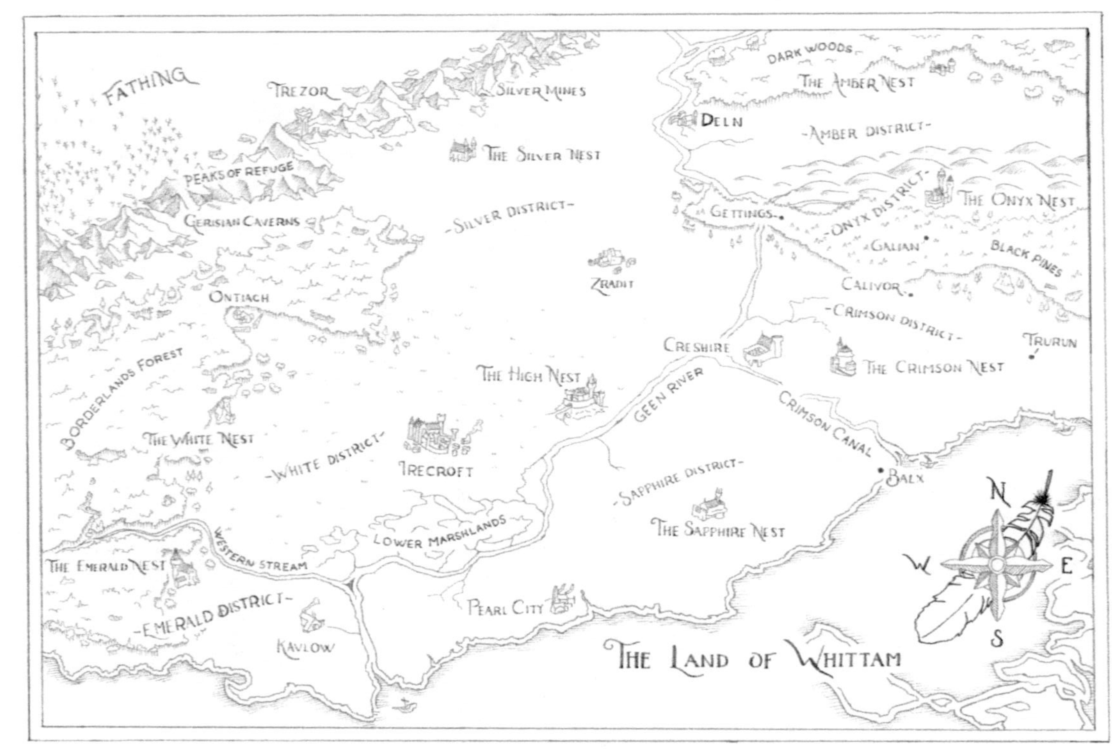

The Land of Whittam
FATHING
TREZOR
SILVER MINES
PEAKS OF REFUGE
The Silver Nest
Gerisian Caverns
Silver District
Zradit
Ontiach
Borderlands Forest
The High Nest
The White Nest
White District
Irecroft
Lower Marshlands
The Emerald Nest
Western Stream
Emerald District
Kavlow
Pearl City
The Sapphire Nest
Sapphire District
Geen River
Creshire
Crimson Canal
Balx
Dark Woods
The Amber Nest
Deln
Amber District
Gettings
Onyx District
The Onyx Nest
Galian
Black Pines
Calivor
Crimson District
Trurun
The Crimson Nest
N
E
S
W

HISTORY OF WHITTAM

In the Anocican year 487, the people rebelled against the emperor, shattering the empire into five nations, in what would come to be known as the Great Split.

Legend says that seven brave men killed the tyrant emperor and stole his jeweled crown, breaking it into seven pieces and giving one to each man. This way, no one could claim the right to rule over the others. They were all equally victorious. Those men founded a new nation, Whittam, and its seven districts based on the colors of the shattered crown: White, Silver, Amber, Onyx, Crimson, Sapphire, and Emerald.

By the year 802, much of the original sentiment of equality among the Seven Noble Families had faded away, and infighting broke out across Whittam. At the height of war, when it looked as if the country would collapse, Geris Aetos, a Prophet of the Creator, called fire down from the heavens and stopped the fighting. He demanded peace, warning of a great destruction on the horizon if the noble families continued in their ways. Fearful for their lives, the lords heeded his warning, and the war ended.

In an attempt to maintain the peace, the Council of Seven was formed; for the first time since the Great Split, the districts were united. Geris Aetos fell in love and married the lady of the White District and, in doing so, eventually took his place as lord and head of the Council.

The Aetos family remained on the Council until the year 1124, when war loomed once again. The country was flooded with refugees from the Oram Islands as the nation of Orik invaded the sovereign archipelago. Warren Tenaris, Commander of the Black Crows, asked the Council to let him lead a force to drive the Oriks out of the Oram Islands. Lord Marcus Aetos, Prophet and descendent of Geris Aetos, refused.

Shortly after, the Oriks invaded Whittam, massacring its people along the coastal districts and pushing inland. One by one, the lords came to Commander Tenaris, pleading with him to lead their armies to defeat the Oriks. He agreed *if*, in return, they pledged their allegiance to him. Desperate for a solution, all the Council members except Lord Marcus Aetos accepted. With their support, the Black Crows led a united Whittamese army to win the war, pushing their enemies back to Orik.

Whittam was safe again, but Lord Marcus Aetos still refused to pledge his allegiance to Commander Tenaris. Then, in the year 1126, Commander Tenaris led the Black Crows into battle once more...

PROLOGUE

For the fifth time that day, Blaze Laskaris was hiding.

He watched from his lowered position in the tall grass as a tiny pair of bare feet stumbled through the meadow. The blooming summer flowers mingled throughout the field snapped and crumpled under the weight, leaving a winding path of matted destruction in the pasture. Blaze rolled his eyes. Catrice would never find him if she kept wandering aimlessly like this.

"Blaze, come on!" Catrice's high-pitched voice filled the quiet valley. "Let me win this time, at least..." She pouted and crossed her arms.

He glanced behind her at the city of Ontiach. Lady Vivian Aetos watched their antics from her guarded position just outside the city gates. Her elegant blue robes flowed around her as she raised a hand, blocking her eyes from the setting sun. It was getting late, and they would have to go inside soon. Aunt Diana would be making dinner, and she would make him wash up before they could eat.

He sighed and straightened from his crouched position, rustling the violet belldrops surrounding him from their resting place. Catrice's face lit up in excitement as she pointed and ran toward him.

"I found you!" she squealed, latching onto his sleeve.

"Not fair!" Izaak's voice rang out from behind him. Blaze turned, dragging Catrice with him as she remained attached to his shirt. His little brother stood a few feet away, fists bunched at his side and face scrunched in a disappointed frown that nearly obscured the bright blue eyes that matched Blaze's own. "It was my turn to find you."

Blaze groaned. It was *always* Izaak's turn.

"I found him first!" Catrice stuck her tongue out at Izaak, and Blaze's sleeve tightened on his arm as she reinforced her grip.

Blaze pivoted toward her, blocking his brother from her gaze, and returned her taunting expression. "Only 'cause it's your birthday, Catrice. If it was any other day, I wouldn't be so nice." He shook her off his arm. "You're too little. You'd never find me by yourself."

"Nuh-uh! You're only ten, Blaze, so you're still little

too." Her bottom lip jutted back out into the familiar pout.

"But not as little as you. Seven-year-olds are *really* little." He tapped Catrice on the head to emphasize his point. She smacked his hand away as if it were a bothersome fly.

"Eight. I'm eight now, Blaze. Same as Izaak." She nodded and, glaring at him, held up eight stubby fingers in his face.

"Yeah!" Izaak held up his hand but added an extra finger, failing to match her number.

"Whatever. You're both still little..." A mischievous grin appeared on his face. "And you may have found me, but you still have to catch me!" He jumped away from their grasping hands and took off deeper into the meadow.

"Not fair!" Izaak yelled after him again.

A flock of birds retreated to the nearby trees and a dozen butterflies took to the air as their chase wound through the meadow. Blaze laughed as the colorful wings encircled him before disappearing in the blinding sunlight streaming over the hill at the end of the valley.

A single dark rider appeared at the top of the hill, momentarily blocking out the bright sunset. His silhouette cast a long, ominous shadow over the field.

Loud bells broke through the silence in the valley.

Blaze skidded to a dead halt. Catrice promptly ran into him, followed immediately by Izaak, and the two bounced off him and fell in a heap into the flowers. Blaze whirled around to face Ontiach, where the large bell in the city hall's steeple flew back and forth, every swing sending a deep *clang* throughout the meadow. More guards poured out of the gates and surrounded Lady Vivian. His heart dropped.

"Let's go, Izaak." Blaze grabbed his brother's hand and yanked him from the ground before pulling him toward the beaten path leading to the main gate. He could hear Catrice's quick, labored breaths behind him as she struggled to keep up. He slowed to a jog, but kept a hard gaze on the main entrance ahead.

Father's words echoed in his mind with every step.

"Take care of your brother, Blaze, especially when the bell rings. I'll be back soon."

Those were the last words he had said to Blaze. Two years ago, Father had left to fight in the war that all the adults refused to talk about. Father hadn't returned, and no one would tell Blaze why.

Guards swarmed around them as they approached the gates, ushering them through the wooden doors in the tall, stone walls surrounding the city. With urgent gestures, the watchman atop his tower beckoned the group further inside. Blaze tightened his grip on Izaak's hand.

Lady Vivian broke through the group and rushed toward them, taking Catrice up in her arms and hugging her tightly. Blaze put an arm over Izaak's shoulders, pulling him close, and turned back to the gates behind him as they slowly began to close.

He stayed focused on the horizon, squinting against the bright sunset as the doors came closer together. The rider remained at his post at the valley's edge and drew his sword. The evening light reflected off the weapon as its long shadow fell over the sea of colorful flowers leading to the gates. A thousand soldiers appeared behind the rider, filling the remainder of the horizon, all drawing their swords and advancing upon his home.

TEN YEARS LATER

I

CATRICE

"Hurry up!" Catrice shouted over her shoulder as she ran through the crowded street.

Bunching up her plain dress around her knees, she ducked under a low-hanging sign jutting out from the side of a fruit stand. Shouts and laughter mingled behind her, followed by the unmistakable *thunk* of Tay hitting his head on the sign.

She kept running, dodging the people walking past different wooden and stone houses and buildings lining the road. Two ladies haggled over a bundle of mixed herbs two stands down. One of their husbands sat against the edge of the stand, wide-brimmed hat slouched over his eyes as if he were napping. A handful of Lord Royn's soldiers made their way from stall to stall, collecting the month's dues, with the local tax collector nipping at their heels. Farther down, a group of children no older than six drew circles in the dirt, taking turns jumping in and out of them in some nonsensical game. Their giggles echoed down the street before disappearing into the breeze.

She blew past them all within seconds, keeping her head down as she passed the soldiers.

"Elynn! Elynn, slow down!" Tay called out behind her.

She rolled her eyes, dropped the skirt of her dress, and slid past two of the large crates lined up between market stands before ducking into an alley on the other side. She skidded to a stop as the alley broke open to another street lined with more wooden stands sporting an array of fruits, vegetables, dried meats, and various goods from across the Amber District. The busy street was less than a mile away from where she and Mother lived, but it often felt like another country, as if they were aliens passing through.

Vendors from across the Seven Districts boasted relics and delicacies from the farthest nations of Anocica. Some wore unfamiliar, patterned robes, head coverings, and shoes that blended in a sea of rainbows before her eyes. Others were dressed in more solid colors and simplistic, layered designs more reflective of the working class of Whittam.

The diversity and sheer population of the city folk allowed her and Mother to blend in most of the time. They had once risked living within another town— village, really—a few years prior, but it hadn't lasted long. Mother had said people ask too many questions when you're close to their home, especially if you're the outsider. The city of Deln, on the other hand, was sizable, large enough to get lost in the crowd and carried away to distant lands as exotic perfumes and spices filled the air, and large enough that Mother felt safe, and that's what mattered.

A storefront on the other side of the road stood out from the otherwise dull buildings. Bright, painted letters dominated the windows, advertising an array of parchment, ink, and writing utensils. Catrice wiped a fresh layer of sweat from her brow and jogged across the road, weaving her way through the flow of strangers. Glancing both ways before stepping up to the entrance, she pushed open the door. A bell rang above her. As she entered, a middle-aged man stood up behind the counter.

"Morning, Elynn." The name everyone knew her by flew from his mouth without any hesitation.

"Good morning, Bard. How's little James doing?"

"Oh, he's on the mend. The doctor said he should make a full recovery." He smiled at the mention of his son's name and picked up a stained towel from the countertop. "Thanks to your mother, anyway. Her herbal tea did wonders for his stomach." A tattered apron hung over his neck. The blotches of ink that marred his hands faded a bit as he dried them off with the cloth. "What can I do for you today?"

Catrice had just opened her mouth to respond

when the door crashed open behind her, sending the bell clanging again. Tay stumbled up beside her, resting his hands on his knees, gasping. She fought to keep a grin from playing at her lips.

She leaned toward Tay. "For the record, I beat you again," she whispered.

"For the record"—Tay paused to take a gulp of air—"you cheated."

"Just like the last seven times?"

"You have to take some kind of short cut. That's the only explanation."

"The only explanation is that I know these streets better after two years than you do after your whole life."

Tay gaped, struggling to find an adequate response. She smirked and turned back to Bard, pulling a drawstring pouch from the belt slung over her hips and placing it on the counter. The dozen or so coppers inside clinked against each other.

Bard nodded, and amusement danced across his features at Tay's lack of retort. "The usual?"

"Yes, please."

She clasped her hands in front of her as he ducked behind the counter. She gazed around the small shop lit up by the morning sun streaming through the thick, dusty windows. The scents of acidic ink and warm, freshly dried parchment wafted from every corner, putting her mind at ease. Bard reappeared and placed an open crate full of parchment, dark ink bottles, and feathered pens on the counter. Catrice inspected the contents inside and smiled before lifting the crate and balancing it against her side.

"Perfect, thank you."

"Of course." Bard emptied the pouch and started counting the coins. He paused and looked up as if considering something. "How old are you now, Elynn?"

"I'll be eighteen next week."

"Well." He scooped the coppers into his hand. "You're a little older than most, but I have an apprenticeship opening up soon. Tay's shown me some of your script work."

"He did?" She spun around to Tay. He was holding a bottle of ink to the sunlight, blush creeping up his cheeks, and he shrugged his shoulders. Catrice's chest warmed, and she turned back to Bard.

"It's good work. It would seem your mother taught you well." He offered her a square of parchment with a scribbled list across the front. "If you're interested, the job is yours. I'll need your family information and a copy of your travel papers for the annual census. As soon as you fill that out, we can get started."

Her heart dropped. Of course. The one thing she couldn't provide. She stared at the parchment and forced herself to continue smiling.

"Thank you." She took the list and dropped it into the crate.

"Anything for the Halvors." Bard beamed and

tossed her empty coin pouch into the crate. He turned to Tay as Catrice stepped back. "I have yours, too."

He glanced at the windows, waiting as a family passed by the store, before sliding a short stack of pamphlets across the counter.

Tay jumped forward, swiping the literature and grinning ear to ear. "Did this just come in?"

"Last night. My boys have been working in the back, making copies all morning."

Catrice wrinkled her nose as Tay flipped through the familiar pamphlets. They were simple and always the same: a small, folded square of parchment filled with complaints against the king, reports of district soldiers and Black Crows abusing their power, and calls to join local rebel groups. A circular seal dominated the front page. The unique image of an owl in mid-flight with talons extended forward had started appearing in the rebel propaganda just a few months earlier, and was already spreading like wildfire.

She swallowed. It was risky for Tay to carry them around, and even more so for Bard to distribute them in his shop. But, then again, who was she to question others breaking the law? She glanced down at the writing materials in her crate that would soon hold illegal messages of their own. After all, she did it every day.

"Elynn, you won't believe this!" Tay bounced on the balls of his feet and shoved the open pamphlet in front of Catrice, pulling her out of her musings.

"Hmm?" She struggled to focus on the bolded message at the top of the page as he continued to bounce, but Tay yanked it back before she could finish.

"According to this, the Northern Hunters intercepted a whole shipment of weapons from Rewon. Stole them from right under Lord Royn's nose!"

"Sounds like they're getting bolder."

"It's about time! This kind of stuff never happened before the White Owl got involved. He's incredible."

Catrice plucked the paper from his hand. "He's also an outlaw we know nothing about."

"At least he's doing something."

"Tay's right about that." Bard chimed in. "It's been a long time since anyone stood up to King Tenaris like the White Owl does. I don't think anyone has since Lord Aetos." He took a deep breath and wiped the counter with the stained cloth. "Not that I'm surprised. Look where that got him."

Lord Aetos.

At the mention of her deceased father, Catrice's heart plummeted to her stomach. A tense stillness settled over the room. She dug her fingernails into the crate's rough wood, biting her tongue and staring at her scuffed, dirty boots. The uncomfortable quiet was something she had become accustomed to whenever people brought up the name of the once-powerful Aetos family. It was yet another reminder of why she and Mother lived under fake aliases and moved from town to town every few years.

She sucked in a shaky breath and shook her head. "I should get going. My mother will be wondering where I am."

Bard jumped as if startled and flashed her a smile. "Of course. Tell Mari I said hello, would you?"

Catrice returned his smile at the mention of Mother's chosen name. "I always do."

She adjusted the crate against her hip and turned to exit the shop. Tay was at her side in an instant, shoving the pamphlets into his leather vest's inner pocket. The bell rang as they pulled open the door and entered the busy street. The remaining pamphlet crinkled in her hand and she scanned the text in the morning light.

"So, the rebels are looking for fresh recruits?" She kept her voice low to avoid drawing attention, even though her words were swept away in the buzz of the crowd nearly the same moment they left her mouth.

Tay ducked under a stack of fabric bolts two men were carrying between them and shot a grin over his shoulder at Catrice. "I know! This may be my chance. I'd be more than just another boy handing out the latest news. I could actually join them. Do something! It says I just need to drop an address and some coin off at one of the old butcher shops on the north side for an invite to their next meeting."

Catrice stepped around the men and shook her head. "I don't know, Tay. It doesn't sound safe. What if you're caught?"

"Then I guess the Crows will lock me up like they did to my brother. At least then I'd have an excuse to finally swing at one."

Catrice slowed her steps, staring at the pamphlet in dismay. Tay's hate for the throne was nothing new, but he was her only friend. She couldn't lose him to something as reckless as joining the most recent disjointed rebellion that had decided to spring up this month. If he did that, he would risk more than a short stint in the local jailhouse. Hadn't the Crows already taken enough from her?

Someone bumped her shoulder, and she jumped, startled. Tay had turned and stopped ahead of her, watching her with a worried expression and forcing the crowd to bubble and flow around them.

"Everything all right, Elynn?" His brow furrowed above his hazel eyes.

"Of course." She swallowed and shoved the pamphlet into the crate between the stacks of parchment. "I just don't think it's a good idea."

"Oh, come on, Elynn. Aren't you and Mari tired of smuggling scraps from that old bakery you live above? Even with me working all day at the stables, my family's barely making it by, and that was before Lord Royn raised the taxes *again*. This is how we change things. Don't you want to make a difference for once?"

Catrice's mind flashed to an image of Mother toiling over a new batch of dough in the kitchen, sweat pouring down her brow in front of the brick oven, and hair caked with flour. Only for Baker Ratton to toss her a few coppers at the end of the day.

"The rest goes toward your rent. And my gracious protection of two single, undocumented *ladies such as yourselves,"* he had rasped out in the heat.

No one would guess Mother was the once-loved Lady Vivian Aetos who, next to her husband, had ruled the prestigious White District with grace and justice. The one who sacrificed everything to protect her daughter and save what was left of her people. Instead, she was just Mari Halvor, the woman in the bakery. If anyone deserved a change, it was Mother.

Sorrow and anger welled in Catrice's chest, and she opened her mouth to respond, but not before a commotion down the street carried above the noise and cut her off. The crowd seemed to split in every direction, disappearing behind her until a furs stand, an angry vendor, and four men became visible.

"What are you talking about?" The vendor crossed his arms. "I already paid my dues this month."

Tay grabbed Catrice's arm and pulled her to the edge of the road, closer to the shops and alleyways, giving them better access to an escape and a view of what was happening.

The soldiers she had avoided earlier stood before the vendor. They wore amber jerkins representing the district, and the leading one had a matching coat, marking him as captain. One of them had an assortment of bags in his hand, weighed down by what

Catrice could only assume were coins. The tax collector stood back with a board of parchment in his hand, counting the number of furs hanging in the stand. Two more soldiers stood at relaxed attention with their swords sheathed at their sides, seemingly bored with their assignment to retrieve a handful of coin from a tired vendor. The captain in front stepped closer to the booth.

"Lord Royn raised the taxes last week. He's had to deal with an influx of rebels in this region, which means more manpower and more supplies if you want us to continue to keep you safe." He glanced over to the tax collector's board. "You owe twenty-four more coppers."

The vendor crossed his arms. "I barely got twenty-four coppers with me this morning. Besides, the rebels don't give us no trouble here." He looked the soldiers up and down. "I can't say the same for you lot."

Catrice's chest tightened as the soldiers gripped their swords. The remaining crowd collectively recoiled, and a murmur rippled through the air. She took a step away from the stand and clutched the crate at her side.

The captain raised his eyebrows. "Do you want trouble, old man?"

Before the vendor could respond, Tay walked forward, placing himself in front of the captain and raising his arms. Catrice's heart raced. What was he *doing*?

"Whoa now, I think this is all just a grave misunderstanding. I'm sure he can get you the dues by the end of the day. It's early, and he still has lots of sales to do."

The captain placed a finger on Tay's chest. "The dues are required now. My men are tired, and we don't have time to deal with you, boy." He shoved Tay back.

Tay stumbled into the stand, pulling down a whole row of dangling furs as his arms flew behind him. Catrice dropped her crate and rushed forward to help him up. Tay stood and straightened his tunic. His bicep tightened under her fingers as he met the captain's gaze. The street grew quiet as the soldiers drew their swords, the screeching metal drawing the attention of the few city folk who had stopped to watch. Catrice stiffened. She shouldn't be here.

"Is there a problem here?" Another voice broke through the silence.

A man dressed in all black walked casually toward the group. As he grew closer, the soldiers quickly sheathed their weapons and lowered their heads, casting nervous glances back and forth as if afraid to make eye contact with the man. Black clothing covered him from just below his eyes to his toes, including a flowing cloak draped over his left shoulder. Strips of black cloth wrapped around his palm and between each finger. Swords the length of his thighs lay secured flush against each hip. An amber pin in the shape of a crow stood out against the dark clothing and held his cloak clasped at his neck. Catrice's breath hitched in her throat.

No. *Heavens, no.* This couldn't be happening.

A Black Crow.

Catrice lowered her gaze and tried to shrink farther back against the stand as her heart pounded in her chest. Out of the corner of her eye, she could see the vendor drop his head. Tay pushed her behind him, and they shuffled to the corner of the booth. Doors slammed shut as any remaining people disappeared from the street, and it took every ounce of her strength not to run. If she ran, they would find her. Or worse, they would find Mother.

The Crow stopped a few feet away. "I *asked* if there was a problem here," he repeated.

The captain cleared his throat. "N-no. We're just collecting the monthly dues. This vendor owes twenty-four more coppers under the tax raise. He was getting it ready for us now."

The Crow glanced over to the stand. His eyes felt hot on Catrice as she tried to focus on anything other than the dark orbs. The black cloth covering the rest of his face masked any emotion or indications as to what he might do next. If she just remained calm, maybe he would move on. His gaze settled on the vendor.

"Well, continue then. I would hate to report any incident to the High Crow of our great district." His eyes flickered back to the captain. "Which, of course, he would then have to tell Lord Royn."

The vendor set his jaw and his face flushed, but he didn't object. With a grunt, he reached under the stand and pulled out a small coin box. The coppers clinked irregularly as he counted them out in his hand, grating on Catrice's already frazzled nerves with every coin that dropped.

"Good." The Crow shifted to the soldiers. "King Warren Tenaris, the Amber Crow, and Lord Royn thank you for your service."

The soldiers nodded as the vendor reached to pour the coppers into the captain's hand. The tax collector counted the coins for himself and jotted down small notes on his parchment. Crinkles appeared at the edges of the Crow's eyes—the only sign he was satisfied with the situation. Good. Now he would leave, and she could go home.

Except the Crow didn't leave. Instead, he turned to Tay. "What's your name, boy?"

Tay swallowed. "Tay Rees, sir."

The Crow cocked his head. "You're strong. Have you signed up for the Calling yet?"

"No, sir. I'm the second son in my family. My older brother Trit was in the draft."

"Very well. I look forward to training with him one day." The Crow glanced over Tay's shoulder to her. "And you are?"

Catrice's heartbeat pounded in her ears. Dark memories of that day ten years ago flooded to the front of her mind. The thick, black smoke of burning houses clouding the streets. Whistling arrows and clashing metal drowning out the screams of her people. And Father, running toward the front gate with the rest of his soldiers—her last memory of him. She and Mother had barely escaped with their lives. All because of Crows like the man in front of her.

She sucked in a breath. *Stay calm.* "Elynn."

"Your family name?"

This couldn't be happening. "H-Halvor."

"Halvor? Where is your family from, Elynn Halvor?"

Her mouth went dry. She tried to swallow, but her tongue felt like a block of sandstone in her mouth. "I... We're from..."

The Crow narrowed his eyes and stepped forward. "I asked you a question. Where are your papers?"

Tay placed his hand over hers. "She's from Trurun, in the Crimson District. Her family's from Rewon. She's my mother's cousin, and she doesn't speak much Whittamese."

Catrice dared to look back to the Crow. With olive skin and dark hair, she would have a hard time passing as Rewonian, and she wondered what Tay had been thinking when he said that. The Crow held her gaze, as if searching her eyes for any betrayal of the story. She couldn't breathe. He broke away and nodded at Tay.

"Make sure she's registered with the Amber District if she's here longer than a month. Wouldn't want her to get mistaken for someone else." The Crow turned away and marched down the center of the street, followed shortly by the group of soldiers as they continued to the next stand. Murmurs grew into the steady buzz of the marketplace again as the crowd returned to their morning shopping. Outside of the beet-red vendor and the occasional passersby shooting scowls in the direction of the soldiers, it was as if nothing had happened.

The tension in Catrice's chest eased as she let out a deep breath. Her knuckles were white around Tay's sleeve, and she struggled to relax them.

"Rewonian?" she finally managed to ask. "That's the best you could come up with?"

Tay shrugged. "Hey, you blanked first. I'll take any gifts of gratitude in the form of free pastries from the bakery."

She rolled her eyes and released his sleeve. "Thank you, but you shouldn't have done that. What if the Crow found the pamphlets in your pockets?"

"Don't worry about it. I'm just happy he bought it." He raised his eyebrows at her and lowered his voice. "Why didn't you just give him your papers?"

Catrice sighed, bracing herself to lie. "I don't know. You're right; I blanked. I'm sorry." She backed up and lifted the crate to her hip again, double-checking the contents inside and thanking the Creator at the sight of all the ink bottles intact. "I've never talked directly to a Crow before," she admitted.

At least that was true.

"Really? I thought you traveled a lot before settling here. You must have gone through at least a few checkpoints between districts."

"We did." Catrice hesitated. "But Mother always handled the talking." Truth be told, they had snuck through the night and stayed in secret basement cellars, avoiding the checkpoints, but she couldn't exactly tell him that. "I should be heading back. Mother will need some help in the kitchen, and I don't want this ink to sit in the sun for too long."

"You sure you don't want to come with me to the butcher's shop tonight? I have enough coin saved up for both of us to get an invite."

So, he was still going. The incident with the Crow must have solidified that. "Tay, I still don't think it's a good idea. Mother would kill me if she found out I was even looking at those pamphlets. I really shouldn't—"

He raised his hands to stop her. "Say no more. I'll pay for both of us. If you change your mind, I'll let you know where the meeting will be."

Catrice rolled her eyes, but relented. There was no changing his mind now.

Tay shoved his hands in his pockets. "You ever going to show me what you're working on with all of that?" He nodded toward the crate.

"You've seen some of my work."

"Only a few random letters and signs for the bakery. There has to be more than that."

Catrice shrugged. "Maybe one day." Another lie.

Never. She meant never. She wouldn't risk his safety like that.

"Well, I'll be waiting patiently for that 'one day,' then. Maybe then I'll finally beat you." He offered her a wink and turned on his heel to disappear down an alley.

"I'll see you later, Tay!" she called out after him.

He lazily waved a hand without looking back. She couldn't help the smile creeping onto her face. Shifting the crate one more time, she slipped through an opening in the crowd in the direction of the bakery.

The morning's events blurred in her mind as she rounded corners, avoided puddles, and ducked under signs almost instinctively on the memorized route she took home every day. When she approached the bakery, smoke was already billowing from the chimney and Baker Ratton was scrambling in the front windows to arrange the fresh pastries.

With zero desire to face his stale breath or temper that would no doubt be the result of a nasty hangover headache this early in the morning, she opted for the back kitchen entrance. The door was propped open for ventilation, which allowed the sweet, maple-rich scent of freshly baked bread to fill the air. Sure enough, Mother was already hard at work kneading piles of dough. She hadn't yet been awake when Catrice had left, so it couldn't have been more than an hour since she started, but a fine layer of flour had already dusted her from head to toe.

Catrice paused, pulling the rebel pamphlet from the crate and shoving it into the top of her chemise under her dress. Mother didn't seem to notice Catrice as she entered the boiling kitchen. Her eyes stayed on the dough between her hands, but a far-off look and the soft, familiar lyrics of a common Follower song passing through her lips hinted she was somewhere else.

"Oh, the Wonders of the Creator . . . on display for all to see. Behold, He shines His face upon us . . . His Prophet will set us free."

Catrice knew the centuries-old lyrics by heart. Many of the Followers believed it was written about her family—the great Aetos Prophet line—while others thought it referred to a future Prophet yet to come. Not that it mattered either way. It was just a song.

Setting the crate on the counter, she laid a hand on Mother's shoulder. The song was cut short as she raised tired eyes to meet Catrice.

"Oh, my dear, you're back already?" Mother dusted her hands off on the soiled apron hanging over her plain brown dress, but only succeeded in transferring another layer of powder to her fingertips. "How was the market?"

"Busy. Same as always."

"And how was Tay?"

Catrice's mouth fell open. Somehow, her mother

always knew everything. She smiled sheepishly. "He's fine."

"Good. Good."

Her smile dropped, and she folded her arms. "Probably would be better if I didn't have to lie to him all the time."

At that comment, Mother narrowed her eyes. "It's for your own safety, and his. You can bring him by for dinner later this week if you like. But I want you to be careful around him. That boy can be trouble. Too much rebel propaganda in his head."

"You say that about every boy I've been friends with, Mother."

"And have I been wrong?"

Catrice mimicked her mother's expression and, instead of answering, motioned to the crate. "I picked up the new materials from Bard's shop."

Mother's eyes lit up, and she gently flipped through the parchment squares and counted the various ink bottles and quills. "Oh, good." She glanced behind her, through the door leading to the front of the shop where Ratton stood doubled over the window displays. "You head on upstairs. I'll get cleaned up and meet you there in a moment."

Catrice nodded and lifted the crate from the counter before going back outside and bounding up the rickety stairs leading to the single room on the second floor. She balanced the crate against her hip and opened the door. Two thin, padded mats covered most of the floor on the other side of the room save for a large water basin, a basket of clothing, and a dilapidated cabinet with more parchment spilling out from the crooked drawers.

Catrice set the crate on the wooden table and knelt, pulling up a splintering floorboard. One of the leather bags from their home in Ontiach sat in a carved-out hole in the packed clay between the floorboards and the ceiling of the bakery below her. She grabbed the worn satchel from its hiding place and placed it on the table. Various documents and scrolls spilled out of the opening.

Creaking behind her announced Mother's entrance, and Catrice continued to sort the scrolls. "Do you need me in the kitchen today? If so, I can wait to start on the Testimonies until tomorrow."

"No." Mother came up behind her and emptied the rest of the bag. "I promised Vina I would have more of the Old Prophets' writings sent to her by next week. This should be enough to get us through at least a few copies. I can help you in the evenings."

"What happened to the copies we sent her a few months ago?"

Mother sighed. "Compromised. The Crows found a few pages on a woman during a checkpoint search between districts."

"What happened to her?"

"She was arrested. Her husband and two young daughters escaped, but the Crows will be looking for them for a while. They traced the Testimony back to Vina's Haven near Calivor and she was forced to burn the rest before they found them or traced them here."

Catrice shook her head. "Calivor? Heavens, I don't know why we still send copies to the Onyx District. They arrest more Followers there than anywhere else."

"They arrest Followers all over Whittam, dear."

She paused her sorting and frowned. "Because of us, right?"

Mother let out a deep breath and pushed her graying hair back. "Yes. Because of the whole Aetos family."

Catrice's thoughts drifted to the pamphlet crumpled against her chest, and what happened in the market flashed across her mind.

"I talked to a Crow today," she said softly.

Mother reacted as if a jolt of lighting had run through her. "What?"

"There was a Crow at the market. He stopped at one of the vendor's stands when the soldiers were collecting the monthly dues."

Mother set down the scroll she was holding and glanced toward the open door. "Did he see you? What happened?"

"Yes. He asked Tay and I for our names and where we're from. I froze, but Tay covered for me, and the Crow seemed to believe him."

"Very well." Mother took a deep breath and placed her hands on the table. "We can deal with this then.

I've been researching other cities closer to the border anyway. After we send the copies off next week, we can start packing."

Catrice whipped her head around to stare at Mother. One of the ink bottles clattered from the crate onto the table. "What? No, Mother. The Crow believed Tay. We don't have to leave."

Mother shook her head. "We can't risk it, Catrice. We have more than ourselves to think about. If there's even a *chance* the Crows suspect us, they will be back. It's not safe anymore." She placed a hand on Catrice's cheek. "I'm sorry, dear. I know you really liked it here. You can say your goodbyes this week sometime."

Goodbyes? She didn't want to say goodbye. Catrice blinked back tears and groaned. "I wish there was something else we could do. Something more."

"We will, one day. For now, you'll continue your studies. When the time comes, the Creator will reveal the next Prophet and lead us to our next steps." Mother combed her fingers through Catrice's curls. "'In my despair, I called out to the Creator, and He answered me.'"

The rest of the Testimony verse materialized in Catrice's head effortlessly. "'He led me through the dark valleys and directed my steps. His presence never leaves me.' From the Testimony of Prophet Yon Reklan. Year 620."

"Good job. You're getting to know your Old Prophets well."

Catrice absently nodded as she stacked the ink bottles neatly along the edge of the table. Mother again wiped her hands in vain against her apron before planting them on her hips.

"Well, I should get back to the kitchen before Ratton gets concerned."

"You mean 'starts screaming at us?'" Catrice grumbled.

Mother pressed her lips into a tight line and tilted her head in a knowing gesture. "That too. I'll be back for lunch. We'll discuss our plans more then." She leaned closer and planted a kiss on the top of Catrice's dark curls before leaving the room.

Catrice rubbed her face and stared at the blank parchment sheets and old scrolls. She had a lot of work to do if she was going to copy the Old Prophets multiple times before the next week. And now they had to pack too? This wouldn't be the first time they had to leave suddenly after nearly being discovered. She knew Followers across the country counted on them for the Testimonies. They couldn't afford to be caught, but it didn't make leaving any easier.

She reached for a sad, half-dried bottle of ink and a splintering quill to start on the first section. By this point in her life she had made enough copies of the Testimonies to quote most of them by heart, which Mother said was a key part in her studies, but she could reference the original scrolls from Ontiach if needed. They were mostly stories of the Creator's

Wonders, the history of their people, and prophecies recorded by the Prophets.

A large portion, the most recent passages, were written by Father. It was one of the few things she still had left from him, and also the reason the king had outlawed the sacred texts in the first place. Father's defiance had been laid out for all of Whittam to see and immortalized in the Testimonies. And now the rest of the Creator's Followers—her people—were paying the price. Simply for wanting to worship in peace.

What was she doing to help? Scribbling, running, and hiding while she waited for the opportunity to follow in Father's footsteps. What *could* she do other than this?

She dipped the quill into the ink and lowered it to the page, stopping before the tip collided with the parchment. The edge of the crumpled pamphlet in her chemise bit into her skin. She set the quill down carefully and pulled out the rebel pamphlet, spreading it on the table next to the Testimonies.

Maybe there was something she could do after all.

2

BLAZE

"BY ROYAL DECREE, PRIVATE GATHERINGS
OF THE CREATOR'S FOLLOWERS AND
READING OR POSSESSION OF THE
TESTIMONIES IS STRICTLY FORBIDDEN." -
THE ROYAL ARCHIVES OF WHITTAM

Lightning crackled across the sky above Blaze, followed by the distant boom of thunder. He ushered his horse into the stable and handed him off to the stablehand. Shaking the raindrops off his shoulders, he pulled the cloak tight over his head and darted back into the storm.

The tall, white stone walls of his castle stood out against the ominous clouds lit up only by another flash of lightning. A servant waited just inside the entrance of the castle, towel in hand. Blaze grabbed it as he passed, drying off the upper half of his face and black mask. The roar of the wind faded away as the door slammed shut behind him, and he continued down the wide hall.

An older, well-dressed man stepped from one of the doorways dotting the hallway and bowed his head.

"High Crow Laskaris," the butler began as he held out a silver tray holding a paper scroll, "we've been waiting for your return."

Blaze adjusted the onyx crow pin securing the cloak around his neck and draped the towel over his shoulder. "My mission took longer than expected. The Rewonian smugglers in the eastern border towns are getting smarter. It took me three days to find their base."

"I would imagine that would be frustrating."

"You imagine correctly. What do you have for me, Harold?" He retrieved the scroll from the tray and turned into his office.

Harold's sure footsteps echoed behind him and stopped once Blaze reached his desk. Tossing the scroll onto the mahogany surface, he unclasped his cloak and offered it to the butler, who took the wet garment and hung it on the rack near the crackling fireplace.

Blaze straightened the various letters and maps that littered his desk and unrolled the scroll, revealing a list of requests and mission updates from Black Crows across the Onyx District. The list continued past where the paper met the wooden rod and he turned over the scroll to read the rest. He frowned.

"Is this all?"

Harold hesitated and stepped away from the fireplace. "Yes and no, sir. There's a few men here as well with prisoners to register."

"This is ridiculous. I don't even have two hundred

Crows in my district. How do they manage to come up with this many problems in the week I'm gone?" He huffed and leaned back in his chair, dropping the scroll on the desk. "Is there anything else I should know?"

A commotion outside his office rang down the stone walls followed by the familiar shouts of a spoiled nobleman. Harold leaned back to peek into the hallway.

Oh, no.

Blaze rolled his eyes. Harold straightened and offered an apologetic expression.

"Sir, Lord Harris Grener is here."

As the words left his mouth, Harold stepped into the hallway, and a young man in layered, flowing black robes marched into the room with a guard flanking him on either side. Blaze sat up and resisted the urge to drag a hand down his face. The lord stopped in front of his desk, face red and eyes bulging.

"Lord Grener," Blaze started, "to what do I owe the pleasure?"

"Don't play dumb with me, Crow—"

"It's *High* Crow, my lord." Blaze kept his tone cool. He didn't want to deal with this right now, but there was etiquette that needed to be followed.

The guards beside the lord straightened their shoulders and left their hands resting on the swords at their sides, but neither dared to look up at Blaze. They knew he was right. Lord Grener bristled regardless.

"Because you couldn't be bothered to respond to my summons, I was forced to ride through the rain and mud today."

That was unlikely. There was definitely a carriage waiting on the covered patio outside. Lord Grener didn't have a speck of mud on him. Blaze held his tongue.

"My apologies, my lord. But your desire to enforce a tax raise for your castle renovations does not require the same immediate attention as many of the other issues I oversee as the Onyx Crow. That is something your own soldiers should be able to handle."

"My soldiers are doing what they can, but it has been over a month and I am still facing resistance in many of the Upper households."

"I am unsure how I am supposed to assist you with that."

"You are the king's men. They will listen to me if you do what I ask."

"My lord, my Crows and I are not a weapon to hide behind, and I will not always be available at your every beck and call."

"Lady Isadore's High Crow enforces her tax laws."

Lady Isadore doesn't add additional towers to her castle just so it's the tallest in her district.

Blaze cleared his throat. "The Sapphire Crow and Lady Isadore have their own agreement."

"Regardless, it's been over a month, and you have

not responded. I am the lord of this district and should be heeded!"

"My duties have kept me elsewhere."

"Your duty is to *me*."

"Lord Grener." Blaze stood, allowing his voice to drop. That was enough. The young nobleman in front of him stiffened, a sudden change in posture Blaze had come to recognize as an attempt to hide a flinch. "Despite what you would like to think, I report to the throne first. Not to you. It is by King Tenaris's *grace* that you have me at your disposal in the Onyx District for protection and order. It is one of the many benefits his rule offers to you." The memorized words flowed from his mouth as easily as any other lesson drilled into his head over the last ten years.

Lord Grener responded as he always did: flushing red and pushing his carefully groomed mane back from his face in an attempt to appear composed. His father had been a far better lord, one Blaze had served under as a standard Crow, but he had neglected his son's discipline, and now Blaze had to deal with the fallout for the rest of his term as a High Crow.

How incredibly inconvenient.

"Now, is there anything else I can help you with?" Blaze crinkled the corners of his eyes in what he hoped would come across as a polite expression above his mask.

The lord's face contorted into a scrunched mess of frustration and anger, but he lowered his gaze. "No.

That will be all." Straightening his robes, he turned on his heel and exited the room, the guards following.

Blaze let out a breath and sank into his chair, raising his eyes when Harold entered again.

"Would you like anything to drink, sir? Water? Tea?" he glanced at Blaze's slouched posture. "Or perhaps something stronger?"

"No, thank you, Harold." Blaze pushed himself up. "Send the next group in."

Harold bowed and stepped back into the hallway. Two Crows entered shortly after, pulling a young woman in with them. Blaze narrowed his eyes. He had been expecting them. His men were rarely able to catch a Follower of the Creator carrying illegal documents on their person, but it certainly made his job easier when they managed it.

"The black crow flies," he said.

"And all fear its cry," the Crows answered.

Blaze nodded, and one of them set a crinkled scrap of parchment on the desk and stepped back beside the prisoner. The yellowed page boasted a scribbled passage from one of the Old Prophets Blaze had heard quoted by Followers and seen copied on hidden messages too many times to count. It was a rather popular passage praising the Creator for His faithfulness, and the fools were often willing to sacrifice anything for it.

"Personal possession of any form of the Testimonies is forbidden," he said.

The woman stood resigned between the Crows, her dark eyes downcast and hands tied in front of her.

Blaze pressed his fists into the wood on either side of the parchment and leaned forward. The black mask around the lower half of his face would hide any expression his mouth betrayed at the reddened eyes or raw wrists of the Follower bound in his office. Not that it mattered. He was used to such sights by now, and he had learned that Followers chose their own fate, regardless of what consequences would befall them or others.

"Do you deny that the Testimony passage is yours?" he asked the woman.

She shook her head.

"Are you aware possession of such documents is punishable by public flogging and imprisonment?"

She nodded, still refusing to meet his gaze.

"Do you know cooperation with us can spare you that sentence?"

No response.

"Let me guess." Blaze frowned and took a deep breath. "You're a peaceful people who only want to worship freely together? Is that right?"

She looked up at him, eyes welling. It was a story Blaze had heard again and again.

"Then *why* do the largest rebel groups come out of your homes? The Markians. The DaggerThorns. The Coastal Harbongers. All of them have roots tracing back to the White District under the Aetos family. And we've found members of all of them hiding in your so-called Havens. Is that just a coincidence?"

"We provide shelter for anyone who asks." Her voice hitched on the last two words.

"Even fugitives? Murderers? Enemies of the throne? The king has been incredibly gracious with your people. He's established public places for you to gather at certain times of the year and read parts of the Testimonies—"

"Parts *he* controls."

"Well, when entire passages were written by Marcus Aetos, what do you expect?"

"Lord Aetos was the Creator's Prophet."

"He was a *traitor*! His rebellion threatened this country and the king." Blaze sucked in a breath. Blasts, he wasn't getting anywhere with this. "And when the time came, he hid behind the walls of Ontiach, and your people paid the price." He rubbed the scar stretching across the back of his neck. "Isn't it time that ends?"

She opened her mouth to respond. Blaze held her gaze, and she closed it, looking away.

He folded the paper before picking it up and walking around the desk. The flames in the fireplace beside him snapped and crackled.

"I understand you have a husband."

She swallowed. Blaze tapped the parchment against his palm.

"And two children. Daughters, right?"

The Follower's eyes flickered up to him. Good. She was paying attention now. He stopped in front of her and leaned back against his desk.

"My Crows are searching for them as we speak. It's only a matter of time before we find them. If you care for them, tell me about the Havens, and perhaps I can spare them as well."

Her lip quivered. Blaze straightened and stepped forward, dipping his head in what he hoped would come across as a compassionate gesture. Then maybe she'd tell him what he wanted to hear.

"All you have to do is tell me what you know. The king will extend grace to those who are loyal to him. You will be able to leave with your family if that is your wish."

She clasped her hands together, squeezing her fingers as her eyes darted back and forth. "All I have to do is tell you about the Havens?"

He nodded. Good. He was getting close. "We just want to know where they are. Who provides you with copies of the Testimonies? Who organizes them? Who corresponds with the rebel groups—"

"We are not part of the rebels."

Blaze raised his hands in defense. "Of course. Very well. Then just give me a name—someone who told you what to do or led your Haven. If you give me that, I'll keep you and your family safe. You have my word."

The Follower raised her chin as her gaze hardened.

"The Creator keeps me and my family safe. Our loyalty is to Him alone."

Blaze gritted his teeth and stepped back. "Very well."

He moved to the fireplace and tossed the paper into the flames. She gasped behind him as the parchment blackened and crumbled in the fire.

Typical. She cared more about the scribbles of a long-dead madman than the safety of her daughters.

He motioned to the two Crows and the door without looking back at her. "Take her away. Send her with the rest of the prisoners to the High Nest for judgment."

The muted sounds of the soldiers placing closed fists over their hearts in salutes faded as they marched out the door. Blaze glanced at their backs as they exited. The woman's soft sobs filled the hallway outside his office, and he closed his eyes.

This was her own fault. Even at the potential cost of her family's freedom, she would choose a made-up belief over betraying the other Followers. It was a choice he had seen again and again. And it was lunacy.

Footsteps entered the room, and he opened his eyes. Harold stood in the doorway, again holding the silver tray in his hands. He moved forward and offered it to Blaze, revealing a folded flyer and a sealed, small scroll on the flat dish.

"These just arrived. They're from the king, sir."

Blaze retrieved the items, unfolding the flyer. The

profile of a young woman was sketched onto the page. On the bottom, the words WANTED: CATRICE AETOS OF ONTIACH were written in bold. Kind eyes and a soft smile stood out on the familiar face and wild, curly hair dominated the rest of the portrait. The royal seal weighed down the corner of the paper and Blaze rubbed his thumb over the wax stamp. His stomach clenched.

Every few years, each of the High Crows received an updated version to keep up with the potential aging of the fugitive. The initial sketch had been based on his own memory. But it had been so many years, and neither Vivian nor Catrice had been found. Still, the flyers remained a painful reminder of what they had done—how they had left him.

For what felt like the hundredth time, he regretted ever meeting the Aetos family.

"Thank you, Harold. Put this in my room with the others."

He handed it to the butler, then broke the royal seal pressed on the scroll. He unrolled it and scanned the message written in red:

Potential rebel gathering located in Deln in the Amber District.

Infiltrate, observe, and report. If needed, eliminate.

High Crow Gideon Askin will accompany you.

- King Warren Tenaris, Commander of the Black Crows

He frowned as he reread the instructions. It was unusual, nearly unheard of, for him to be sent on a mission in another High Crow's district. But he understood why the Commander had chosen him. He had the best record for flushing out and arresting rebel groups. And from what he had heard, the Amber District was overflowing with them.

Blaze sucked in a breath and glanced at his butler.

"Prepare my horse and supplies for a journey to Deln in the morning. My father has a new mission for me."

3

CATRICE

"ALL COMES FROM THE CREATOR. BUT WITHOUT HIM, ALL IS DISTORTED AND BROKEN." - TESTIMONY OF PROPHET RIAH CHARIS

The sweet song of birds as they flitted from rooftop to rooftop filled the room. Catrice groaned and straightened from her resting place at the table. She stretched out her arms and rubbed her eyes as the rising sun shone through the single window looking out over the empty street, warming her face. She rotated her neck and immediately regretted falling asleep in her seat the night before. This wasn't how she imagined starting out her eighteenth birthday.

The completed copies of the Old Prophets lay stacked neatly inside the half-packed crate on the table. In just a week, she had managed to finish all but one. She had stayed up most of the night in a half-hearted attempt to complete it, the evidence of which was the drool pooling on one of the pieces of parchment and ink blotting her arms and staining the sleeves of her chemise. Mother had managed to finish any backed-up pastry orders, scrape together enough coppers to purchase fresh traveling supplies, and pack up the room in a few days. Not that there was much to pack up. Catrice was less enthusiastic about doing so, and her few belongings lay scattered throughout the room as a result.

Drool stuck to the corner of her mouth as she stood and shuffled over to a small water bowl in the corner. She splashed cold, stale water against her face as she knelt over the cracked basin, washing away the drool and any dirt leftover from the previous day. Dark circles—no doubt a result of forsaking her bed in favor of completing the Testimonies—rested under her brown eyes in the tarnished mirror hanging crookedly on the wall. Her hair was tangled, and the chestnut locks fought her wooden comb as she pulled it through the matted curls before tossing it in an open bag next to the basin.

A soft snore broke through the birds' song and Catrice turned to see Mother still asleep on one of the mats; it must have been earlier than she originally thought. She snagged her brown dress draped over the chair and pulled the garment over her fitted chemise. Matching stockings hugged her thighs and peeked out from under her dress as she tied the hem up just below her right knee. She secured her frizzy hair in a loose bun and slipped a fraying pair of socks and buckskin boots over her cold feet.

The floorboards creaked beneath her as she straightened out the table and wiped down the wash-basin. Catrice always liked to do small favors for Mother on her birthday to thank her for another safe year of life. Mother did what she had to do to protect them, and so far, it had worked. For that, Catrice was thankful.

A roll of bread sat on the table next to the money purse slung over her unbuckled belt and Catrice scooped up all three, nibbling on the stale bread as she opened the door to the stairs. The purse felt danger-ously light as she wrapped the belt around her waist. It held the last of the coin they had budgeted for supplies, but hopefully, it would be enough to make it to their new home.

The warm summer breeze pushed the loose strands of hair away from her face as she stepped down the stairs and rounded the building to enter the street. She was out a little earlier than normal, and the city was mostly quiet. Only a few stands were set up in the street for the market. Tay would still be at the stables finishing up his morning tasks.

She shoved the last bite of the roll into her mouth as she passed a few more city blocks toward the stables. Sure enough, Tay was hauling hay bales off a wagon just inside the low gate. He paused and wiped the sweat off his brow as she approached. The fence creaked as he leaned against it and smiled up at her. She smiled back, amused at the trail of dust that coated his forehead where he had brushed his hand over a moment earlier.

"Better patch up that post next. I'd say it's likely to give way any minute now." She nodded toward his support.

Tay raised his eyebrows. "Of course, Queen Elynn." He made a wide sweeping motion at the post and bowed. "Anything for you." He straightened again, grinning. "I didn't expect to see you today, let alone this early. To what do I owe the pleasure?"

Catrice clasped her hands in front of her. When she opened her mouth to respond, she couldn't seem to find the words to say goodbye, and a lump formed in her throat. She shook her head. "It's my birthday."

Tay's eyes widened, and he stepped closer to the gate. "Really?" He slapped a hand against his forehead. "Of course! Happy birthday."

"Thank you."

"I can't believe I forgot. I'm so sorry." He patted his pockets as if looking for something. "I didn't get you anything."

"Tay, it's fine. You didn't know until I told you last week."

"I guess, even after two years, we're still learning stuff about each other. Who knows what we'll find out in the next two?" He wiggled his eyebrows and opened his arms as if welcoming the prospect.

Catrice fought to match his playful demeanor. They wouldn't have a 'next two years.' She was leaving tomorrow. And she hadn't told him yet. She'd even neglected to extend the invitation for him to come to dinner. She opened her mouth to begin, but not before Tay spoke up again.

"So, what did you learn about me this week, then?"

"Uh…" She blew air out of her mouth as her mind searched for an answer. "Well, I didn't know your older brother was chosen in the Calling. I thought he was arrested by the Crows."

Tay pushed himself away from the gate, his cheerful demeanor disappearing as if Catrice had told him his mother had died. "He was. Our family name was picked two years ago in the draft, and he was sent to the High Nest to train. If you think I'm trouble… I'm nothing compared to how Trit was." Tay grabbed the pitchfork leaning against the side of the stable. He paused and looked down at the wooden tool. "He didn't even like the Crows, let alone want to become one. He never came back from training."

Catrice leaned against the fence. "I thought most people who fail the Calling are just sent back as soldiers to their home districts?"

Tay planted the pitchfork into one of the hay bales. "They're supposed to be. If they're not a threat. I guess Trit was too much trouble. We never got word about what happened, but we know. He's either rotting in a jail cell somewhere… or worse."

"I'm sorry." Her words felt empty against the

weight of the conversation, but she couldn't think of anything else to say. Tay shrugged.

"He used to send us letters when he first arrived at the High Nest. Did you know over half of the Called volunteer or are handpicked by Crows? They just fill the rest with random drafts from the lower families. I understand it pays well, but I can't imagine spending my life doing the dirty work of the king."

She watched as Tay used the pitchfork to gather any loose hay from the wagon bed and tried to ignore the pang in her gut reminding her this would be one of their last conversations. Shifting her weight off the fence, she opened the gate and stepped closer to the stable.

"Tay..." she started.

"Yes?" he said without stopping his work.

She bit her lip. Heavens, why was this so hard? "I'm leaving."

Tay continued to clean out the wagon. "Oh, all right. When will you be back?"

"No, Tay. I... we're moving away."

He sunk the pitchfork into the ground and stared at Catrice. "What do you mean?"

"My mother and I are moving. Tomorrow."

"Where? I'll send letters. I can come visit."

Catrice looked away. She had a whole script written out by Mother explaining they were moving in with a long-lost cousin along the coastal region, but staring into Tay's earnest eyes, she couldn't do it. "...I can't tell you."

Well, that was better than lying.

"What?" Tay's expression darkened. "Elynn, what's going on? Are you in trouble? Is it Ratton? I knew he was a no-good, drunken, creep—"

"Tay," she cut him off. "No. We're fine." No, they weren't. "Mother and I just need a change. I wish I could tell you more. But I need you to trust me." That was true.

Tay settled down, but his face remained downcast. "I can do that. Can I ask you to do one last thing with me before you go?"

Catrice smiled. "Of course. Anything."

He reached into his pants pocket and retrieved a tightly folded note. Glancing around him first, he unfolded the parchment and held it out for her to read. Inside the folds lay two fabric swatches embroidered with the image of an owl with outstretched talons. "The rebels are meeting tonight at an abandoned tavern by Falon's Square."

Catrice gasped. "You got through to them?"

Tay nodded. "It was just like the pamphlet said. I dropped off a few coppers and my address, and they slipped this note and the patches under my door this morning. I had to give them the bakery's address, too, so I could get two patches—they said they only give out one per family. But I asked them to leave anything at my house so your mother wouldn't know." He stepped forward and grabbed her hand. "Go with me? I don't know what's happening, Elynn, but maybe the rebels can help you and Mari."

Catrice chewed on the inside of her cheek and dropped her gaze. She wished it was that easy. Mother didn't trust the rebels. Said they were just as lost as the Crows. But what if she was wrong? What if they could offer some kind of protection to their family? After all, Lord Aetos was hailed as a hero by most for standing up to the king and protecting his people. Maybe they could even use the smuggling networks the rebels set up to send the Testimonies throughout Whittam. At the very least, she and Mother wouldn't have to look over their shoulder every second and lie about who they were anymore.

A spark of hope rose in Catrice's chest. She could tell someone her name. No one outside of Mother had said her name in ten years.

"Elynn?" Tay's voice broke her train of thought, but it didn't matter. She had already decided.

"Yes." She breathed, excitement swelling within her at the word.

"Yes, what?"

"I'll go with you to the rebel gathering tonight."

WHEN TAY HAD MENTIONED the rebels would be meeting at an abandoned tavern, Catrice had imagined maybe a dozen people gathered around a table introducing themselves and grilling the new recruits. What she hadn't expected was a crowd of what must have been close to a hundred strong packed wall-to-wall on the ground floor of the tavern.

A narrow balcony lined three walls, framing a raised stage against the fourth wall. Large, iron fixtures hung from the ceiling, casting a decent amount of light from the candles burning within. Most of the crowd was pressed in toward the empty stage, although a dozen or so had managed to make it to the balconies and spread out there or climb on top of the bar adjacent to the stage. It had been difficult to even get in the building, but now she didn't think she could turn and make it back out even if she wanted to.

Rebel guards had started to appear a few blocks away from Falon's Square. Tay and Catrice had presented their patches with the owl insignia at every stop, and again when they had entered the building. Like the tavern, the other buildings surrounding Falon's Square were mostly abandoned, making this the perfect location for such a meeting. Lord Royn's soldiers rarely patrolled this part of town, as there wasn't much to patrol.

Mother had believed her when she said she wanted to spend their last evening in Deln at the market with Tay. Although it wasn't a complete lie, it still left a sour taste in Catrice's mouth. She would come clean when she got back—hopefully with the good news that the rebels would protect them and they wouldn't have to leave after all.

Catrice jolted forward as someone bumped into her. Tay caught her arm, stabilizing her, right before her face collided with the shoulder blade of the person in front of her. She hated how close everyone was, how little she could see above the heads of those surrounding her. If something happened, would she even be able to get out, or would she be trampled as people ran for the exits? Maybe showing up tonight wasn't such a good idea after all.

She pulled her dark cloak closer around her and was about to suggest to Tay that they should try to leave when the doors on each side of the building slammed shut, momentarily silencing the low hum of the crowd. Catrice shrunk closer to Tay's side, buried in her cloak. Now she was definitely trapped.

Slowly, the hum returned as grumbles about the slow start to the night and excited voices discussing who would be speaking mingled together. Someone tapped her on the back, and she jumped, turning around. A boy—several years younger than her with ears he hadn't quite grown into yet—grinned at her and Tay.

"Did you hear?" he asked eagerly.

Tay draped his arm over Catrice's shoulder and cocked an eyebrow. "Hear what?"

"They're saying the White Owl himself might be coming tonight."

Tay dropped his arm and bounced on his heels as he grinned back at the boy. "Seriously?"

The boy nodded, and his oversized ears wiggled in sync. "I've been to a few of these, but never like this. Look how many of us there are! No way the king can ignore us now."

"Well, I don't exactly *want* him to find us," Catrice mumbled under her breath to Tay.

Tay stifled a laugh behind a fake cough. "Have to agree with you there."

Catrice bumped him with her shoulder and didn't bother hiding her mirth. Tay and the boy stepped closer and continued their conversation. She pressed her toes into the ground to lift herself a few inches higher. With the extra height, she could just make out a few people setting something up on the stage. Whatever was going to happen, it was obviously going to start soon. A nervous excitement ran through her body, and she shivered. She could understand why something secret and dangerous like this attracted so many people. And for it to make a potential change for the better too? The energy was contagious.

Another stranger brushed against her side, causing her to drop back down to her heels and turn as a hooded man passed her by.

"Excuse me," he whispered, avoiding her gaze.

His plain clothes and brown cloak blended in with the rest of the crowd seamlessly. A dark green scarf was pulled over his face, masking him from the eyes down.

But those eyes.

Catrice barely caught a glance before he turned away. Strikingly blue and oddly familiar beneath thick, dark brows. She continued to watch him as he wove his way through the crowd effortlessly, slowly making his way toward one of the staircases that led to the balconies. An odd, nostalgic warmth rose in her chest as he climbed the stairs and disappeared into one of the shadows that blanketed the walkway's corners.

Then, as quickly as it came, the warmth was drowned out by the deep, piercing coolness of dread.

4

BLAZE

Blaze slipped into the shadowy corner on the tavern's balcony, giving him a clear view of the entire room and stage area below. He adjusted the green scarf around his face and leaned over to Gideon. The other High Crow was nearly two full heads taller than him, but he hunched his shoulders to meet Blaze halfway.

"The black crow flies," Blaze said in a low voice, not that anyone else would hear them over the buzz of the crowd below.

"And nothing escapes its sight," Gideon responded, letting Blaze know he was open for conversation.

"This about what you expected?"

Gideon nodded, folding his beefy forearms across his chest. His tall frame and ebony skin were consistent with his Fathinian heritage, which was one of the reasons he had been appointed as High Crow over the district bordering the neighboring country. "We've been tracking this group for a few months. They've been garnering steady support from the people in town and the surrounding villages, but this is their biggest turnout yet."

"Why haven't you done anything before this? Taken out the group before it could get grounded?"

"We're playing the long game. Got a man on the inside now. He told us they were expecting someone big to show up tonight."

Blaze's heart raced, and he scanned the room again. "The White Owl?"

Gideon shook his head. "No way. He wouldn't expose himself like this. But we may see a close member of his circle. If so, we plan on getting him tonight."

"And after that? What about all these people?"

"Don't worry, Blaze." Gideon reached into his cloak and retrieved a list. The creamy parchment stood out against his palm in the shadows. "I had my inside man get a copy of all the names and addresses of everyone who signed up to attend. My Crows are stationed outside, and we have soldiers at each of their homes to make arrests the moment I give the word. This uprising will end tonight."

"And how many more do you have to quell still?"

Gideon shifted his stance and sighed. "Despite

what you think, I have the Amber District under control."

"Hmm." Blaze propped a foot up against the wall behind him. "Is that why Commander Tenaris sent me to oversee this?"

The giant of a man beside him craned his neck to look down at Blaze. In the shadows, Gideon's expression was hidden, but Blaze could imagine a scowl marring the bearded face. He brought down a massive hand to clap Blaze on the shoulder and gave it a little shake.

"You really are the worst. You know that?" A deep chuckle reverberated from his body.

Blaze raised his arm to clasp Gideon's bicep and joined in his laughter. "Someone has to keep you humble."

"The question is, who is doing that for you? Tell me, does that ring still fit around your finger with all that hot air inside you?"

Blaze flashed a grin beneath his scarf and patted the necklace under his shirt. "Like a glove. You got yours on you somewhere, I assume?"

Gideon nodded and pulled back his sleeve, revealing a leather bracelet woven through a black ring with a vein of amber running through it. On the band were the bold words *The Amber Crow* engraved in the metal. Blaze's was identical, save the amber vein, and his own engraving read *The Onyx Crow*. When the ring wasn't strung on his necklace while he was undercover, he wore it proudly on his left hand, signifying his position and authority in the guild.

"You know," Gideon thumbed the ring at his wrist, "Izaak should have been the one to wear this."

Blaze bowed his head, and his smile dropped at the mention of his brother's name. "He would be happy you have it."

"It would have been an honor to serve him in this district."

"He would have said the same thing about you."

Gideon pulled his sleeve back down. "I'm sorry. It was a tragedy what happened. I'm sure you don't hear that enough."

Blaze sniffed and lifted his head again. "Don't need to. It was a long time ago."

Gideon seemed like he wanted to respond, but Blaze was glad when he didn't. He didn't need to talk about his dead brother. Not now. Not when they were so close to finding his killer.

He shifted his gaze back to the crowd. It mostly consisted of men ranging in age from boys too young to be away from their mothers to elderly men leaning on canes for support. The rowdiest ones were near the front of the stage, cheering as a few makeshift soldiers lined up in the back carrying a rolled tapestry. He had tried to get an idea of how many weapons there were when he walked through the crowd earlier, but everyone was standing so close together that it was hard to tell.

Toward the center of the room, a young lady caught his eye. Unlike the others, she was facing away from the stage and staring up at the balcony as if looking for someone. He instinctively leaned further into the shadows, but there was no way she could see him from there. He must have passed her earlier because there was something eerily familiar about the wild curls framing her face.

"Do you know her?" He turned to Gideon and pointed to the girl.

Gideon glanced down at his notes and shook his head. "No. There's only a handful of women on my list. Most of them have attended events like these before, but I don't recognize her. This must be her first time." He turned over his sheet. "Denith Jons, maybe? No. Elynn. Elynn Halvor. She lives with her mom above a bakery on the south side of town. I couldn't dig up much more on the two of them other than she had her patch delivered to another boy's house. Must be undocumented. Probably refugees from Rewon or the Oram Islands."

"Yes." Blaze squinted, trying to get a better look at her face. "Must be."

What was so familiar about her?

His attention was pulled back to the stage as the rebel soldiers unrolled their tapestry, revealing a giant emblem of an owl with its talons outstretched. The crowd cheered. Blaze gritted his teeth. The White Owl.

A tall, lean man with dark bronze skin and black

hair pulled into thick braids stepped on stage. His garb was strikingly similar to a Crow's traditional outfit, except every item was lined with bright red thread and the mask was missing. Blaze's mouth fell open.

"Is that...?" he started.

"A Rogue." Gideon let out an exasperated sigh. "Makes sense. If the White Owl has a few former Crows on his side, it would explain how he seems to predict our every move."

Gideon leaned back and stuck his arm out a window beside him. The small, circular mirror in his palm caught the light from the hanging iron fixtures as he twisted it back and forth. When he returned the mirror to his pocket, he rubbed a hand over his bald head.

"Just alerting my men. This changes the game." He pulled two wooden whistles from another pocket and handed one to Blaze. "If anything goes wrong, use this."

Blaze agreed. Rogues were notoriously unpredictable, which was one of the reasons many of them had been kicked out of the Crows in the first place. He took the whistle and nodded. "We should split up. I'll head over to the opposite balcony."

He double-checked that the scarf was pulled above his nose before making his way across the balcony as the room quieted. The few commoners around him relaxed against the wall or casually leaned against the railing, paying Blaze no heed. On stage, the Rogue leaned forward, bowing as if he had just performed for an audience.

"Well, this is an awfully good turnout, wouldn't you say?" He raised his arms, gesturing to the room, and it exploded in shouts and back-slapping. "The White Owl, unfortunately, couldn't make it tonight, but he thanks every one of you for coming. Without new faces like you, our brothers and sisters across the country would have died out years ago." He dropped his hands and clasped them behind his back. Raising his chin, his voice took on a solemn tone. "King Tenaris thinks we're few in number. Just some angry peasants from the lower families he can't control. And what he can't control, he wipes out."

The crowd echoed their agreement.

"As you can see, we are more than just a few. But he's right about one thing." The Rogue seemed to pause for dramatic effect. Blaze rolled his eyes as the crowd collectively leaned forward. "He *cannot* control us!"

Applause echoed off the walls as the room again burst into cheers. Blaze leaned back and halfheartedly clapped along. He would be happy when this was over. Half of these people didn't know any better. They were just caught up in the lie that the White Owl offered something better for them. Blaze knew firsthand the only thing the White Owl offered was death.

At the Rogue's behest, the room quieted again. The men around Blaze seemed to shift as if anticipating something; the hair on the back of his neck bristled. What was going on?

"Now," the Rogue continued, "I've already thanked you all, but there's someone else here tonight I still need to acknowledge."

He glanced up at the balcony, and the men near Blaze pushed back their cloaks, revealing rope and daggers secured in their belts. Blaze stiffened as adrenaline coursed through his veins. Something was happening.

"You see, the king seems to think he's always one step ahead of us. In reality, the White Owl sees everything. Including our *special* guest hiding up in the rafters."

The Rogue smiled—a sinister, dark expression. Terror jolted thought Blaze's body. "Ladies and gentlemen, would you join me in welcoming the Amber Crow here tonight?"

Gideon. No. This couldn't be happening. They shouldn't know he was here.

The dozen or so commoners on the balcony rushed toward Gideon as the crowd on the floor burst into a frenzy of anger and fear. When they reached the shadowed corner, all Blaze could hear was fists hitting flesh and pained shouts. He started forward, but stopped as Gideon burst from the corner, tossing the men left and right like they were nothing. It wouldn't last though; they were slowly overwhelming him, and a fresh round of rebels was running up the stairs toward him.

One of the men on Gideon's arm stumbled back, crashing into the thin railing on the balcony and falling into the crowd below. In response, any remaining cries of terror morphed into shouts of anger. They were turning into a mob. This was about to become a blood bath. Blaze had to do something. But he couldn't reveal himself, not in his common garb. They didn't know he was there yet.

Through the flying fists and sprawling bodies, he caught a glimpse of Gideon's bleeding face. The Amber Crow jerked his head toward the window, barely managing to reach for his pocket before another man jumped on him.

But it was enough. Blaze darted toward the closest open window and pulled the whistle from his pocket. Pressing the wooden instrument to his lips, he released two full lungs worth of breath, and a shrill note rang through the night.

For a moment, nothing happened, and Blaze panicked. Where were Gideon's men? Had they even heard him?

Then, as if on cue, tens of them crashed through the windows above the balcony and stage.

Fresh screams erupted from the floor below as smoke bombs flew through the room and people ran for the nearest exits. Blaze whirled around, scanning the chaos below him. Some men were standing their ground, throwing wayward punches and drawing swords on the Crows, but most of the people were desperately trying to get out. He focused on the stage where the tapestry lay trampled and forgotten, and the rebel soldiers fended off a handful of Gideon's men. Blaze narrowed his eyes as the room filled with smoke. Where was the Rogue?

A disruption behind one of the bar counters caught his eye. A black cloak with red thread slipped through one of the shattered windows. *Blasts.* He was getting away.

Blaze growled and ducked under a rebel's punch before leaping over the railing and grabbing onto one of the balcony's support beams. He slid down the pole, dodging past more screaming people and jumping over trampled bodies before darting through the same broken window the Rogue had disappeared through.

Once outside, his eyes struggled to adjust to the darkness but managed to catch the edge of a cape disappearing behind a building across the square. He broke into a run, clearing the abandoned courtyard and passing dozens of fleeing citizens in a matter of seconds.

The Rogue was in his sights, running full speed down a dark alleyway riddled with trash and deeper into the city where he could disappear. Blaze doubled his stride, closing the distance between them. He reached for the cloak, ready to grab it, when the Rogue tripped. Blaze didn't have time to stop and collided with the falling body, sending the both of them tumbling to the ground.

He cursed through his teeth as loose rocks dug into his skin, and his scarf was ripped from his face. He jumped to his feet, drawing one of the daggers at his side and crouching, ready for the Rogue to attack. But instead of launching to his feet like Blaze, the cloaked figure groaned, leaning on the wall for support as he tried to stand. When he succeeded, his hood fell, revealing a mess of dark curls, and a pair of pretty brown eyes turned to Blaze.

His heart dropped. Not the Rogue.

And suddenly, it made sense why she had been so familiar: the wild curls adorning her head. The image of the crude sketch on the wanted poster flashed across his mind. It had been close, but not exact. But now that he saw her up close, he wondered how he could have ever overlooked her in the tavern. How could anyone overlook a face like hers?

He lowered his dagger and let out a deep breath as he spoke the name he thought he would never say again.

"Catrice?"

5

CATRICE

"WHO WILL CALL ON THE CREATOR IN TIMES OF NEED? HE COMFORTS THOSE WHO HURT, AND LIGHTS THE DARKNESS WITH THE DAWN." - TESTIMONY OF PROPHET BENIAH AETOS

Catrice stared at the stranger before her. Her lungs burned as she struggled to take a deep breath. She leaned against the wall for support and tried to get her bearings. She hadn't run that fast in years, and she must have hit her head hard... because she could swear the stranger had just called her by her real name.

The stranger blocked the path in front of her, brandishing a dagger that caught the moonlight when he moved. She shifted her feet and kicked the crate she had tripped over with her toe. The splintered wood would make a good enough weapon. At least then she wouldn't be completely defenseless. She dropped to a knee and yanked a loose board free from the crate before stepping back, wielding the splintering plank in front of her.

He took a step toward her, weapon lowered but

still unsheathed. She jerked back, and the world spun around her.

"Catrice, it's me."

There it was again. He said her name. Heavens, how hard had she hit her head?

The stranger returned the blade to his side and raised his arms in a non-threatening gesture. "Hey, it's all right."

Catrice kept the plank brandished between them. "Who are you?"

The stranger raised his eyebrows. "You really don't remember?"

"Answer my question." There was something familiar about him, like the distant memory of a dream. She scanned his basic garb: a plain white shirt, brown trousers, and matching brown cloak and boots. Nothing remarkable. Her gaze stopped at the green scarf hanging around his neck. "You were at the tavern."

He nodded. His eyebrows were slightly furrowed, and his eyes were entirely focused on her, like he was testing something. She could turn and run again, but where would she go? If he knew who she was, she couldn't lead him back to Mother until she knew what he wanted.

"Why were you chasing me?" She resented that her voice wavered ever so slightly when she spoke.

He cocked his head to the side. "I thought you were someone else. My apologies if I scared you. But I'm glad you're all right." His gaze flickered to her forehead. "Well, mostly."

Catrice touched her brow and winced as a sharp pain shot through her skull. She drew her hand back to see dark liquid staining her fingertips. So she had hit her head after all.

The stranger stepped forward again while reaching for something in his pocket. She stumbled back and extended the plank.

"Stay back!"

Concern crossed his features, and he paused. "Don't worry." He pulled a handkerchief from his pocket and extended it to Catrice. "For your cut. It was my mother's, but you can have it."

"Why would you do that? I don't even know you."

The stranger's eyes crinkled. "Because it's your birthday, of course. If it was any other day, I may not be so nice."

As the words left his mouth, Catrice's eyes widened. Dark memories from ten years prior came flooding back, and she looked down as her mind sorted through that day. One name stood out from the rest. She flicked her gaze back up to him.

"Blaze?"

He smiled. "Hello, Catrice."

She screamed and threw the plank at him. He raised an arm to block it and it bounced off.

"Ow! What was that for?"

"You're supposed to be dead."

"Obviously, I'm not."

"We lost you at Ontiach. We never heard from you again."

"Well, when the Crows pulled Izaak and me from the rubble and forced us to serve for our district's crimes, we didn't exactly have time to write."

Catrice backed up. "They forced you to do that?"

Blaze turned his head. "Yeah. Not all of us had the luxury of running." He took a deep breath in. "I got out two years ago and have been searching for our people ever since. I figured joining the rebels might not be too bad of a start." He glanced over the alley. "Where is Vivian?"

"She's—" Catrice's words caught in her throat. What was she doing? She couldn't just tell him where they lived. That was supposed to be a secret. But her name was supposed to be too, and he knew that already.

"Catrice?" Blaze had taken another step toward her, only leaving a few feet between them. "Is Vivian safe? Did something happen?"

"No, she's fine." Catrice shook her head. What was she worried about? Of course she could trust Blaze. They had known each other since they were babies. He offered her the handkerchief again, and she winced as she pressed it against the wound on her brow.

"Hey!" a deep voice rang through the night. Catrice jumped and spun about. A Crow ran towards them in the alleyway.

Before she could react, Blaze grabbed her hand and pulled her away from the Crow. In an instant, the two of them were sprinting around corners, over trash piles, and under laundry lines toward the marketplace, but their pursuer was gaining on them.

As they turned down another street, Blaze stopped suddenly, bending over at the waist and resting his hands on his knees as he panted. Catrice's heart pounded faster as she stopped beside him.

"What are you doing?" She scanned the closed shops and empty road.

Blaze cast a look around the corner and grimaced. "We can't outrun him."

"We have to try!"

He shook his head, sweat dripping down his nose. "You hide." He pointed to an empty vendor stand across the street. "I'll take care of this."

"Blaze, he's a Crow. You can't—"

"Trust me." He turned her shoulders and pushed her toward the stand.

She dug her heels in the dirt before relenting. Fighting Blaze wouldn't help, and she couldn't do anything. Her heartbeat thudded in her ears as she ducked behind the stall. Between the various signs and paneling, she could make out Blaze pressing his back against the wall near the corner of the shop, listening for the approaching footsteps of the Crow.

For a moment, it was silent.

Then the Crow came barreling around the corner.

Blaze launched from his position, tackling the Crow to the ground. They grappled in the dirt, kicking up dust that obscured what little Catrice could see in the moonlight. She couldn't tell who was on top, just that they were both still fighting. Finally, after what seemed like minutes, one of them stopped moving. Blaze stood from the ground over the still body of the Crow.

Catrice moved from the stand slowly. What had happened? Was he dead? Had Blaze killed him? Just as she was sure she knew the answer, the Crow's chest rose in a deep breath, but he remained on the ground.

"What did you do?" Catrice kept her distance behind Blaze.

He turned and wiped his brow. "He'll be fine. Just knocked him out. It won't last long." Blaze jumped into a jog as the Crow began to stir. "Do you have a safe place we can go?"

"Uh…" Catrice hesitated, still glancing at the unconscious Crow as she instinctively matched Blaze's pace.

"Catrice!"

She didn't have a choice; she had to trust him. "Yes. Follow me."

Changing directions, she led him through the roads and alleys she took every day to get back home. It was different at night, somehow peaceful and unsettling at the same time. She wondered if Tay had made it back to his home yet. Had he been trampled beneath the crowd or, worse, captured by the Crows? The thought made her sick. She would have to go check on him after she touched base with Mother. He would do the same for her.

By the time they reached the bakery, her legs ached and it hurt to breathe. She slowed to a walk as they approached the storefront and made their way to the back, freezing in place when she saw the kitchen door ajar. It was supposed to be locked. No one should be in the bakery this late. A tarnished sword lay near the entrance.

Blaze stepped in front of her and held a finger up to his lips. He picked up the weapon and snuck up to the door, pushing it open more with the tip of the blade.

Silence.

Then a stench like a butcher's shop on a hot day smacked Catrice across the face. She covered her nose and gagged as the foul smell made its way into her mouth. Blaze pulled the scarf over his nose and stepped into the kitchen. Catrice followed, stopping at the doorway. But she could see enough from there.

Mixing bowls and utensils lay scattered haphazardly throughout the kitchen. Blood splatter ran along the lengths of the counters and stained the floor. Ratton sat propped up against one of the counters. A broken sword protruded from his back, and thick, sticky blood covered his torso.

Catrice recoiled as another gag rushed to the front

of her throat. Blaze stood in the destruction, surveying the room and Ratton's body. A deep set of wrinkles lined his forehead when he turned back to Catrice and exited the kitchen.

"What happened?" Catrice managed to squeak out while her stomach fought to expel its contents.

Blaze frowned. "I don't know. Where's your mother?"

Catrice glanced up at the staircase attached to the back of the building. Their door creaked open in the wind.

No. *Please, Creator, no.*

Catrice darted toward the stairs, nearly tripping on the first three. She vaguely registered Blaze warning her to stop as she reached for the doorknob. Flinging the door wide open, she gasped at the scene before her.

Parchment and ink were strewn throughout the room. What few items had been packed away lay broken at her feet as if someone had thrown them at intruders. The sleeping mats were cut open and piled in a corner, and the table was split in two. Covering it all, splattered along the walls and every piece of furniture, was bright, red blood.

No. This couldn't be happening.

Catrice didn't remember falling to her knees, but she was suddenly on the floor as a guttural scream worked its way up from her stomach.

"NO!"

She was shaking. Crying. Sobbing. Grabbing the broken pieces of pottery and throwing them across the room. What was happening? This couldn't be real. This *couldn't* be real.

"Catrice." Blaze's calm voice barely made it past the panicked, strange noises coming from her mouth. He knelt in front of her and placed his hands on her shoulders. "Catrice, deep breaths. Deep breaths."

He lifted her chin to look at him and exaggerated his breathing as if for her to copy him. What was he doing? She didn't need to breathe. She *was* breathing. Where was Mother? She should be here.

Catrice jerked her head to see past Blaze, scanning the mess surrounding them. Mother had to be somewhere. Maybe she was hiding under the mats. Waiting for Catrice to find her.

"Catrice." Blaze gently directed her gaze back to him again. "I need you to breathe."

Breathe. Her hands shook. Right. Mother would want her to breathe. She took a deep breath in. Tears pooled in her open mouth. Blaze nodded and she breathed out.

"Good." He patted her on the shoulder. "Again."

Deep breath in. This time she held it for a few seconds as he directed. Deep breath out. The tears slowed, and she hiccupped.

Blaze grabbed her hands and squeezed, pulling her to her feet. She wobbled, and he slipped an arm around her for support.

"Do you know what happened here?" he asked her softly.

"No." She hiccupped again. "Mother was just finishing the last of the letters to send out to..."

As she scanned the room again, her eyes landed on the broken table. While their quills, ink, and unused parchment were scattered about the room, the copies of the Testimonies, all sealed and ready to send out, were gone. She stepped forward, shuffling through the materials on the table.

"They're gone," she whispered.

"What's gone, Catrice?"

"The Testimonies. I don't understand. Who would take them and kill—" She froze as she focused on a metal pin peeking out from under one of the torn parchments. She knelt, picked up the crow symbol, and turned back to Blaze. "The Crows. They must have found us. But how? We don't have our address listed anywhere..."

Tay. She covered her mouth. A fresh round of sobs threatened to burst forth as her eyes welled with tears.

"Oh, no." She turned to Blaze. "This is my fault."

"What do you mean?"

"I had to provide my address for the meeting tonight, but the Crows were there. They had to have known about the meeting. They must have gotten a copy of it somehow."

Blaze scanned the room. "You think the Crows did this?"

"Who else would it be? Who else would take her body and the Testimonies? They've been after us for years. Ever since they attacked Ontiach. I thought we were safe here for once." She choked back a cry. "I did this."

"Catrice." Blaze moved toward her. "This is not your fault."

She shook her head. "Mother always told me I should be more careful. Said I shouldn't hang around the rebels. I thought they could protect us."

Blaze bowed his head. "I'm sorry, Catrice." He surveyed the destruction. "Do you have anywhere you can go?"

Did she? If the Crows had come for her mother, they were bound to come back for her. She couldn't stay in town, and she wouldn't risk Tay or his family. There was only one place she could go. One place she knew would offer her shelter.

"Yes. There's a Haven south of here in the Silver District. No more than a few days' ride away."

"You know where the Havens are?"

"Mhm." She bit her bottom lip. "But I don't have papers. Or a horse."

Blaze paused and looked away as if he was considering something. "I do."

"What?"

"I told you, I've been searching for our people for two years. I know how the Crows work and what to do to avoid them. We can go together."

"Really?" She narrowed her eyes at him.

She had longed for a moment like this; for someone to offer to come along side and help them. With Blaze, she would never have to lie about who she was. But now, as she stared at him and his eager expression, anxiety gripped her heart.

Mother had always said to ask the Creator for direction in times of doubt. She closed her eyes and took a breath.

Creator, did you send him?

Silence. This was up to her to decide.

Opening her eyes, she extended her hand to him. "Can I trust you?"

He took her hand, flashing her a smile, and the deep sense of dread she had felt in the tavern returned. "Always."

6

BLAZE

"A BLACK CROW PLEDGES TO SERVE THE THRONE FOR FOUR YEARS. UPON COMPLETION, THEY MAY ELECT TO RENEW THEIR TERM, OR STEP DOWN FROM THE BLACK CROWS." - THE ROYAL ARCHIVES OF WHITTAM

When Blaze had accepted the mission to infiltrate the rebel gathering, he had anticipated many different scenarios.

Quite literally, running into the daughter of one of the most wanted families in the country and maintaining his cover to convince her to trust him was not one of them.

But now here he was, sweating in a stinking stable and hooking up his warhorse to a rickety wagon to prove he was really a traveling merchant and not the High Crow of the Onyx District. He dragged a hand down his face and sighed.

This was *not* how he had imagined spending the next few weeks.

After convincing a rather stunned Catrice to leave the bakery, he had put her up at a local inn for the night while he decided what to do next. He had never been so thankful for the mandatory backstories all Crows were required to come up with before going undercover. It had made convincing her to trust him that much easier. And, like every good lie, it was mixed in with a bit of truth that Catrice would be able to verify.

He *had* been Called in Ontiach after the city was attacked. The feather tattoo on his forearm proved he had served at one point. Plenty of Crows quit after one term. She would have no way of knowing he was still serving, let alone a High Crow. He *was* looking for their people, the Followers, just not for the same reasons she would be. But again, she would have no way of knowing that. If he was smart, she never would. Not until it was too late.

He double-checked the tack's various buckles and tightened the breeching strap to ensure the wagon was attached to his horse's harness. The tall, buckskin gelding had served him well during his years as a Crow, although Blaze could tell Ace wasn't a fan of the restrictive harness straps. Blaze rubbed the horse's broad, muscular neck.

"I know it's not fair, Ace. But it's just for a few weeks." He gave the horse one last pat and moved to the front of the wagon.

Catrice would be getting restless at the inn. He had convinced her to stay put overnight while he retrieved his belongings, which gave him enough time to procure the wagon and miscellaneous goods a traveling merchant would have. More importantly, it gave him enough time to touch base with Gideon. The sun was starting to rise, and he would have to be back soon. He glanced at the entrance of the stable as Gideon limped through the open doors.

The Amber Crow was once again in common garb, most likely to avoid raising suspicion or unwanted attention, but his right eye was nearly swollen shut, and his left arm was tucked under his cloak in a sling.

Blaze grimaced at his dismal appearance. "Looks like you had quite a night."

Gideon offered a small smile and winced at the movement. "You should see the other guys."

"Do we know what happened? How did they know you were there?"

Gideon stopped a few feet from Blaze and leaned against the wall for support. "We found the Crow we planted in their ranks this morning."

"He ratted you out?"

"If he did, there's no way to know now. He's dead. Either way, they figured out who he was." He drew a hand over his beard. "The Rogue got away too."

Of course.

Blaze ran his hands through his hair and clasped them behind his head. "I'm sorry, Gideon. I've lost a few of my own men this year."

"It's part of the job." Gideon let out a deep sigh and shifted. "I understand you had a surprise of your own last night."

"Ha!" Blaze let out a pained laugh and dropped his arms. "Did you know the Aetoses were hiding here in town?"

"No. But, from what I've read, the Aetoses are resourceful, and their connections run deep. They've been on the run longer than either of us have been Crows. Doesn't surprise me they went unnoticed for so long." Gideon shook his head. "Vivian is gone?"

"And most likely dead. You should have seen how much blood was in that room. It wasn't your men, I take it?"

"My Crows would never be that sloppy. They were up all night cleaning it up. Someone else must be a part of this."

"That's what I was afraid of." Blaze shoved a hand into his pocket and retrieved the crow pin Catrice had found the night before.

Gideon reached for the pin and blew a hard breath from his mouth. "Where did you find this?"

"Where the Aetoses were staying. Someone went through a lot of trouble to make it look like the Crows killed Vivian."

"The Rogue, maybe?"

"I'm not sure."

"Well, whoever it was, I want them out of my district." Gideon pocketed the pin and scratched his beard. "You know, Derek's pretty sour about that beating you gave him in the alley. He's been nursing a headache all night."

Blaze chuckled. "I had to sell it for Catrice. She wouldn't trust me if I didn't. Tell Derek I'll make it up to him next time I'm in the Amber District."

"Will do." Gideon nodded toward the wagon. "You got everything you need?"

"Almost." Blaze reached into his pocket and retrieved a piece of parchment. "From what I understand, Catrice and her mother were the ones providing the Followers with illegal copies of the Testimonies. Most of them were gone, but we gathered what we could, and I managed to swipe this last night when she wasn't looking. If the Commander compares the script to the ones we have on record, it should be a match."

Gideon took the page from Blaze and studied it. "If we can prove the Aetoses are the ones who have been organizing the Havens and providing the Testimonies, then we can tie the Followers to last night's rebel gathering and the White Owl."

"Exactly."

"Are you sure you want to do this? Once we open that door, we can't close it."

"I've been waiting years to prove the Followers are nothing more than a treacherous cult. This is the proof we need."

Gideon raised his eyebrows and tapped the parchment against his leg. "Very well. I'll send it to the Commander and update him on the situation. You're staying undercover, then?"

"If Catrice can take me to the Havens, she's worth more roaming free than in chains at the High Nest."

"Where's your first stop?"

"Down south. Zradit."

"The Silver District? Oof. Have fun with Nikita."

Blaze rolled his eyes. Seeing the Silver Crow was one aspect of this mission he was *not* looking forward to. He clapped a hand on Gideon's good shoulder.

"Take care of yourself."

Gideon forced another small smile and winced again. "You, too."

Blaze climbed on top of the wagon's seat and grabbed Ace's reins, directing him out of the stables. As he made his way back to the inn, the city woke up around him, and he became painfully aware of how little sleep he had managed to get while waiting for the wagon. His head pounded and shoulders ached as he straightened his back; the pile of hay in the stable was a far cry from his bed.

Hopefully, Catrice had slept better. He would need her awake and aware if she was to lead him to the Zradit Haven.

After he tied Ace to one of the posts at the front of the inn, he bounded his way up the stairs, bypassing the early morning travelers and housekeepers in the halls. Knocking gently, he pushed the door to Catrice's room open.

The small, single room wasn't much bigger than the room she and Vivian had been staying in, and it boasted more furniture. They must have been scraping by, which benefited them in the long run. If there wasn't a lot of coin going missing from a shop or bakery, the less likely it was a soldier would be called to investigate the books. Vivian had been smart, but apparently, not smart enough.

He stepped past the door to see Catrice asleep above the covers on the bed, shoes still on, and blood still smeared on her fingers from the night before. Blaze had convinced her to pack a bag of items and supplies for their travels. It turned out she didn't have much more than a bag's worth of possessions to her name anyway. The worn sack was slung over the bedpost, and Blaze imagined she hadn't even bothered to unpack anything before passing out.

So this is what had become of the great Aetos family. The thought gave him an odd sense of satisfaction. They got what they deserved.

Glancing over her again, something else caught his eye. She had a bundle of parchment gripped tightly in her hand. Most likely the few passages of the Testimonies she had scavenged. Blaze shook his head. They were nothing more than stories, and yet Catrice clung to them in her sleep like holding them was a matter of life or death.

A ten-year-old memory of Vivian and Catrice riding away from his childhood home, clutching the bag of Testimonies like Catrice did now, forced its way to the front of his mind. They had taken those cursed scrolls, but left him and Izaak.

Left them to be buried under a burning house as their city fell.

He could hardly believe the sleeping girl in front of him with rosy cheeks and drool pooling on her pillow was capable of such a thing, but he had the scars to prove it. When he had seen her the previous night, for the first time in ten years, she had taken his breath away, but it didn't matter.

Appearances could be deceiving.

The Followers said they took care of people. That they were called to help the needy and hurting. But it was the Crows who had saved him and Izaak from the rubble and given them a new life. Not some all-knowing Creator or His Followers. The fact that anyone would claim otherwise was lunacy.

Catrice stirred from her resting place, and he busied himself by straightening his cloak. When she opened her eyes, they wandered about the room, dazed, for a moment, before widening.

She launched from the bed, frantic, and focused on Blaze again. Fear blanketed her expression, and Blaze held his hands up in a non-threatening gesture.

"Hey, Catrice. It's all right. You're safe. We're at the

inn I dropped you at last night." He took a step toward her, and she shrank back.

"So, last night..." She reached a shaking hand up to her mouth. "That was real?"

"I'm afraid so."

She took a deep breath and reached to push her frizzy hair back from her face, stopping in horror when her bloodstained hands passed in front of her eyes. Blaze grimaced.

"Why don't you get washed up?" He gestured to the washbasin across the room.

She nodded absently and shuffled to the vanity where the clay bowl sat.

Blaze grabbed her sack and set it on the foot of the bed. "I have my horse and wagon ready downstairs when you are. If we leave soon, we can make it to Zradit within three days."

Catrice remained silent as the water sloshed in the basin. Blaze walked up behind her, but her eyes remained glued to the red-tinged water.

"Catrice? Did you hear me?"

"I don't know." Catrice squeezed her hands in the bowl. "Maybe we should leave."

"Leave town?"

"The country."

Blaze raised his eyebrows. Where was she going with this? "I thought we were going to the Haven to meet up with our people."

Catrice dried her hands and paced across the

room. "My family's caused enough trouble for the Followers. It would probably be better if I disappeared."

"For them or for you?"

She paused, wrapped her arms around herself, and chewed on her lower lip. But offered no response.

"You would just leave them?" He tried to infuse a measure of shock in his voice, but he should have expected this. It wouldn't be the first time an Aetos left their people to ruin. But he couldn't let her do it this time. Not if he wanted to find the Havens. "Catrice, our people need you. They looked to your father when he was still here. And now they will look to you for direction."

"But I don't even know what I'm doing. All I ever did was write copies of the Testimonies. My mother was the one who sent them out and helped organize the Havens when we were on the run after Ontiach. What am I supposed to offer them? How am I supposed to help?"

Blaze frowned. She couldn't help. It was her family's fault they were in this situation in the first place. But he wasn't about to tell her that.

"Well, you're willing to do what it takes to make a change. Why else would you go to the rebel gathering last night? That's what the rebels want, isn't it? Change?"

"I guess." She grabbed her bag. "But that's what I was hoping the rebels would be able to give me. A change from the constant running and hiding. I can't offer that to my people."

"Maybe one day you will." She wouldn't, but the false hope seemed to have motivated her enough to move; that's what he needed.

"Thank you."

Her sudden gratitude caught him off guard, and he tilted his head to the side, waiting for her to continue.

"I realized I never thanked you for saving me last night."

Save her? When had he saved her?

"I have to admit"—she swung the sack over her shoulder—"when you told me you were a former Crow, I was nervous. But after you stopped the other Crow from catching us..." She paused, seemingly overcome with emotion.

Ah. That was right. He had saved her from Derek.

She took a deep breath and continued. "I remembered how you always protected Izaak and me when we were little. Even if it was just from wandering too far in the meadow when we would play. You always gave yourself up before we'd get lost."

An odd mix of pain and anger swelled in his chest as if someone had punched him in the gut. She didn't get to bring up Izaak. Not now.

He reached up to rub the scar on the back of his neck and cleared his throat. "Of course. As I said, I've been looking for our people since I got out of the Crows. I'm just glad I found you."

"Is that from Ontiach?" Catrice pointed to his neck.

He dropped his hand. "Yes. Our home collapsed. I nearly burned to death."

"How did you get out?"

"The Crows found me."

Catrice paused, her expression darkening. "You said you and Izaak were Called by force."

"Yes." Why was she pushing this? "To pay for the sins of our people. Or at least that's what they told us."

Another lie, but it had happened to others in Ontiach. And it was better than admitting that the Commander was his father.

"And Diana?"

At the mention of his aunt, Blaze allowed a small smile. "She's alive. She lives with me in the Onyx District. Maybe after we're done with all this, we can go visit her."

Catrice smiled. "I would like that. I would like to see Izaak too. Does he live with you also?"

"No." *He was killed by the rebels you seem so desperate to align yourself with.* "He died a few years ago."

Catrice's jaw dropped at his blunt statement, but she quickly composed herself again. "I'm so sorry."

"And I'm sorry about your mother."

As much as he didn't want it to, the statement rang true within him.

Vivian's death may have resulted from her own actions, but no one deserved to be murdered in their own home. At least if the Crows had found her, she would have had a fair trial.

He extended an arm toward the door and inclined his head in a slight bow. "Are you ready?"

"Yes." Catrice adjusted the strap on her shoulder. "Are you?"

Blaze grinned. He had waited ten years for this. Oh yes, he was ready.

7

CATRICE

"IF THE FUTURE KINGS AND QUEENS OF ANOCICA WISH TO RULE, THEY MUST BE ANOINTED BY THE CREATOR'S PROPHET. THEN ALL SHALL KNOW WHO THE CREATOR HAS CHOSEN." - TESTIMONY OF PROPHET MERIB BEKAN

Catrice couldn't remember the last time she had covered so much ground in one day of travel.

When she and Mother had fled Ontiach, they had a horse and enough coin to get them settled while they waited for Father to join them in the Silver District. But when he never did, they had been forced to sell their horse and what few possessions were worth something just to eat and clothe themselves. They had found a few other Followers, and they all pooled their resources to buy a small building so they could live and cook together and care for each other. Thus, the first Haven was born in Zradit. But it wasn't long before Mother told her they had to leave for the sake of the others. The new king was looking for them.

The king who had killed Father.

So, Mother had committed to providing for the

Followers in other ways. Organizing the Havens, providing copies of the Testimonies when they were outlawed, and praying the Creator would send another Prophet to set the king straight and save their people. Catrice had helped where she could, taking over the responsibility of copying the Testimonies when her skills had developed enough, but it was never enough. Their people still couldn't worship freely, many were jailed for owning the Testimonies, and the Creator had failed to send another Prophet.

Now, Mother was dead too, and this time, it was Catrice's fault.

She blew a stray curl from her face and shook her head, attempting to clear any more negative thoughts so they wouldn't spiral out of control. Blaze had gone to relieve himself in the forest, leaving her alone with her thoughts. She distracted herself by digging into one of the crates that dotted Blaze's wagon in search of something to eat.

They had stopped near a stream to allow the horse to drink and rest. As they had traveled south, the landscape had revealed a brighter, richer hue of colors and flowers dotting the fields and forests. Whenever she took a deep breath, dozens of new and familiar scents flooded her senses. But right now, all her senses demanded was food.

Since they had left Deln two days before, they had camped under the stars, waded through the shallows of the Geen River to avoid a checkpoint, and slowly made their way through Blaze's stash of salted meats and dried fruits. In the past two years, she and Mother had sustained themselves mostly on deformed pastries and stale bread from the bakery, so the tough, savory snacks more than satisfied Catrice's rumbling stomach.

She snagged a rather large piece of salted fish from the bottom of one of the crates and unwrapped the paper around it to take a bite as Blaze appeared from behind a tree. He took his time walking back to the wagon, stopping to stretch and do various athletic feats Catrice had become familiar with over the last several days. Leaning forward, he fell into a push-up, completing several before moving on to a different exercise.

"Do you really have to do that every time we stop?" Catrice asked through a mouthful of food. "I'm exhausted just watching you."

Blaze shrugged and walked the rest of the distance to the wagon. "Old habit."

She swallowed the dry meat and grimaced. "From when you were a Crow?"

"I may have hated it, but I did pick up a few skills."

"What?" Catrice scoffed and bit off another chunk of fish. "Like killing people?"

The bite in her words surprised her, and guilt settled in her chest. Blaze pursed his lips and looked away.

Catrice sighed. "I'm sorry. You didn't deserve

that." She grabbed another filet from the crate and offered it to him. "When you were a Crow… did you know the king?"

"Not really." Blaze shook his head and took the food. "The Commander primarily corresponds with the High Crows over each district. The rest of us just reported to them."

"Is that what you called him? The Commander?"

"All the Crows did. In the guild, he's not just the king but also our commanding officer. Everything we learned was from him."

Catrice furrowed her brow and took a step back. She didn't like the sound of that. What could King Tenaris possibly teach that would be good? "Did he ever command you to hunt our people?"

Blaze paused at her question, unwrapping his filet slowly, as if he was weighing his answer. "There are a lot of things I did that I'm not proud of, Catrice. But when you're a Crow, when you're living in that environment every day, you just do what it takes to survive." He bit the fish. "And I had Izaak to think about too."

That was fair. In a lot of ways, she and Mother had been forced to do the same. Hiding her identity and lying to her best friend had never been her desire, but it was what she had to do to survive. She couldn't imagine what Blaze had been forced to do for the sake of his own life or Izaak's. Had he ever considered running like she had?

The memory of her own moment of weakness—confessing that she had wanted to leave to Blaze just days earlier—set a sour taste in her mouth. How could she have even considered such a thing? He was right. Her people needed her. Much like Izaak had probably needed him in the Crows.

She swallowed the last bit of fish and wiped her hands on her dress. "I'm sorry you had to go through that."

"It's fine. It's not like it's your fault." Blaze said the words without hesitation, but there was an edge to his voice she hadn't expected.

"But it was my family who brought the king's wrath on our city."

Blaze's eyes widened as if she had revealed a dark secret.

"Don't look so surprised." Catrice forced a laugh. "It's the truth. Even though the king is wrong, it's still the Aetoses' fault he hates our people."

"Why do you think that is?"

Catrice clasped her hands together. It was a story she knew by heart. "The Old Prophets foretold that any future ruler of Whittam had to be ordained by the Creator and anointed by one of His Prophets."

"And Lord Aetos was a Prophet..."

She nodded. "The last that we know of. But he refused to anoint Tenaris. Our people followed his lead, and thousands refused to acknowledge the king's rule, including most of Ontiach and the White District."

"Do you know why?"

"Why what?"

"Your father refused to anoint Tenaris?"

Catrice sighed. "I don't. That's one thing he left out of his portion of the Testimonies."

"Do you think he made the right choice?"

Had he? Catrice paused and studied her hands, which were folded neatly in front of her. "I don't know. I like to think he did, but Tenaris is still king, our people are scattered, and my father is dead."

Blaze chewed his lunch quietly, leaving Catrice's words to fill the silence. Had Father made the right choice? She didn't know. He must have had his reasons, and Mother had trusted him, along with most of the White District. Would he have changed his mind if he could see where they were today? What had happened to their people? What had happened to Mother?

She swallowed the last piece of fish and tossed the paper back into the wagon. It did no good to dwell on questions she didn't have the answers to. It's not like she could ask him. Better to ask questions she knew could be answered.

"How far away is Zradit from here?" Catrice knelt to adjust the buckles on her boots.

"About ten miles." Blaze finished his own filet and wiped his mouth. He lifted the water skin off his chest and over his head before offering it to her. "We'll make it by the end of the day."

Catrice took a swig of the warm liquid and handed the water skin back. "You said you know an inn we can stay at in town? One that's safe?"

He nodded and climbed onto the bench. "I still have some old contacts who owe me a favor or two. It would help if I knew where exactly we were going in the city."

Catrice climbed up next to him and folded her hands in her lap. "You will. When we get there."

"You know... this partnership thing only works if you trust me." He cast her a side-eye.

She met his gaze. She supposed that she did trust him, to an extent. But trust only went so far.

"Well, we're not going to make it to Zradit by tonight if you don't start driving the wagon." She motioned to the field in front of them.

Blaze smiled, holding her gaze with his blue eyes until she looked away. She brushed some dust off her lap and could feel her cheeks flush. She had *never* told anyone the location of a Haven. Mother had drilled that lesson into her from a young age. And she wasn't ready to start now.

I'll wait to tell him until I absolutely have to. At least that way, I'll honor Mother's wishes as much as I can.

She knew it didn't make sense, but the thought brought a measure of peace to her mind.

"Of course. Whatever you say, milady." Blaze flicked the reins and pulled the wagon into the field.

Catrice gripped the bench beneath her, and Blaze yanked the reins as the wagon dipped into a puddle, nearly diverting them off the over-traveled road and into one of the buildings lining the street.

She pulled her cloak tighter around her shoulders and kept her eyes down as they rode further into the city. The sun had set almost an hour earlier, leaving their path lit by the oil lamps perched on posts on either side of the road and the flickering candles spotting the various windowsills they passed.

Despite the darkness, the people of Zradit were anything but asleep. Drunken laughter and scandalous whispers echoed through the alleys and doorways. Shadowy figures skulked by, their dark eyes leering at the wagon as if she and Blaze were the laden table at a feast. Catrice resisted the urge to shiver.

When she and Mother had first moved here after Ontiach was attacked, Zradit had been a thriving metropolis—the crown jewel of the Silver District—but the past decade had apparently given rise to crime and illegal trades. As long as the money flowed, Catrice couldn't imagine Lord Denari cared about much else. He never had before. But his oversight had allowed the Haven here to exist in peace, and for that, she was thankful.

Blaze straightened and leaned toward Catrice, pulling her from her thoughts. "Is the Haven close?"

She nodded. "It's just a few blocks away."

"Which way?"

"Turn right up ahead."

"And after that?"

Catrice shrugged. "I'll tell you then."

A sigh escaped his lips. "You're really going to drag this out as long as you can, aren't you?"

"If there's one thing my mother taught me, it's that you can never be too careful." She turned to him. "I just wish I had listened to her sooner."

A stumbling drunkard careened out of a tavern to their left and slammed into the wagon. The hairs on the back of Catrice's neck stood on end as the drunk slurred profanities in their direction before wandering into the street.

"Perhaps it would be best for us to visit your Haven tomorrow... in the daylight," Blaze whispered.

She raised an eyebrow. "Are you scared, Blaze?"

He cleared his throat. "Not at all. But it wouldn't be the best idea for us to be wandering the alleys of Zradit at this hour."

"It wouldn't be the first time. I used to sneak out and run these streets at dawn when we first moved here." She frowned. "It wasn't this bad back then."

"Yeah, well, things change over time... usually for the worse."

Catrice opened her mouth to respond, but was interrupted by a crash from a dark alley ahead of them, followed by the dull sound of fists hitting flesh as a woman wailed. Catrice whipped her head around, but no one else in the street seemed to respond. She scanned the dark as they passed the alley. The beating stopped, but the soft sniffles proved that whoever was crying a moment earlier still lay in the shadows. The bench beneath her creaked as Catrice shuffled just a few inches closer to Blaze on the seat.

This time he raised an eyebrow. "Are *you* scared, Catrice?"

"What? No." She straightened, her cheeks flushing. "But maybe we should head to the inn you spoke of after all. The Followers are probably already asleep at the Haven now anyway."

Blaze let out an awkward cough as if stifling a chuckle. "Of course."

"So, how far is the inn?"

"Just a few blocks. We'll turn up ahead."

"And after that?"

He glanced at her. "I'll tell you then."

She narrowed her eyes at him. He pulled the scarf over his nose, but it was too late; she had already seen the smile teasing at the corner of his mouth.

They rode further into the city in silence as Blaze directed Ace through the streets.

Turning another corner, the wagon dipped to the side again as one of the front wheels slid into another pothole. Catrice lurched forward at the movement, and Blaze grabbed her elbow, pulling her against his side to keep her from falling off the bench. Their shoulders collided, and she turned, suddenly realizing how close they were. He released her arm slowly, but didn't move away.

The heat returned to her cheeks.

"We're here." He nodded to the building in front of them.

Catrice blinked and followed his gaze. Rowdy conversation and loud music sounded from the swinging doors at the front of the well-lit building. The stench of alcohol and sweaty men radiated from the bustle. Catrice's mouth fell open.

"I thought you said this was an inn."

Blaze shrugged and hopped down from the bench. "Inn. Tavern. Same thing."

He stepped around the back of the wagon and reached out a hand to help her down from the stand. She stared at the tavern and took his hand. Mud splashed onto the hem of her dress as she landed in the puddle. She shook her head.

"I can't go in there."

Blaze furrowed his brow. "Why not?"

"Because I'm a woman."

"And?"

"And it's a tavern. They'll be drunks and thieves."

"Different drunks and thieves than the ones we've been passing for the last hour? You didn't seem to have a problem with taverns when you went to the rebel gathering."

Had he always been this sarcastic? She gave him a look, teasing another chuckle from his lips. "That was different. It was abandoned. And frankly, that didn't turn out too well."

"Don't worry." He led her out of the puddle. "You'll be with me. They won't try anything."

She scoffed. "Because you're a man?"

His gaze hardened. "Because I won't let them."

8

BLAZE

"BY ROYAL DECREE, THE SUCCESSOR OF KING WARREN TENARIS WILL BE CHOSEN FROM AMONG THE HIGH CROWS OF THE SEVEN DISTRICTS. MAY THE FUTURE RULERS OF WHITTAM ALSO COMMAND THE BLACK CROWS AS TO NEVER FALL TO INVADING OR INTERNAL ENEMIES AGAIN." - THE ROYAL ARCHIVES OF WHITTAM

Blaze blinked, slightly taken aback by the seriousness in his own voice. He quickly shook off the unexpected feeling, releasing Catrice's hand. Thankfully, she didn't respond. He had no idea where he would have gone with that conversation.

He grabbed their travel bags out of the back of the wagon and slung them over his shoulder. Moving to the front of the wagon, he grabbed Ace's bridle to lead him to the stable across the street. Catrice followed at his heels.

A scrawny stablehand sat at the front of the stalls, flipping a coin over in his fingers. Blaze whistled, nodding to the horse and wagon behind him. The boy jumped up, his eyes wide.

"How much for the night?" Blaze asked.

"For one horse?" He scratched his head. "Four

coppers. But it'll be extra to guarantee the goods in the wagon."

Blaze dug into his pocket for the coin. "That's fine." He pulled out half a dozen coppers and dropped them into the boy's hand. "This enough?"

The boy smiled and turned away to count the money. A dark stallion in one of the stalls caught Blaze's attention, and he narrowed his eyes. A fine leather saddle lined with bits of silver rested on the stall wall and an engraving of a silver crow stood out on the pommel. Blaze sucked in a breath and bit the inside of his cheek.

"Hey, boy," he called out. "Where's the owner of the black stallion?"

The boy pointed to the tavern across the street. "She went in there earlier today. I'd be careful if you're looking for her, though. I don't mess with those Crows."

Catrice gasped beside him, and Blaze groaned. *Blasts.* He didn't need this. He couldn't risk any Silver Crows blowing his cover.

"Thanks." He turned away as the boy moved to take Ace and the wagon into the stables.

Catrice pulled on the edges of her cloak nervously. "I thought you said this inn was safe," she whispered.

Dark clouds gathered in the distance above the rooftops and a strong gale whipped through the streets, catching Blaze off guard and ruffling his hair.

He adjusted the packs on his shoulder and started across the road.

"It is. Listen, how about you just go straight to the room tonight? If there's a Crow here, they're bound to be downstairs in the tavern. There's a back entrance you can take to avoid the bar. I'll grab the room key from the bartender and meet you upstairs."

Catrice frowned. "You won't be too long, right?"

"Of course. Now come on. Looks like a storm is rolling in." He placed an arm on her shoulder and directed her to the side of the tavern where a wooden staircase was built against the stone wall. He swung the bags off his shoulder and handed them to her. "There's a little common area at the top of the stairs you can wait in. I'll be up soon."

Catrice took the sacks and scampered up the stairs, pausing at the top to glance back at him. Blaze forced a reassuring smile, hoping it would translate to his eyes above the scarf, and she disappeared into the doorway. His smile dropped, and he turned to the front of the tavern.

The doors swung open as he pushed through the entrance. He kept his head down and rested his hand on one of the hidden daggers at his side as he made his way through the tables. Conversations stalled, and the heat of a dozen eyes landed on his back. The bartender stood at the back of the room, drying a glass. Blaze slid onto one of the stools at the bar and pulled another bunch of coppers from his pocket.

"I need a room for the night."

The bartender counted the coin on the bar top and, after nodding, grabbed an iron key from behind the bar and placed it on the counter. Blaze swiped it and tucked the key into his pocket. He mumbled a thank you and turned away, nearly colliding with a woman dressed in all black.

He backed up, his stomach dropping as he stared into Nikita Dali's cool eyes. He should have known it would be her.

"Blaze…" she cooed. "It's been a long time."

He took a deep breath, steeling himself. He scanned the tavern. Aside from a few cautious glances, no one seemed to pay any heed to him now, likely out of fear of catching the eye of the Silver District's High Crow.

Nikita cocked her head to the side, and a strand of fine, silver hair, uncommon even amongst the diversity of Whittam at her young age, fell over her shoulder.

"The black crow flies," she spoke.

"And nothing escapes its sight," Blaze responded. He swallowed. It was too late to turn and run upstairs now.

She took a seat on the stool beside him and leaned back against the counter. "I heard you were in my district. Thought I'd stop by and say hello." The black mask covered half her face and set off her clear, alabaster skin, but Blaze could imagine a knowing smile that didn't quite reach her eyes hiding beneath the cloth. She raised an open hand toward him in a questioning gesture. "Well, aren't you going to say hello?"

He cleared his throat and dodged her gaze, settling back on the stool behind him instead. "How'd you know I'd be here?"

Nikita dropped her hand. "You're predictable, Blaze. You've stopped at this tavern every time we traveled through the Silver District."

"I like consistency."

"Huh," she laughed. "I guess you could call it that." Nikita motioned to the bartender behind her. He placed two tankards of warm ale on the counter, and she grabbed one. "How are things in the Onyx District?"

Blaze calculated his answer. Nikita never wasted time with small talk. She was searching for something else, and he didn't like not knowing what it was. He mimicked her relaxed posture and took the other drink from the bar top. Two could play this game.

"Same as always. Lord Grener remains too preoccupied with his new building projects and chasing young skirts to run things. But that's why we're here, right?" He raised his tankard to her.

"Tell me about it." She clinked her cup against his. "Denari delegates the law enforcement to my Crows, and we've run most of the rebels out of the district, but I feel like there's another Rogue every time I turn a corner. Commander Tenaris should just extend the conscription length another four years. I know bounty hunting isn't illegal, but there's too many young Crows getting out too soon and trying to make their own way with the skills *we* taught them."

"I remember a time you thought about joining the Rogues when your term was up."

Nikita chuckled. "Yeah, when I was a child. I'm in this for life now." She glanced down at her drink, her voice taking on a serious tone. "It's my family. Who knows, I may even be the next Commander."

Blaze bit his tongue to keep himself from making a bitter remark. He would sooner become a Follower than see Nikita on the throne. He placed his untouched ale on the counter. "So, why are you really here, Nikita?"

She raised her shoulder, eyes gleaming, and the coy countenance returned. "What? We can't just catch up for old times sake? When was the last time we worked together? Our last assignment was the Baron of..." she mused.

"...of Gettings, yes," he finished her sentence and stiffened as memories from that day rose to his mind. Nikita knew better than to bring that up.

She clicked her tongue. "Of course, our final mission with Izaak. See, now that's why I don't work with you anymore. The mortality rate is just too high."

Blaze gritted his teeth. How *dare* she talk about his brother.

Nikita patted him on the thigh, and her touch set his nerves on edge. He resisted the urge to pull away.

Almost as if she could read his mind, she gave it a little squeeze. "That has to have been two years ago already. I thought you would have quit after that. But now here we are, both High Crows of our own districts. How time flies..."

Blaze grabbed her wrist, pulling her hand off his leg. The game was over. "What do you want, Nikita?"

She glanced at her captive hand, and he knew the sly smirk rested just beneath her mask again. "Who said I wanted anything?"

"You always want something." He set his jaw and lowered his eyebrows.

She pulled her arm back, breaking his grip. "And you always knew me best, Blaze. Besides Izaak, you were the only one I could never beat, too. I always blamed it on you being Commander Tenaris's son, but now I can see you're quite fine on your own." Her gaze roamed over his body, setting his nerves on edge.

"I still report to the Commander."

"Ah, yes. The favored one. No, wait. That was Izaak. I guess you're all that's left though," she needled.

"What do you want, Nikita?" he repeated himself before she could continue.

She was baiting him. Controlling the conversation like she did everything. Trying to get him to react. And he hated it.

She sighed. "You're no fun. You know that, Blaze?"

He waited. She rolled her eyes.

"Fine." She leaned forward and clasped her drink with both hands. "But you answer my question first. What brings you to the Silver District?"

"I'm on a mission, Nikita. But I'm assuming you already know that."

"Really?" She feigned surprise. "What kind of mission would call for you to be out of uniform? Undercover?"

He pressed his lips together.

"Come on, Blaze. We're friends, right? If the Commander trusts one of us, it's definitely me." She swirled her drink. "After all, I'm not the one who got his favorite Crow killed."

That was enough. Blaze lurched from his seat, causing the stool to screech across the floor behind him and crash into the bar.

Dozens of eyes landed on him again, and the rowdy chaos of the room fell to a low hum. Even the small band in the corner stopped playing to stare at the common merchant who dared challenge a Crow. His fingernails pricked into the soft skin of his palm as he balled his hands into fists.

Nikita reclined in her seat, unamused. She took a breath and placed her drink back on the counter.

"By all of Whittam, calm down." She waved a finger at the band, and they picked up their music again. "I'm here on an assignment from the

Commander too. I received a message from him earlier today. He wanted me to check in on you for an update on your progress. Apparently, whatever you have going on is pretty big."

Blaze set his jaw. Father had sicked Nikita on him? He wasn't a child who needed watching. He could handle this on his own.

Nikita eyed him. "I thought you were with Gideon in the Amber District hunting a new group of rebels. Why are you here now?"

"There were... developments."

"What kind of developments?"

He hesitated. Nikita let out an overexaggerated sigh. "Come on. I can help you if you let me. A mission for one Crow is a mission for us all. You know that."

Blaze unclenched his fists. Leave it to Nikita to spout off brotherly philosophy about the Crows like she wouldn't stab him in the back for a shot at being the next Commander. But, then again, he would do the same. And if Father wanted an update, Blaze would be happy to oblige. He was fine with Nikita singing his praises to the Commander. He lifted the stool off the ground and sat again.

"I found the Aetos family," he said under his breath.

Nikita's eyes widened. "Marcus's wife and child? Where were they?"

"In Deln in the Amber District. They've been moving around since the attack on Ontiach. Planting

Havens and smuggling copies of the Testimonies across the country. Even managed to set up a thriving base right under your nose here in Zradit." He resisted the urge to smile as unchecked shock registered across Nikita's face. She quickly regained her composure.

"That's impossible."

Blaze shrugged. "Vivian is dead, and Catrice is taking me there tomorrow."

Nikita whipped her head around to study the tavern. "She's here?"

"Waiting for me upstairs."

She stood. "Why don't you just take her in now? The Commander would execute her for treason. We could eliminate the last of the most influential Follower family tonight. The Aetoses would no longer pose a threat to the throne."

"And give up the chance to find the dozens of Havens across the country? Come now, Nikita." He ran a finger over the rim of his drink. "Besides, the Commander wouldn't kill her. She'll have a fair trial. Even you know the Followers and rebels would just use the Aetoses' execution as another excuse to rebel, and my father is smarter than that. We have to uproot these people from within."

"And you think *you're* the one to do that?"

Blaze flashed her a smile. "Catrice is starting to trust me. I can use that to my advantage."

Nikita scrutinized him. "Sounds like something the Commander would say."

"I'll take that as a compliment."

"Fine." Nikita adjusted the silver pin across her neck. "I'll report back to Commander Tenaris with your status, but I want to know the location of the Haven tomorrow. I can't have those cultists in my district."

Blaze nodded. "You can trail behind us in the morning. I'll leave a message for you after I confirm the location." He paused, holding her gaze. "But you'll stay away from Catrice."

"Of course." For a moment, it looked like she actually cared. "Now, you better run upstairs before she starts to miss you. The last thing I need is for you to screw up another mission."

The moment was gone.

She sidestepped him, swiped her drink from the bar top, and sauntered towards the tavern's back door.

"And Nikita," Blaze called out after her. She turned and glanced up at him innocently. "This is my mission. Anything else you find, you report to me."

Whether Nikita would listen to him or not was unpredictable, but she would respect the Commander's orders. She was the perfect Crow in that regard. She smiled again, bowed her head ever so slightly, and disappeared out the door.

9

CATRICE

"SAGE, COUNSEL, JUDGMENT, INSIGHT, SEER, AND WONDERS. THESE ARE THE SIX GIFTS OF THE CREATOR, DESIGNED FOR HIS PEOPLE TO EDIFY EACH OTHER AND BRING HIM GLORY." - TESTIMONY OF PROPHET LEVI JADAN

Catrice rolled a loose thread hanging off the end of her cloak between her fingers and stared at the door. The dimly lit common area sat at the end of a hallway between two doors. One was the door she had entered through from outside, while the other, based on the loud music echoing through the walls, led to the bar downstairs. More doors marked with carved numbers one through seven lined the rest of the hallway and remained closed. Two oil lamps next to rooms three and six flickered silently. So far, no one else had entered the small space, and she prayed it would remain that way until Blaze came up.

She repositioned herself in the cushioned chair. The piece of furniture was pitifully low on stuffing and, no matter which way she wiggled, one of the wooden bridges underneath her seat managed to attack her tailbone. Blaze should have been here by now. After another unsuccessful readjustment left her behind sore, she huffed and stood. The bags stacked at her feet toppled when she moved, and she shoved them under the chair. She focused on the door in front of her.

It had been too long. Something must have happened. What if he ran into the Crow? What if a fight broke out and he was injured? What if he decided this wasn't worth the trouble and left? She had basically asked him to help her do the same. Her heart raced in her chest as the possibilities continued to swirl in her head, each one worse than the last.

She shook her head in an attempt to clear the intrusive thoughts. She needed to calm down, but in order to do so, she needed to put her worries to rest.

"Come now, Catrice," she whispered to herself. "Blaze is just downstairs. Probably getting something to eat or talking to the innkeeper... or barkeeper... whoever runs this place."

With the little bit of mustered-up courage that thought gave her, she reached for the handle and twisted it, wincing at the creak from the rusty hinge. There was no point in turning back now. She took a deep breath, stepped forward, and yanked the door open, nearly squealing when she spotted Blaze standing on the other side, arm extended as if reaching for the handle. He raised an eyebrow at her.

"Everything fine?" he asked.

Catrice released the knob and stepped back, willing her heart to slow its racing in her chest. "Yeah, everything's fine. You just took so long... I thought something might have happened."

Blaze walked through the doorway and closed the door behind him. He shook his head. "No. The barback was just extra chatty tonight. Wanted to know how much I'd be willing to trade for a crate of Trium pastries."

"Oh." Catrice bit her lip. "What'd you tell him?"

"I said I don't move fresh goods. They spoil too quickly on the road."

"Ah, that explains the stale rolls we've been gnawing on for the last four days."

Blaze chuckled. "Yeah. I was supposed to offload those near the border of the Onyx District."

"I'm sorry you didn't get to." Catrice frowned. "You must have lost quite a bit of coin."

He tilted his head, looking down at her. "Some things are more important."

Her eyes widened, and she turned away as her cheeks grew hot, chastising herself for her easy embarrassment. He meant finding the Haven and reuniting with their people. Clearly. That was the obvious answer. Before she could respond, he stepped past her, metal key in hand.

"This is the key to our room. Number, uh..." He glanced at the leather tag hanging from the end of it. "Five."

Catrice swallowed. "*Our* room?"

He nodded. "I'm saving my coppers. I can sell some goods at a market tomorrow after we stop at the Haven, but I figured it would be a good idea to budget what I have left in case I can't find one... if that's fine with you."

"Of course." Catrice blinked. That was perfectly logical. A wise, prudent decision. Then why was her stomach tying itself into knots? "That makes sense."

She dropped to her knees and retrieved the bags she had shoved underneath the chair. Gripping them in her arms, she strutted down the hall to room number five. Blaze trailed behind her with the key, and she let out a slow breath, willing her cheeks to cool down.

Sleeping outside under the stars was one thing. Staying in the same room was another she hadn't expected. In many ways, Blaze was still a stranger, and she resented how easily he flustered her. It's not like she had never spent time with a boy before. But traveling together? Staying in the same room? Mother would have never allowed it. But Mother would've never allowed her to trust Blaze in the first place either. Guilt settled in her chest, and she frowned.

Blaze jammed the key in the lock and turned, releasing a single *click* as the door unlocked. He pulled it open, and Catrice peeked her head in the room, nearly falling over in relief when she saw two separate beds. At least now she wouldn't have to sleep on the floor.

She stepped forward before she could second-guess herself and glanced at the bed directly in front of the entrance. An identical bed lay underneath the single window, through which the moon cast cool light into the room. The door clicked behind her as it closed, and the knots in her stomach tightened.

They were alone.

Like, *really* alone.

Blaze wandered over to the window as Catrice plopped the bags in front of the single dresser, which separated the beds, and chose the one closest to the door. A cold fireplace dominating the wall adjacent to her bed had fresh firewood piled inside. Unlit candles in tarnished candlesticks were scattered across the hearth and dresser, and the small desk next to the door sported more candles, a cracked mirror, and a wash basin.

The room was simple, but it was more than she had lived with for the last two years. In an odd way, it felt luxurious, and the guilt returned. Did she even deserve this while Mother lay rotting somewhere? Did she even deserve this after what she had done; after she had considered leaving her people? She swallowed the bit of bile that rose in her throat at the thought and shook her thoughts away.

The bed's straw mattress bent under her weight as she sat. She pulled her cloak closer as a shiver ran up her spine. The sun had set several hours prior, and the foggy window Blaze stared out of proved it would be a cold night. Just as the thought entered her head, thunder clapped above them and she jumped. The moonlight faded as soft raindrops pelted the glass pane and the roof above them. Blaze turned to the center of the room.

"I'll get the fire going. You should make yourself comfortable for the night." He moved to the fireplace and grabbed a piece of flint from the top of the hearth.

Catrice focused on unpacking the few belongings she would need for their stay as Blaze struck the flint against a dagger he had pulled from his side over the wood. She paused and watched him with the tools. Did he always keep that knife on him? From what she had heard, a Crow could have up to a dozen different blades on them at one time. How many other weapons lay hidden within the folds of his clothes?

She turned away, unbuckled her boots, and placed them at the foot of her bed. Blaze wasn't a Crow anymore. He traveled for a living. It was only practical that he had some kind of weapon with him in case of bandits on the road. At least that's the best answer she could come up with to dispel the anxiety that had gripped her at the sight of the blade.

Sparks crackled behind her, and the warm glow of fire settled over her back. She took a deep breath in and tried to relax. What mattered was that they had made it. They were safe. And tomorrow, she would be with her people. Their people.

Blaze stood from where he was blowing into the wood and backed up from the fireplace, admiring his work as the flames grew. Catrice grabbed one of the candlesticks from the dresser and brought it close to the fire. She eyed his dagger as he slipped it back to his side, hiding it from view. The candle's wick caught quickly and she cupped the flame with her other hand.

"Thank you," she said. "I never could start a fire that fast. Mother would make me practice on the road when we'd move towns—" the image of Mother waving goodbye in the kitchen the day of the rebel gathering interrupted her thoughts. Catrice had never told her the truth about where she and Tay were going. She had thought she'd have the opportunity to later that night. She sucked in a breath and blinked back tears. "...but I never got the hang of it."

Blaze folded his arms and leaned against the stone frame of the hearth. "Why did you stay?"

Catrice swallowed and tried to focus on what Blaze was asking. Better that than the blood-splattered room lingering in the back of her mind. "What do you mean?"

"You and your mother. Why did you stay in Whittam? I'm sure you could have found sanctuary over the mountains in Fathing." He nodded to the burning wood. "Maybe even work on your fire-making skills."

"My fire-making skills are perfectly fine, thank

you. You just do it so much better." She forced herself to smile. She didn't want to talk about this. "I think Mother hoped the day would come when we didn't have to hide anymore. She used to say the Creator would lead us to our next steps when the time comes, but for now, our duty was to our people and making sure they had access to their history and the Testimonies so they wouldn't forget what the Creator has done."

"You haven't spoken much about her."

Catrice bit the inside of her cheek and turned back to the bed. Why was he bringing this up? "I don't see the need to. She's gone, and the best thing I can do is continue our work." She set the candlestick on the dresser and sat down.

Blaze was silent for a moment, and she hoped he would stay that way. She didn't want to talk about Mother. She had enough guilt building in her chest already. He walked to his bed and sat facing her.

"You know," he began. "When my mother died and my father left, I didn't want to talk about it either."

Catrice scoffed. "Yeah, well, you were also eight. And you had Izaak and Diana. I don't think it's quite the same." The harshness in her words pricked at her heart, and she bit her tongue. "I'm sorry. That's not what I meant."

"No, you're right." Blaze removed his scarf and set it on the dresser. He leaned back against the wall at the head of his bed, propping a leg up on the mattress while the other hung over the edge. "It's not the same, but it was still hard. At least you had all these years with your mom. I hardly remember mine." He shrugged. "But maybe it's better that way."

Catrice pulled her knees up to her chest. She wrapped her arms around them and rested her chin on top. "I remember her."

"What?"

"She used to bake fresh honey rolls before each of our Fellowships. The sweet scent would fill up the entire living area as my father read through the Testimonies. Sometimes she'd even sneak us a few pieces before we were done with the readings."

"You remember that?" Blaze's eyes were soft and vulnerable, unlike Catrice could remember ever seeing them before.

"Of course. I mean it's probably because I thought I'd starve to death before the meetings ended and your mother was sent from the Creator to bring sweet sustenance in my five-year-old mind, but..." Catrice trailed off, and Blaze let out a low chuckle. She found herself laughing along, and the heaviness in her chest lightened. "I always thought you had her smile."

"Most people would say I favor my father."

A flash of lightning lit up the small room, and thunder clapped above them again. Catrice tilted her head to the side. "Did you ever find out where he went? What happened to him?"

Blaze hesitated, and the softness in his eyes disappeared, replaced with the same cool, neutral edge that had masked his features for the last few days. "He was a soldier. He joined the army during the Orikan War after my mother was killed. I guess you could say he wanted to avenge her."

"Oh. Did you ever reconnect? Is he still alive?"

"No." Blaze looked away. "My father died in the war a long time ago."

"I'm sorry." Catrice relaxed her arms and let her feet drop back to the floor. She wanted to say something else, but everything she came up with felt trivial at the moment. "I guess we're both orphans, then."

Blaze sniffed and straightened. "It's getting late. We should get some rest for tomorrow."

Catrice frowned but didn't object. He was right. She rolled over and pulled the worn quilt back, slipping under the covers. Bits of straw sticking out of the stuffed pillow tickled her nose and she resisted the urge to sneeze. The sweet, woody smell was faint but reminded her of the stables in Deln and long talks with Tay. How was he? Had he made it back home safely after the rebel gathering? Was he thinking about her as well? She pulled the quilt over her shoulders and snuggled closer to the pillow, pushing away the unanswered questions and closing her eyes as Blaze continued to move around behind her.

They would have a long day tomorrow, and she dreaded breaking the news to the Haven about Mother. They would take it hard. Mother had been a matriarchal figure to the Followers for as long as she could remember. Would they look to her now that Mother was gone? The heaviness returned and settled in her gut at the thought of filling those shoes. She doubted they would if they knew she had tried to run just a few days earlier. Would they even welcome her after hearing it was her fault Mother was dead?

"Goodnight, Catrice." Blaze's voice broke through her thoughts and the constant pitter-patter of the rain.

She didn't move, feigning sleep. Mother would never have trusted Blaze with the location of one of the Havens. She had rarely trusted anyone. But if she and Mother had had someone to watch over them—someone to come alongside them in their work or protect them like the rebels—then maybe she would still be alive. Lightning lit up the room again, flashing the back of her eyelids a bright red, and a deep rumble from the heavens shook the building. For once, she hoped Mother had it wrong and trusting Blaze wouldn't be a mistake.

ALL THINGS CONSIDERED, Zradit was rather pleasant in the daylight. Catrice sidestepped a murky pothole like the one that had nearly knocked her off the wagon seat the night before in the bustling street. An early morning market boasting hundreds of vendors lined either side of the road; it was full of exotic foods and cultures and reminded her of Deln. Blaze had opted to leave his horse and wagon at the stable for the morning while they searched for the Haven.

After they found it, Blaze would return to the market to sell some of his goods. If they were smart, the funds he earned could last them for the next several weeks—at least, that's what Blaze had said.

Despite their need to be careful with their coin, Blaze had given a few coppers to Catrice in case anything caught her eye at the market. Her purse sat low on the back of her hip, hanging around the belt slung over her dress but under her cloak. Blaze had suggested she tuck it out of sight, just as his pouch was hidden under his cloak. There were too many greedy eyes and wandering hands in the crowd.

A tall shoulder collided with her own, knocking her off balance and into the puddle she had so carefully avoided a moment before. Her brown boots sunk into the muddy water and splashed dark droplets and soggy leaves onto her stockings and tied-up skirt. Blaze placed a hand on her elbow and gently led her out of the slippery ditch.

"You all right?" he asked.

Catrice sighed and brushed bits of mud off her front. "I'm starting to wish I had more than two changes of clothes. These are my only pair of stockings, and I'm down to one clean dress now."

Blaze peeled a wet leaf from the puddle off her arm

and shrugged. "That's what your coin is for. If you don't see anything now, we can visit a few more shops this morning. I'm sure there's someplace nearby where we can wash and hang the clothes to dry, or at least pick up some new ones."

"No." She shook her head. "It's fine. I just want to make it to the Haven."

"Catrice," Blaze tilted his head towards her. "It's good to rest a little. We've been traveling for five days straight."

"I've gone longer. Really, I'm fine." Catrice walked forward, leaving Blaze to trail behind her in the crowd. She didn't need to rest. She needed to find the Haven. Then she would be with her people. She would be safe, and everything would be fine again.

Bright, colorful fabrics to the right caught her eye as the scent of sweet incense drifted from one of the stalls before her. If they had been here under other circumstances, she would have loved to slowly wander the booths, taking her time to admire each piece of art or taste each baked treat that even now made her mouth water. She and Mother had never had the funds to do anything like that in Deln. Any extra coin had gone toward materials for the Testimonies. Maybe she would be able to enjoy such things now with the Zradit Haven. She felt a twinge of guilt. How could she think of enjoying herself when Mother never would again?

"So…" Blaze said from behind her. "Are you going to tell me where we're going yet?"

Catrice pivoted as a large family rushed by, careful not to bump shoulders with any of them and fall into yet another puddle. "You'll know soon enough."

"Fine. Can you at least tell me how far it is?"

She scanned the buildings around them. Her eyes searched the stone walls and what little she could see of the alleyways between the stalls. "Not far."

"That is not helpful."

"You asked."

Blaze stepped beside her. "Do you even know where we're going?"

Catrice hesitated and stared at the dirt between her feet. *Not exactly.* Blaze groaned at her lack of response. He pulled her off to the side of the street between two booths.

"Are you serious?" he asked.

"Everything looks so different now. They didn't even have this market when my mother and I lived here."

Blaze rubbed his hand over his face. "Do you know what road it was on? Any landmarks we could search for?"

"I know the general location of where it was in town. It has to be around here somewhere. And usually, the Havens are marked."

"With what?"

Catrice hesitated again. The dove was one of the

sacred symbols of her people. Blaze should remember it. And if he didn't, she wasn't prepared to share it yet.

Blaze leaned one arm against the wall beside him. His eyes held her own. "Catrice, you have to start trusting me if we're going to do this."

She dropped her gaze. Did she? They had made it this far without her giving up all her secrets. Why was he pushing for more?

She drifted her gaze to the stall behind Blaze. Wood carvings decorated the small booth and hung from the edges of the tent. A faint memory of a man carving something into a door frame flickered to the front of Catrice's mind, and she walked past Blaze.

An older man sat in the back of the booth with a large straw hat flopped over his features. In his hands was an unfinished block of wood and a carving knife scraping away at the piece. Among the wooden ornaments dangling above the table was the image of a small dove with its wings outstretched in flight. Catrice's heart pounded as she pointed to the bird and struggled to catch a fleeting memory of an old Follower code.

"How much is this one?"

The man tipped his hat up and glanced at her. "That one's not for sale."

Catrice smiled. "Because it's a free gift?"

His hands froze at her words, and he stood slowly. He glanced at Blaze beside her and lowered his voice. "Are you together?"

"Yes." Catrice nodded. "He's with me."

The man gestured behind him. "This way."

He stepped out the back of the booth and into the alley. Catrice glanced around, a nervous energy building within her, before following. Blaze stayed close to her side.

"What's going on?" he whispered

"I think we just found the Haven." Catrice's voice was giddy with excitement, and she struggled to keep it low in the small alleyway. She had done it. They'd made it.

The man stopped at one of doors carved into the building's wall. Above the entrance, the same image of a dove was carved into the stone. He rapped his knuckles against the wood in a rhythmic pattern, and the sound of scurrying footsteps could be heard on the other side before the door creaked open. An older woman peered through the opening and smiled when she saw the man.

"Tali, it's me. And I have two friends with me," he whispered.

The woman pulled the door back and ushered the three of them inside. Catrice entered a large living space furnished with a long table on one end and dozens of chairs and cushions scattered throughout the room. A short wall divided a third of the room into a kitchen area furnished with a fireplace, wash basin, and cupboards. Curtained windows dotted the stone walls and several lamps spaced strategically throughout the room lit the open area and casted a warm glow that reflected off the ceiling. A pile of scrolls and bundled parchment sat in a basket against the wall, and a few lay sprawled out across the table. Children's laughter echoed from behind a door on the other side of the room and added a sense of joy to the already comforting space. The woman moved behind the wall into the kitchen and returned with a steaming kettle and three mugs as the man shut the door behind them.

"Welcome, welcome," she said as she set the items on the table and pushed the open scrolls away. "I apologize for the mess. We weren't expecting anyone this morning. Fellowship doesn't start until later tonight." She brushed a tight, dark curl from her round face and motioned for them to sit. "I'm Tali, and you've already met Wyatt."

The older man tipped his hat again at the mention of his name. Catrice paused. They hadn't recognized her yet. What would they do when they did? Tali's kind face triggered a faint sense of familiarity, and Mother had mentioned both of their names before, but it had been so long since she had been here.

"It's so nice to be here again." Catrice placed her hands on the back of a chair at the table. "My mother always spoke well of you and this Haven."

Tali raised her eyebrows in an unspoken question and Catrice's cheeks flushed. She shouldn't be this nervous. These were her people. She could trust them.

"I'm so sorry. We haven't even introduced ourselves." She motioned to herself and Blaze. "This is Blaze Laskaris, and I'm Catrice Aetos."

Tali's mouth fell open, and she lowered herself to a seat across from Catrice. "Of course. I'm surprised I didn't see it sooner. My, how you've grown! You look just like your mother." She smiled and glanced around the room. "Where is Vivian?"

A lump formed in Catrice's throat, and her stomach knotted again as the guilt returned. "That's, um... that's actually why I'm here."

What would they do when she told them what happened? When they learned it was her fault? She squeezed her fingers in her lap and took a deep breath, but the words fell silent on her dry tongue.

After a few awkward moments, Blaze spoke up from behind her. "Vivian is dead."

Because of me.

The smile dropped from Tali's face and Wyatt grunted under his breath.

They know.

"Oh, no," Tali muttered. She shifted her gaze to Catrice. "What happened?"

"The Crows attacked our home five days ago. My mother was alone," Catrice forced the words out.

"I'm so sorry." Tali hesitated and furrowed her brow. "But I don't understand. Vivian was always so careful. How did they find you?"

They know it's my fault.

"I—" Catrice froze. Her heartbeat pounded in her ears. These were her people. Fellow Followers. What was she afraid of? They had always been loyal to the Aetos family.

Will they still be loyal when they find out I'm the reason Mother is dead?

"I don't know." She turned her head, avoiding Tali's gaze, and caught Blaze casting her a curious look out of the corner of her eye. She swallowed and raised her chin. They didn't need to know. Just like they didn't know she had almost abandoned them. "But if it wasn't for Blaze, they would have found me too. He saved me."

"Praise the Creator, you're safe, then." Tali paused, seemingly buying the story. Catrice breathed a sigh of relief. "I didn't expect to lose such a dear friend as Vivian so soon. May the Creator welcome her into His arms." Tali glanced at Blaze. "Thank you, son. Do you follow the Creator, then?"

Blaze shifted where he stood beside Catrice. "My mother did, and after she died in the Orikan War, my aunt raised me and my brother."

"Blaze lived in Ontiach before we were attacked." Catrice reached for one of the ceramic mugs and Tali leaned forward to pour steaming tea into the cup. At least they weren't talking about her anymore. "After that, he was lost for a while, but he wants to reconnect with our people."

"It's a miracle you both made it out alive, then. We

lost a great many brothers and sisters that day." Tali offered a mug to Blaze, but he held out a hand to decline it.

"Are you from Ontiach, too?" Blaze asked.

"Oh, no. I've lived in Zradit my whole life. When we heard about the first attack, I opened my home to those needing sanctuary. So few actually made it here." She poured herself a cup of tea and returned the pot to the table. "When Catrice and Vivian arrived, and we realized we would receive no aid from Lord Denari, we saved up some coin to buy this building so we could continue Fellowships and provide sanctuary to refugees or anyone who needed it. We converted the front of it into Wyatt's wood shop as a cover. My girls and I live just a block away, but we spend most of our time here now." Tali sat down and cupped the mug in her hands, casting a motherly glance at Catrice. "You are welcome to stay with us as long as you need."

Catrice took a deep breath and sat across from Tali. "Thank you. If it wasn't for the Havens, I would have nowhere to go." Except fleeing the country. Which she had wanted to do. She bit the inside of her cheek and nodded to the scrolls laid out on the table and piled in the corner. "I see you have some partials of the Testimonies here."

"Yes. Mostly copies of some of the Old Prophets and your father's recordings. We share passages during Fellowship, but we're still missing quite a bit, and we've lost some portions simply to wear and tear.

I was going to reach out to Vivian in a few weeks about sending us new copies."

Catrice perked up, straightening her back. Maybe there was a way she could help after all. She would have a purpose. A reason to stay. "I can help fill in the gaps. I've spent the last ten years memorizing and copying the Testimonies."

"Really?" Tali's smile returned. "That would be such a blessing."

"It will take me a few days to go through the portions you have and fill in the missing pieces. Then, after that, I can start making more copies of the whole Testimonies." Catrice paused, blushing. She was getting ahead of herself. "If that's all right with you, of course."

Tali leaned back in her seat, observing Catrice with a content expression. "Hmm. You have your mother's spirit. I know she would be so proud of you."

Catrice's chest tightened. "That's all I want."

"You're an Aetos, my dear. And a Follower. You are welcome to stay as long as you like. The other Havens will need to know where to reach out for their Testimonies now. I'm assuming you know how to contact them all?"

"Yes, of course. You don't?"

Tali shook her head. "Vivian thought it would be best if no one else knew the locations of all the Havens. That way, even if one was discovered by the king, the others would remain safe. If we needed to contact another Haven or send something to them, we always went through your mother."

"I didn't know that." Catrice frowned.

That couldn't be right. Their people should be connected. But surely Mother had known what she was doing. After all, the Havens had stayed relatively hidden and safe for a reason. She knew Mother had often worked late into the night on letters to send with smugglers and projects she had said she didn't want to bother Catrice with, but had she really taken all that on herself? She had done so much to keep their people safe. She had given up so much.

And now she was gone.

Who would that responsibility fall to now?

Wyatt slapped his knee and stretched his arms above his head, startling Catrice from her spiraling thoughts. "Well, I'm in. I have some clean parchment and ink in the back of the shop. One of my boys can watch the booth out front for a bit."

Catrice smiled and took a long drink of her tea. "Thank you so much."

She heard Blaze step forward behind her. She turned her head to see him grab the back of her chair and lean against it.

"What time does the morning market close?" he asked.

Wyatt scratched his beard. "Usually around midday. We have a couple of hours."

Blaze furrowed his eyebrows, and Catrice placed a

hand on his arm. "You can go. We'll start on the Testimonies here, and you can come back when you're done." He nodded, and she turned to Tali. "Blaze is a merchant. He's going to sell some of his goods at the market."

"Of course." Tali nodded and waved to Blaze. "I'm assuming I'll see you back here for Fellowship tonight?"

Blaze pursed his lips. "Will there be enough room for us with everyone else? I wouldn't want to impose."

"Oh, yes. It's no trouble. We have about thirty come every week. It's a little tight, but we always make room."

He smiled. "Then I'll be here. Thank you for your hospitality."

Wyatt grunted and adjusted his hat. "I'll walk you out." He opened the door for Blaze and the two moved into the alley, closing the door behind them.

Tali stood and poked her head through the door leading to the front of the shop. "Gleena, Rey! Clean up your toys and come help your mother!" she called out.

The laughter morphed into happy squeals, followed by the pitter-patter of running feet as the children darted through the shop on the other side of the wall.

Tali shook her head and planted her hands on her hips. "My girls are at the age where they do everything at high speed and then crash into tired tantrums at the end of the day. We don't get too many new faces around here anymore, so I'm sorry if they crawl all over you."

Catrice laughed. "I don't mind. My father used to call me his little whirlwind. Probably because our house looked like a storm had rolled through every time Blaze and his brother and I had to play inside."

Tali retrieved her mug and the tea kettle from the table. "That sounds like something my husband would have said." She reached for Catrice's mug.

Catrice handed her the dish and frowned. "May I ask what happened to him?"

"Same thing that's happened to a lot of us." She stacked the cups and made her way back into the kitchen. She paused at the sink as sorrow overcame her expression. "We lost our son. He was three years old. And after that, my husband lost himself. Started doubting the Creator and His ways. He didn't think the risks were worth it. It was hard, but I was determined to stick it out. Then one day, I woke up, and he was gone."

"I'm so sorry." Even as the words left Catrice's mouth, they felt flat, but it was all she could think to say.

Tali returned the kettle to the hearth and placed the dishes in the sink. She brushed her hands off on the front of her dress and sighed. "We've all lost something, but the Haven supports me, and the Creator takes care of me. It's tougher for the girls. I still pray he'll find his way back to the Creator."

"Do you think he will?"

"I hope so. Loss can change someone; it was his choice to walk away, but the Creator always waits with open arms. No matter how far gone we think someone might be. Even the king could change his ways if he wanted to."

Catrice adjusted her position in her seat. "I don't know about that."

Tali narrowed her eyes. "Be careful."

"Of what?" She crossed her arms.

"Hate. It can change someone just as much as, if not more than, loss can. The difference is we have no control over our losses, but we do over our hate."

"Seems like the king has a lot of hate towards our people."

Tali nodded. "Yes, and that hate came from his own loss."

"What do you mean?"

"He lost his wife. Some would say at the fault of the Followers. The king doesn't know the Creator, and so he doesn't know the healing the Creator can provide." She paused and tilted her head toward Catrice. "'The grace I am given is as endless as the Great North. As numerous as the Trium leaves. How, then, could I withhold the same from others?'"

Of course, she would quote a Testimony verse. Catrice couldn't argue with that. "From the Testimony of the Prophet Presyn Aetos. Year 942." She uncrossed her arms and slouched in her seat. "I can see why my mother liked you."

Tali winked at her. "Your mother was a smart woman, and an excellent judge of character." She pulled out an armful of scrolls from the basket and set them on the table. "Now, let's get started."

IO

BLAZE

"IN THE ANOCICAN YEAR 1126, ON THE
22ND DAY OF THE 8TH MONTH, THE
COUNCIL OF SEVEN APPROVED THE
STATIONING OF BLACK CROWS
THROUGHOUT THEIR DISTRICTS TO CARRY
OUT THE WILL OF THE THRONE." - THE
ROYAL ARCHIVES OF WHITTAM

Blaze counted the coppers as he dropped them into the leather pouch. The morning market had all but disappeared from the street around him. The few remaining merchants were packing up their booths while the last customers wandered off with full arms and heavy packs slung over their shoulders. He dropped the last coin into the pouch and pulled the drawstring tight, testing the weight in his hand.

It would be close, but it should last the next few weeks; hopefully, enough time for Catrice to reveal the location of the rest of the Havens. When she and Tali had discussed contacting them all, he had resisted the urge to laugh. He wouldn't even have to travel to the other districts. Catrice would hand over the locations and Elders of the Havens on a silver platter. It was too easy.

He secured the purse to his side and turned to the wagon and the waiting horse behind him. Ace would have an easier time pulling the wagon now that there would only be their bags and a few crates full of food and basic supplies in the bed.

Judging by the sun beating down on his uncovered neck, it had been a couple hours since he left the Haven, and Catrice would be waiting for him. He removed his green scarf from his back pocket and dabbed the sweat beading his forehead. The wagon's bench creaked as he gripped the edge, readying himself to climb up.

"Leaving so soon?" The familiar voice sounded behind him, and he sighed.

Blasts.

He released the bench and shoved the scarf into his pocket again. Rolling his head to the side, he cast an unamused look at Nikita. She had been trailing him all morning, but Wyatt had stuck by his side through most of the market. Now he was finally alone, and impatience and eagerness shone through her steel eyes as she approached.

"Aren't you forgetting something?" she asked, arms outstretched at her sides.

She was in casual garb—a loose gray blouse and fitted black trousers. Most women wore skirts or dresses when out of their Crow uniform, but Nikita was never one for following tradition. Her silver locks were pulled from her bare face in a long braid, save a few wispy tendrils around her ears, giving her a youthful, innocent aura. The only item on her person validating her position as a High Crow was the black and silver ring wrapped around the first finger on her right hand; at a distance, it could easily be mistaken for an ordinary band.

If he passed her in a crowd, he almost wouldn't give her a second thought, let alone assume she was the deadliest figure in the Silver District, which was the point. The traditional Crow garb and mask were iconic for a reason; when not wearing it, Crows could easily blend into crowds and complete covert missions without being recognized. But he knew, underneath the folds of plain fabric and carefully plaited hair, there were hidden blades Nikita could pull out at a moment's notice.

The measure of comfort his own concealed weapons normally gave him was gone.

"The black crow flies." Blaze crossed his arms. If nothing else, he could make her follow proper procedure.

She dropped her hands to her sides and shifted her jaw. Good. He liked getting under her skin. "And all fear its cry."

He nodded in approval. At least she acknowledged him as the lead on this mission.

"You found the Haven?" she asked.

He glanced over his shoulder at the empty road. "Yes."

"Is it the woodcarver's shop? You went in the back." She stepped closer to him and lowered her voice, but the eagerness rang clear in her tone.

Blaze avoided her gaze, keeping his voice just above a whisper. "It's owned by an older man named Wyatt. They're supposed to have their weekly Fellowship meeting tonight. Most of the Followers belonging to the Haven should be there."

"Good. Good. How many are there?"

"There was only Wyatt and another woman with her kids this morning. She said they'll have about thirty at the meeting."

"Were any of them armed? I need to know how many Crows to bring with me tonight."

"What do you mean?"

"When I take down the Haven."

Blaze scrutinized her. What was she talking about?

"Oh,"—that sly smile he knew so well crept across her face—"you didn't hear? The Commander has ordered the immediate seizure and eradication of any known Havens. The Zradit Followers will be arrested tonight."

"What?" Panic gripped his chest. That couldn't be right. "No, I'm still undercover. I need more time."

"Too bad. It would seem he's taking the fight to them now that we know the Followers are in league with the rebels. We can't afford for the White Owl to gain any more support."

"Catrice is about to reveal all the locations of the Havens. You can't attack tonight."

Nikita shrugged, her smile widening. She was enjoying undermining his plans. "It's not up to me."

"No. I need to talk to my father. He'll understand."

"Fine. But until you do, I'm following orders. And without a messenger crow, I'm afraid he won't receive any letter you send for days." Nikita spoke the words as if she was sorry for him, but her smug smile and squared shoulders said otherwise. "Thanks to you, the Commander will hear that the Silver District was the first to flush out the Followers cult. Besides, I'm sure you can convince Catrice to tell you about the rest of the Havens after you rescue her from the Crows again tonight. Don't worry. I'll go easy on you. In reality, I'm doing you a favor."

He clenched his jaw so tight his teeth ached. She was relishing this.

"Now." She shoved her hands into her pockets. "Back to the weapons. How many were there?"

"None." Blaze sighed. "I didn't see any."

Nikita rubbed her nose. "That doesn't mean they won't bring any tonight." She looked down as if calculating her own numbers and plans in her head.

"Havens are typically mostly women and children, Nikita. I don't think you need to use much force. It's not like you're going to execute them all on sight."

"I will if I have to." She shrugged, and the casual tone in her voice sent a chill down his spine.

The Followers may have been delusional, but they didn't deserve to die. Certainly not in their own place, or at the hands of someone as ruthless as Nikita. If the guild were to do that, then they were no better than the rebels.

"We're not permitted to perform executions without explicit orders."

"I won't. Don't worry." Nikita waved a hand and shook her head. "But I'm not taking any chances tonight." She flicked her gaze up to him again. "How did Catrice identify the Haven?"

Blaze raised a shoulder. "I'm not sure."

"So much for gaining her trust, then." Nikita rolled her eyes. "Did you notice anything out of the ordinary or something she may have said?"

The memory of Catrice asking Wyatt about the dove carving at the booth flashed through Blaze's mind. The exact exchange was fuzzy, but it was some kind of code. And the same image of a dove had been carved into the doorframe. He kept his eyes on Nikita.

"No."

"You must have seen something."

"Well, I didn't," Blaze snapped.

The scar on the back of his neck throbbed, and he fought to keep his tone level. She had already compromised his mission for the sake of her reputation with the Commander. And he certainly didn't need her rampaging through the Silver District and tipping off the rest of the Havens that someone had betrayed them.

"You didn't see anything. Really?" Nikita brought her eyebrows together. "Did you even bother looking? We know they use secret messages and symbols to communicate. If I knew what they were, my Crows wouldn't have to keep guessing. We would save so much time and resources and be able to focus on more important things, like dispersing the rebels and improving the district. Think about what that would mean for the guild!" She threw her hands up and stepped forward.

Blaze scoffed. Surely she didn't expect him to believe that. She only cared about proving herself to the Commander.

Nikita swept her gaze over him again. Her arms dropped as her lip curled in disgust. "Right. I remember. You only care about yourself. My fault for thinking that would change after what happened to Izaak."

He held her gaze, anger boiling inside him. She was on thin ice, and the way her hand moved to the dagger's hilt at her belt proved she knew it. But she wasn't stupid enough to challenge him, and he didn't have time for this.

"Are we done?"

"Yeah." Nikita stepped back. Her demeanor had changed from her typical coy, calculated countenance to a reserved, hostile one. And though she hadn't drawn her weapons, the daggers in her eyes had already killed him a hundred times over. "We're done. Make sure you're out of my district by tomorrow."

"If Catrice leads me to another Silver Haven, then I'll have to go there."

"I can take care of my own district," she spat. "And I don't want to see your face in it again."

"Fine." Blaze swallowed. "But you're the one who has to explain to the Commander why I'll be extending my mission." He pulled himself onto the wagon and sat on the bench.

"Oh, don't worry. I will." Nikita smiled—a cold, lifeless expression that failed to reach her eyes. "I have *much* to report back to him anyway."

Blaze steeled himself, willing his face to remain neutral as a heaviness settled into the pit of his stomach. She was right. Any message he would try to send to the Commander would take days to reach the High Nest. Meaning anything she wrote in her report would reach him first, and Blaze would be left to clean up any mess and correct any lies she left in her wake. By then, the damage would be done. But he wouldn't give her the satisfaction of watching him squirm, and he certainly wouldn't let her make him regret standing his ground.

He gathered the reins into his hands and nodded. The fake smile remained plastered on her face as he turned away and urged the horses down the street.

~

BLAZE GLANCED at the dove carved into the doorframe as Wyatt repeated the rhythmic knock outside the Haven. His horse and the wagon were parked in the alley behind them, and one of Wyatt's boys stood by Ace with wide eyes and his neck craned back to look into the gelding's eyes. Ace bucked his head and shook his mane, but the boy remained gob-smacked as he placed a single hand on the horse's thick neck. Blaze stifled his chuckle. Ace was larger than most of the regular draft horses filling the streets of Zradit. He was bred for war, even if his playful demeanor suggested otherwise.

"You know where to take him?" Blaze asked the boy.

"Uh-huh. The stable on Frit Street. Papa's going to help me drive him."

"That's right. He's a big horse, but he's steady. Just take it slow."

"Yes, sir." The boy kept his eyes on Ace.

Blaze refocused his attention in front of him as the door swung open. Tali stood in the gap and offered them a wide smile.

"Come in." She rotated to the side. "We're just cleaning up now."

Wyatt gestured for Blaze to enter, then shut the door behind him. Two young girls lay sprawled out on the floor between the cushions as they played with a few blocks and dolls scattered in the space. Their whispers and giggles filled the room as they stared in his direction.

The Haven would be packed with Followers in a few hours, completely oblivious of the danger coming their way. The girls wouldn't be playing then; their laughter would be replaced by cries. He swallowed to clear the sour taste filling his mouth. They had chosen this path. It wasn't his fault where it ended.

Catrice stood by the table, crouched over various scrolls and documents as she rolled them up and divided them into piles. Ink dotted her hands, and a few smear marks marred the otherwise clear skin on her face. She wiped a hand across her forehead, and another streak appeared over her tanned brow. She straightened and planted her hands on her hips, admiring her work. When she turned to Blaze, her dark eyes sparkled with excitement.

"Tali's Testimonies were almost complete, although a few portions are on their last leg. I've sorted them into sections based on the Prophet who wrote them." She placed a hand on the scrolls. "Tomorrow, I'll start filling in the gaps, and then we can begin contacting the other Havens to see what they need."

He forced a smile. Nikita would have her hands on those Testimonies by the end of the day. They would never be complete, Catrice's work today would be for nothing, and Tali and Wyatt would be behind bars.

His expression faltered. "That's great news."

Catrice frowned and stepped toward him. "Is everything all right?"

"Yeah." Blaze nodded, but the concern on Catrice's face remained. The sour taste returned. This was what he had wanted, wasn't it? "It's fine. I'm just a little tired."

"You can rest a little before Fellowship tonight. I'm going to help Tali clean up." She placed a hand on his arm.

Warmth radiated from where her skin touched his own. The sudden sensation threw him off guard, and he resisted the urge to pull away. Instead, he covered her hand with his own and smiled. "That sounds good."

Catrice smiled back and lingered longer than he expected. Confidence radiated from her as she held his gaze and gave his arm a comforting squeeze.

"Well, then..." Tali's voice broke through the moment, and Blaze cleared his throat.

He released Catrice's hand, breaking their contact. The faintest bouquet of fresh parchment, ink, and warm sugar wafted from her hair as Catrice stepped back. Her eyes fluttered, and the blush he had grown accustomed to crept up her face.

Tali's eyes flickered between the two of them, and a knowing smile teased at her lips. "I'll go grab a few extra bags to sort the Testimonies."

She disappeared through the door on the other side of the room, leaving Blaze to fill the silence on his own. He scratched the back of his head. Catrice took a deep breath and fidgeted with the scrolls.

"How was the market?" she asked, finally.

Blaze scrambled to grab the purse from his belt and held it up. Anything to distract from the awkward space between them. "Good. I sold most of the supplies. This should be enough to hold us over for a while."

"That's good. I don't want to burden the Haven with supporting us for too long, but it may take me a few days to find another source of income. Tali said she had some contacts that might be able to help and that she'll reach out to them this week."

Blaze looked away, his eyes falling on the girls playing across the room. Tali and the other members of the Haven wouldn't be doing anything after tonight. She would be left on her own, the girls taken away. At least she wouldn't have to worry about taking care of anyone while in a jail cell.

Tali strolled into the room with a few packs draped over her arm. She dropped the empty sacks on the table and wiped her hands against each other.

"Blaze." She smiled at him. "Why don't you help me with dinner?"

"Me?"

"Yes. I caught up with Catrice while you were gone, but I know hardly anything about you. We can talk while we cook."

"I—" The words caught in his throat. He wasn't

prepared for this. He could fight a dozen Rogues with one arm tied behind his back. But *baking*? He swallowed. "I'm not sure I'll be much help in the kitchen, Tali."

"Oh, nonsense. Follow me." She turned and strutted around the corner of the short wall.

He looked to Catrice, channeling every ounce of desperate pleading he could into his eyes. She avoided his gaze as she started placing the sorted Testimonies into the bags, but a mischievous smirk fought its way to the corner of her mouth.

"Blaze, are you coming?" Tali called out.

He dropped his shoulders and groaned before following in Tali's footsteps. He could almost swear Catrice giggled behind him.

When he entered the kitchen, Tali was already gathering an assortment of dry goods, bowls, and eggs onto the small counter space. The fireplace smoldered in the wall behind him, and he scanned the divided-off kitchen for any weapons. Aside from a set of tarnished cooking knives and a rusty fire poker, there was nothing for the Followers to defend themselves with. They must have truly believed they were safe here. Nikita wouldn't face any resistance tonight.

"Do you always provide dinner for Fellowships?" he asked.

Tali emptied a cup full of butter *and* cracked a few eggs into a large bowl. "It's part of our tradition as laid out by the Prophet Geris Aetos. We share a meal together, which meets people's physical needs, before we move on to reading the Testimonies and praying for each other to meet our spiritual needs. A Haven needs to do both to truly serve others." She pointed to a wooden spoon on the other side of the counter and Blaze handed it to her. "Catrice told me you participated in Fellowships in Ontiach. Didn't someone provide the meals there?"

"My mother did." A warmth spread across his chest as he remembered his conversation with Catrice the night before. "She used to make honey rolls for everyone."

"And you didn't pick up anything from watching her bake every week?" Tali beat the eggs with the spoon and raised an eyebrow at him.

"Well, I—" Blaze stammered. Why was she even asking about this? "My brother was normally the one to help her."

"Hmm." Tali dumped a cup of water into the egg and butter mixture, then a smaller bowl filled with flour. "We've all lost someone we care about, I'm afraid."

Blaze stared at her. Was she talking about Izaak? What had Catrice told her?

"The question is"—Tali mixed the colorless goop until a thick, soupy dough started to form—"how do we respond to that loss?" She nodded to a bag of salt. "Catrice is still figuring that out for herself. But have you?"

He passed her the bag and kept his expression neutral. Did she know Catrice had lied to her about Vivian? He wondered how she would react if she did, but there was no way he was talking about Izaak with her. She had no right to question him about anything.

"Do we let it change us for the worse"—she sprinkled a handful of salt into the dough and continued to mix—"or do we heal and learn from it to help others do the same?"

"I'm afraid I don't know what you're talking about, Tali."

She beckoned him to come closer. Once he was within range, she wrapped her arm around his shoulder. "You were brought here for a reason, Blaze. Or do you think it was a coincidence you found Catrice when you did? The Creator has great plans for both of you. You just have to trust Him."

Blaze bowed his head solemnly, keeping his tone serious as if he believed her cryptic words were more than the ramblings of a delusional, albeit well-meaning, woman. "Of course. I will."

Tali's eyes met his own, and a pang of unfamiliar guilt hit his gut. She frowned as if she could see through all of his lies. "You can't run forever, son. May the Creator open your eyes," she whispered.

The guilt grew hot in his gut, and his heart pounded beneath his ribs. He pulled away as Catrice entered the kitchen.

"Almost done?" she asked.

Blaze hesitated, and his eyes flickered up to Tali again. Her motherly gaze remained on him, full of sadness and... pity? What did she know?

He shook his head and turned to Catrice, breaking off the connection. "Yes, at least, I think so. Do you need me for anything else, Tali?"

She smiled and pointed to a stack of ceramic pans on the ground in the corner, any heaviness from their conversation gone from her face. "Yes, could you grab those for me? We'll pour the batter inside and then cover them and let them sit in the hearth for an hour or so. When they're done, the girls will help me top them with more butter and some sugar and fruit."

Catrice inhaled deeply through her nose as if already smelling the treat. "Oh, I can't wait!"

Blaze assisted Tali with the rest of the baking in silence as she and Catrice rattled on about various recipes and the meeting tonight. He hadn't seen Catrice with this much life since they were children. She was happy and free, and he often found himself smiling along as her laughter filled the kitchen.

A part of him, a *very* small part, wished he could do the same. How simple life would be if he could believe what these Followers did about an almighty Creator watching over them.

But life wasn't that simple. It was hard, ugly, and broken. *People* were broken and, unlike Tali would like to believe, sometimes there was no growth or change. Sometimes loss just caused pain. The best he could do was to stop people from causing more pain, even if they meant well.

The Followers surely didn't *mean* to hurt anyone, but their beliefs encouraged rebellion. Defiance. If the Aetoses had truly just wanted peace, they would have turned themselves in years ago. Not run from district to district distributing passages written by the very man who had denounced the king's rule.

By the time the food had finished cooking, Wyatt had returned and started arranging the various cushions and chairs in the large room. His two boys, no older than fourteen, soon followed and went to work sweeping the floor and cleaning up the toys.

Blaze resigned himself to a wooden stool tucked away in the corner behind the table. He mapped out the exits of the building in his mind. Nikita and her Crows would seal off the doors, and he needed to determine a route where he and Catrice would encounter enough resistance to make her believe they were actually escaping, but not so much that she would suspect the Crows were letting them go.

He glanced at Catrice. She was lifting one of Tali's girls up to the counter so she could drop a messy handful of crushed berries into the pan. The little girl promptly stuck her juice-stained hand into the bowl of sugar before rubbing it across the front of her dress. Catrice scrambled to find a towel to wipe it off with while Tali laughed.

They were happy here. Despite Tali raising the girls

on her own. Despite living under constant threat of discovery. There was a peace that covered the place. A sense of security and belonging.

But tonight, it would all come crashing down, and he would be the one to blame.

Blaze shifted in his seat in an attempt to relieve the knots that had formed in his stomach. Surely it was just nerves before the raid. He had conducted dozens of raids during his time as a Crow. This should be no different. But, then again, he had never been on the receiving end of one.

It was nearly dusk when the first knock sounded on the door leading into the alleyway. Wyatt answered it, and the same encoded exchange Blaze had observed at the booth earlier that day occurred. A family of three, all sharing the same long, slick raven hair, entered the room smiling and embracing the children. The mother and son signed back and forth, their hands moving faster than Blaze could keep up with.

Triumites. He knew very little of the native language of the western country, but he had seen it enough in his travels to recognize it. Other members of the Haven seemed to have picked up enough sign to communicate with the family as easily as they did anyone else.

Like most Triumites, the wife and son were deaf, and they introduced themselves to him through the husband's interpreting with the same warmth that Tali and Wyatt exuded. The young couple and their four-year-old were immigrants from Trium, having settled in Zradit a few years prior, and found assistance from the Haven. After a few months of attending Fellowships, they had participated in the Reclamation Ceremony, which was also outlawed, to announce their decision to become Followers.

Blaze returned their smiles and hugs with as much enthusiasm as he could muster, but avoided explaining his own story, instead welcoming more Followers as they arrived.

The room filled with people from all ages and backgrounds until laughter echoed off the walls and Tali served dinner. Catrice wove through the crowd like she was at home, while Blaze did his best to stay glued to the wall. He didn't have the energy to engage with every person in the room. Not when he knew they would be in chains within a few hours.

"It's a lot to take in, isn't it?" Catrice slid against the wall beside him, pulling him from his observations.

"Mhm. Do you know how long this usually goes?"

"No idea. It always varied depending on what district we were in and who was running the Fellowship."

Great. He crossed his arms and nodded toward Tali, who was engaged in lively conversation across the room. The cryptic words she had said to him about running from the Creator still rattled uncomfortably in his mind. "Tali is... an interesting character."

Catrice laughed. "Did she Sage you?"

"Did she *what* me?"

"Tali has one of the Gifts." Catrice stared at him like he was supposed to know what that was. When he stared blankly back, she rolled her eyes. "One of the Creator's Six Gifts. Do you seriously not remember *anything* from Fellowship when we were little?"

He remembered Mother's honey rolls and hiding under the table with Catrice and Izaak. Did she expect him to remember every monotonous reading of the Testimonies the adults had done? He shook his head.

Catrice sighed. "Well, you know the Creator made all things, and that includes a set of Gifts He gives His people to help us help each other and understand Him more. My mother's was Insight, which essentially meant she could interpret messages from the Creator He gave to her or others. Being away from other Followers during the past few years meant she couldn't use it much, though." She turned toward Tali. "Tali has Sage. The Creator reveals things to her about people or situations beyond her own knowledge so she can help them, warn them, or keep others safe... that particular Gift has a lot of purposes."

He eyed the Elder as she made her rounds throughout the Haven. No way Catrice seriously believed that. But Tali had known about Izaak, and it was almost as if she knew when he had lied to her too. The knots tightened in his stomach. He dropped his gaze. What was he thinking? It had been a lucky guess.

That was all. Maybe she was just really good at reading people. That was the only explanation that made sense.

He inclined his head toward Catrice. "Did you get one?"

"Not yet, but it comes out at a different time for everyone. Some people's Gifts are stronger, or I guess I should say more sensitive, than others. Not everyone knows how to use them either, especially now that we're so scattered. The Gifts work best in community with others. I'm hoping for Judgment or Counsel, but Mother always said I shouldn't pick favorites."

"And anyone can get any of these Gifts? It's just... random chance?"

"No." She smacked his arm. "The Creator gives them out for a purpose. It's Him lending a part of His power to us. And two of them, Seer and Wonders, are only given to Prophets. That's one of the ways we know when He's chosen someone as His Prophet."

Sounded like random chance. "And no one's received either of those since your father?"

"That's right." She shrugged and offered him a folded-up napkin. "Cake?"

He unwrapped the square cloth to reveal a clear, sticky coating on the piece of dense cake. "What is this?"

A bashful smile lit up her eyes. "I found a little bit of honey in the kitchen. I know this isn't the same as your mother's honey rolls, but I thought it might bring back some good memories since we're at Fellowship again, and we're together—" her eyes widened, and a blush filled her cheeks. "Not *together*, together. I just meant we're here, in the same place, as friends. Physically together. I—oh, dear heavens…"

Blaze laughed, a deep, genuine laugh that rumbled in his chest and dispelled any tightness in his stomach. "Thank you, Catrice."

He raised the cake to her in a mock toast and bit into it. The sweetness of the honey flowed from the roof of his mouth to the base of his tongue, and he closed his eyes, savoring the bite. An image of Mother helping Izaak drip honey over the top of a pan of rolls in their small kitchen filled his mind. A wave of unexpected sadness rose within him, and he swallowed. He opened his eyes to see Catrice bouncing on her toes and staring up at him expectantly.

"So? How is it?" She chewed on her bottom lip, and wrinkles lined her forehead.

"It's perfect." He pushed the memory away. "Thank you."

Catrice beamed at him and clapped her hands together. "I can make it whenever you visit for Fellowship. I know you'll probably have to go back home soon, but next time you can bring Diana. I'm sure Tali would love to meet her."

The honey turned bitter in his mouth. He wrapped the cake up again and slipped it into his cloak pocket. "Of course. That sounds great."

An older Follower man came up and handed him a small wicker basket. Blaze took it and coppers rattled together on the bottom. Before he could say anything, the man walked away, and Blaze turned to Catrice for answers.

"Oh, that must be for the Fellowship funds." She grabbed the basket from his hands and nodded to the purse around his waist. "Could we drop a few coppers in?"

Blaze slowly reached for his purse. They were collecting funds? This coin could be going anywhere. Was this how the rebels were being funded? He frowned. "What is it for?"

"The coin helps purchase food and supplies to give out to the community, as well as take care of any Followers who may need it, like Tali and her girls."

"Doesn't Lord Denari have something like that? There should be programs across the Silver District to help the poor."

Catrice shrugged. "Maybe. But it clearly isn't enough. Does Lord Grener in the Onyx District help those who need it near your home?"

Blaze closed his mouth and dropped a few coppers into the basket. His answer would only confirm Catrice's statements.

Under the Commander's rule, all nobles were supposed to set up systems and funds in their districts that would offer assistance to the lower families, but it was rarely regulated to the standard it should be, and soldiers often took advantage of the funds they were supposed to distribute for their own gain. It was an area he had no control over as a High Crow—no wonder it was failing.

"That's what I thought." Catrice passed the basket to a woman next to her. "Besides, it's through the funds that Followers get to connect with others and invite them to Fellowship."

"Aren't you worried you'd invite the wrong people?" He crossed his arms. "What if someone reported a Haven to the king?"

"It hasn't happened yet. Most are grateful for the help. Besides, we're careful, and the Creator keeps us safe."

Apparently not careful enough.

Blaze opened his mouth to respond, but the crowd suddenly quieted as Tali moved to the end of the room. As she passed, people took their seats on cushions, chairs, or benches scattered throughout the room. Blaze reclaimed his stool in the corner, and Catrice settled on a cushion beside him.

"*Oh, the Wonders of the Creator,*" Tali sang out in a strong voice, silencing any lingering whispers in the room.

"*On display for all to see.*" The entirety of the Followers joined in. Blaze jumped, taken aback by the sudden boom of voices around him. "*Behold, He shines His face upon us! His Prophet will set us free.*"

Tali retreated to a seat along the back wall as the notes faded from the air.

Wyatt replaced her, holding up a scroll, and began to read a portion of the Testimonies aloud: "From the Testimony of Enna Res, the Creator's Prophet, in the Anocican year 1033..."

The story was vaguely familiar to Blaze. It was from one of the few newer portions that weren't written by an Aetos prophet, allowing it to be read on occasions as the throne allowed. The story recorded one of the 'Creator's Wonders' as the Followers called it. Essentially meaning it was a myth about some impossible feat the Creator did or ordained through a Follower. Which he now knew was apparently also a Gift reserved for Prophets. He couldn't keep track of all this nonsense.

This particular story was about the healing of a young boy. According to the Testimonies, he had wandered away from the field where he and his father were working and off a cliff. His parents searched for him for hours, and when they finally found him, he was said to be dead, but they carried him back to town, where Enna Res was called to pray over him. The Creator healed the boy, restoring him back to life, and the entire town became Followers as a result of witnessing the Wonder.

Blaze raised his eyebrows as Wyatt finished the story and rolled the scroll back up. People didn't come back from the dead. Clearly, the boy, if he had even existed, had simply been unconscious, and Enna Res had been there at the right time to claim a Wonder when he woke up.

Yet, the Followers in the room around him leaned forward in enraptured silence, as if they were seeing it for themselves. He glanced at Catrice out of the corner of his eye—she was in the same engaged posture. Surely they couldn't all believe something so outrageous.

Tali stepped forward again, and the room seemed to let out a collective breath. She opened her arms as if welcoming them all to the Haven. "Does anyone have a word from the Creator tonight?"

Blaze leaned over to Catrice and asked in a low whisper, "What is she talking about? I thought only the Prophets heard from the Creator."

She shook her head. "The Prophets are the Creator's mouthpiece, recording His words and bringing judgment or warnings through Seer and Wonders, but He can speak to anyone as He chooses."

Blaze resisted the urge to roll his eyes. "Like, He actually *talks* to them?"

"Not always. Sometimes it's through another Follower, a passage of the Testimonies, or even a dream."

"Which is then interpreted by someone with Insight?"

"There you go." She grinned at him. "I knew you'd catch on."

Blaze leaned back and frowned. That didn't make any sense. *Anyone* could hear from an all-powerful Creator? That didn't seem likely, even if He did exist. "Has He ever spoken to you?"

Catrice's smile faded. She lifted one shoulder in a halfhearted shrug. "He will. One day."

So she believed in something she had never even experienced? Poor, poor Catrice. She was brainwashed and didn't even know it.

The room remained silent. Some Followers bowed their heads, while others opened their hands in front of them as if receiving some invisible gift. But no one spoke. Catrice had started humming the song Tali had opened the meeting with quietly beside him, her eyes closed and shoulders swaying back and forth ever so slightly. Blaze resisted the urge to squirm in his seat. The silence was uncomfortable, unnatural even.

A movement out of the corner of his eye caught his attention and he looked to the window. Through the sliver of glass between the two curtains, he caught a glimpse of something dark moving in the alley's shadows.

The Crows were here.

The hairs on the back of his neck stood on end, and goosebumps shot down his arms. The knot in his stomach returned.

He turned to Tali, who still stood at the end of the room as she roamed her gaze over the Followers. She stopped, closing her eyes and taking a deep breath in as if processing something. They had no idea what was about to happen.

Her eyes flew open, landing on him and Catrice at the back of the room. She opened her mouth to speak, and a jolt of lightning ripped down his spine. "We have a Prophet among us."

Then the world exploded.

II

CATRICE

"THE CREATOR IS LIFE. GIVING IT TO ALL AND WITHHOLDING FROM NONE. HIS GIFT OF LIFE IS SACRED." - TESTIMONY OF PROPHET ENNA RES

Catrice couldn't see. Her cheek burned, and her arm ached, and through a piercing cacophony of screams, she had the distinct realization that someone was shouting her name. She blinked, and through the thick haze of smoke, she could just make out a pair of boots next to her head. What was going on?

"Catrice!" Blaze's face came into view as he dropped to the ground next to her. "Catrice, come on!" He grabbed her arm, lifted her to her feet, and dragged her across the room.

"Blaze?" she mumbled. Was her head always this heavy?

The Haven was filled with smoke. Flames licked at the curtains along the walls, and shadowy figures ran through the haze. Glass crackled beneath her feet. She struggled to line her legs up under her body, but Blaze continued pulling her forward with her arm slung over his shoulder and his arm across her back.

"Blaze, what's happening?" She shook her head and took a deep breath, only to immediately fall into a coughing fit. Somewhere in the room, one of Tali's girls was crying. Catrice jolted upright, whipping her gaze across the Haven as she was dragged into the kitchen. "Blaze, where's Gleena? She's crying."

A door slammed open, and the smoke began to clear. Her eyes burned, and the shadowy figures in her vision became clear.

Crows. They were everywhere.

In the darkness, Followers lay scattered on the floor, their hands above their heads, while others cowered in corners and under the table. A few Followers still stood, wrestling with Crows across the room. The windows were shattered, and most of the lanterns were in pieces on the ground. Where was Tali, and why wasn't she with Gleena?

Catrice jerked toward the main room, only for Blaze to yank her back into the dark kitchen.

"What are you doing?" he hissed. "We have to run."

"But Tali—"

"Catrice, there's no time!"

No sooner had the words left his mouth than a Crow burst through the door at the end of the kitchen. Blaze shoved Catrice behind him, keeping a firm grip on her arm, but placing himself between her and the exit. This Crow was different, with long silver hair and steel eyes set on her.

"Stay behind me." Blaze drew a dagger from his side and ran toward the Crow. In a flurry of strikes and moves lost in the dark haze, Blaze and the Crow collided.

Catrice launched herself toward the fire poker at the hearth to her left. She gripped the metal stick and swung it in front of her, but by the time she reached Blaze, he had the Crow pinned against the counter. The door was wide open on the other side of him.

"Run!" he yelled at her, straining against the Crow.

She hesitated, spinning around to her people trapped in the room behind her. She couldn't leave them. Not like this. Not like she did Mother.

Lifting the makeshift weapon, she started back toward the room.

"CATRICE!" Blaze shouted.

Another Crow stepped out from the haze, blocking her from the rest of the Haven. She raised the fire poker again, and the Crow drew a sword from his side.

"No!" Wyatt appeared out of nowhere, launching himself toward the Crow and tackling him against the wall.

The two wrestled on the ground, and Catrice froze. What was she supposed to do? Wyatt was going to die. The Crow was going to kill him. This was their Haven, a place of peace, and he was going to *kill* him.

Creator, what do I do?

The only response was the screams of her people.

Rage boiled within her, lighting her veins on fire, and she tightened her grip around the poker. The Crow grappled for his sword, and she lunged forward. The fire poker met resistance, then gave way into a mass of cloaked torso. He cursed, and she withdrew the weapon.

"Run, Catrice!" Tali shouted from somewhere in the darkness. "Run!"

Catrice released the fire poker, and it clattered to the ground as she turned on her heel and dashed out the door.

Blaze's heavy boots thudded against the ground behind her as she continued running. Her lungs stung with every breath, and tears streamed down her cheeks, but she didn't stop. What had she done? She had never killed anyone. But her people were hurting and in danger; she had no choice.

"Catrice!" Blaze called out behind her. "Catrice, slow down."

Her legs throbbed, and she gasped for breath as she came to a stop in the middle of a dark, empty road. She didn't know how far she had run, only that she could no longer hear the screams of her people. She doubled over and pressed her backside against the wall of a building. The sickening feeling of the poker giving way against the Crow caused her stomach to turn.

"Catrice, are you all right?" Blaze stepped up beside her.

She opened her mouth to respond, but the contents of her stomach rebelled against her. She turned away, losing her dinner to the dirt road. She coughed, heaving until there was nothing left to give, and wiped her mouth. The tears dried on her cheeks and left a crusty film against her skin. Her legs shook, and she slid down against the wall until she was sitting on the ground.

"I didn't mean to kill him," she whispered.

"What?"

"The Crow." Fresh tears gathered in her eyes, and she covered her face. "I didn't mean to! I just wanted to stop him. He was going to kill Wyatt, and I just wanted to stop him."

"Catrice—"

"I've never even used the long bread knives at the bakery. But the fire poker was right there... I didn't mean to kill him—"

"Catrice," Blaze knelt in front of her and grabbed her wrists, gently pulling her hands from her face and cutting her sentence short. "You didn't kill him."

"W-what?"

"Crows wear a thick layer of leather under their cloaks. It's going to take more than a fire poker to the side to take one out."

"But Wyatt—does that mean...?"

Blaze shook his head and released her wrists. "The

Crows don't kill people on standard raids. Especially if the people are unarmed. I'm sure he's fine."

"*That* was a standard raid?" She swung her arm out to gesture down the street. "They nearly burned the Haven down."

"They come through the windows and doors with smoke bombs to take out the lights and disorient like they did in Deln. You were knocked out when one of them crashed through the window."

"I don't understand." Catrice placed her head in her hands and leaned forward, resting her elbows on her knees. "We're not the rebels. We've never had a Haven attacked like that before. How did they know we would be there?"

"I don't know." Blaze sighed and stood. "But we're not safe here anymore." He reached out a hand for her to join him. "Do you know of another Haven we can go to?"

"No. I mean—yes." She rubbed her forehead. How was he asking about that right now? "But the Crows knew we were here. If they know about this Haven, how do we know the others are still safe? What if they aren't anymore? What if they've found all of them somehow?"

The world spun around her as her thoughts continued to spiral. What was happening? She had just been at Fellowship with her people. They had been praying and worshiping together. Now she was sitting alone in an empty street next to a pool of her own vomit. This couldn't be happening.

"All right, all right." He dropped his hand. "But we need to keep moving."

She shook her head. Her people were probably in chains right now. And what had she done to help them? "I should have done something."

"It's not your fault, Catrice."

"I could have done something. The rebels fight against the king every day. Tay would have done something. All I did was stand there and kill a man, then run."

"You *didn't* kill him."

"But I wanted to." The words slipped from her mouth before she had a chance to process them. Heavens, did she just say that out loud? She waited, expecting to feel some kind of guilt at the statement, but there was only hate. She swallowed and looked up at Blaze. His eyes were wide, and his mouth hung open.

"*What?*" he breathed. He was more shocked at her words than she was.

"I wanted to kill him." She blinked, and hot tears rolled down her face. "I asked the Creator what I should do. And I heard nothing. So I just attacked."

"Catrice..."

"How could I think that?" She pushed herself to her feet and wrapped her arms around herself. "How could I *do* that? That's not me. Why didn't the Creator stop me?"

Blaze closed his mouth, pressing his lips together and furrowing his brow as if in deep thought. He offered no answer, but simply waited.

After another moment of tense silence in the dark street, he opened his arms and stepped forward, pulling her into an embrace. She rested her head on his chest, letting her tears flow freely as his heart pounded under her cheek. His warmth calmed her racing mind, and she took a deep breath. The fragrance of old leather and pine filled her senses.

For the first time since Mother died, she felt safe.

"Good, now breathe out." Blaze's deep voice rumbled against her ear.

She snorted and smacked his ribcage. Pulling away, she craned her neck back to face him. A playful smirk commandeered his mouth, but concern shone in his azure eyes. He lifted one hand and his thumb grazed her cheek, wiping away a falling tear. Her heart raced, and she suddenly realized how close they were. When had she put her arms around him?

Catrice cleared her throat, and he released her, taking quite a few steps back and looking anywhere but at her. She brushed the remaining tears from her face. When she lowered her hand, she saw soot covering the tips of her fingers. She needed a bath and a place to change.

What was it that Blaze had asked her earlier?

About going to another Haven? No. She couldn't do that. Not now. Not until she knew how the Crows had found them.

"We should go. The Crows will be searching for us." Blaze gestured behind him. "Ace and my wagon should still be at the stable a few blocks away."

"How do we know they're not waiting for us there?"

"I can go ahead and check if you want, but it should be safe if we get there soon."

Catrice nodded. "But where do we go after that? I need to contact the other Havens and warn them about what happened tonight."

Blaze ran his hand through his hair. "Uh... the Onyx District is the closest to here, and I know somewhere we can set up a temporary base and get you some new clothes."

"Where?"

He shrugged. "My home."

12

BLAZE

"WHITTAM WELCOMES PEOPLE FROM ACROSS ANOCICA SEARCHING FOR A BETTER LIFE. IF THEY ADHERE TO THE WAYS OF OUR NATION AND OFFER LOYALTY TO THE THRONE, THAT LOYALTY SHALL BE EXTENDED TO THEM AS WELL." - THE ROYAL ARCHIVES OF WHITTAM

Blaze took a deep breath of fresh, evening air as he strolled down the street alone. Catrice had been reluctant to travel to his home, but he had insisted. After two days of travel, they had stopped at an inn just inside the border of the Onyx District for the night.

His district.

The thought usually brought a sense of security to his mind, but now all he could think of was what would happen if Catrice found out he was the High Crow here. Obviously, that wouldn't exactly be beneficial to his mission, but it was more than that. He thought of the sweet honey cake she had prepared for him and the way she beamed when he had thanked her. If she knew he was still a Crow, what would she think of him? Would her eyes still sparkle when she looked at him, or would they stare blankly through him like they had after the raid?

He shook his head and turned a corner toward the blockade of soldiers at the edge of town. It was exactly those kinds of questions that would blur his judgment. It didn't matter what she thought. What mattered was that she stayed in the room while he met one of his men, and so far, she had. He had told her he was making arrangements at the upcoming checkpoint so they could pass through undetected. Which was true. He was meeting with the Crow stationed at the border checkpoint, but not to bribe her for safe passage—like that would actually work with his Crows. He needed to send a few messages—messages he had written by candlelight while Catrice slept—before he arrived home.

Stopping short of the blockade, he leaned against the building that housed the soldiers' quarters. His Crow should be here somewhere overseeing the checkpoint. He glanced at the soldiers standing on either side of the wide gate blocking the road. A crowd of people waited in line before the checkpoint, pulling out their papers and preparing any goods in their carts for inspection.

Catrice didn't have any papers, and they had managed to skirt around the last checkpoint between the Amber and Silver Districts, but there were no such backroads leading to his district. He had made sure of it. His district was the most secure in all of Whittam, despite bordering the collapsing neighboring country of Rewon, which was another reason he'd decided to bring Catrice here.

The idea of bringing her to his home had been rather spontaneous, but his plan had become more detailed as they traveled. He wouldn't have to worry about rival Crows or unwanted surprises in his district. If he was lucky, he wouldn't even have to step foot in another Haven until he was arresting those inside. Catrice could contact all the Haven Elders from the confines of his house. He would have all their names and addresses delivered to him on a silver platter, and she would be none the wiser.

He rolled his shoulders, shoved his hands into his pockets, and propped a foot against the wall behind him, trying to ignore the growing pit in his stomach at the thought of turning over the locations of the Havens to the Commander.

The discomfort had started small, no more than a nuisance when he had revealed the Zradit Haven location to Nikita. But over the past few days, it had steadily grown to a constant heaviness in his gut that kept him awake at night and made it difficult to eat. There was no reason he should feel guilty about the Haven being raided. There was no reason he should feel remorse over Tali and Wyatt being behind bars somewhere. It didn't make sense. He was doing what he needed to do to keep Whittam safe. The Followers were a threat to that.

Blasts. He kicked a stone resting on the path and groaned. Where was his Crow? Normally he enjoyed being left alone with his thoughts, but at the moment, it was driving him crazy. He couldn't think straight.

He stretched his neck to peek above the crowd. Half a dozen of Lord Grener's soldiers worked the gate, but his Crow was nowhere in sight. He would have to write her a reprimand when he got back home. Suddenly, the door to the quarters beside him swung open, and a woman dressed in all black with a mask covering half her face stepped out of the building.

Finally.

Blaze grunted, and she turned to face him.

"The black crow flies," he said under his breath.

Her eyes widened, and she placed a closed fist over her chest in salute. "And all fear its cry," she responded, the faintest remnant of an accent hanging off the edge of her words. She dropped her fist and bowed her head. "High Crow Laskaris, my apologies. I wasn't expecting you—"

Blaze raised his hand to stop her. "Just 'Blaze' right now. I can't stay long." He pulled out three letters from his pocket and held up two of them. One held a message for his aunt, and the other was a warning to Harold that Catrice would be coming soon and instructions for how to prepare the household for their arrival. "I need you to send these through air note to the Onyx Nest. They must arrive by tomorrow night. You have a few messenger crows here, I assume?"

She nodded and took the letters. "Of course. They're upstairs in my quarters."

"Good." He passed her the third letter containing his report addressed to the Commander. Hopefully, it would clean up any damage Nikita had tried to inflict against him. "This one goes to the High Nest."

The Crow took the last note. "Yes, sir. I will send these out tonight."

He nodded to the line of people waiting by the checkpoint. "Any incidents I should be aware of here?"

"No, sir. Outside of the occasional drunk or smuggled goods, this has been the dream post for me." She smiled.

"What kind of goods?"

She hesitated and brushed a strand of copper hair behind her ear. "Mostly *sapid*, but nothing more than a few pinches."

Blaze sighed. The Rewonian drug was nothing new in his district, but it had become more common in the last two years, which meant coin was being funneled to the cartels and mercenaries running the war-torn country. He nodded at her unique hair color.

"You're Rewonian?"

"Yes, sir. My family fled here when I was a child. I can smell *sapid* a mile away. One of the reasons I'm so good at my job."

He chuckled. At least she was honest. "You joined the Crows last year. If I remember correctly, you specifically requested the Onyx District."

She shrugged. "The Crows here helped my family when we were still just refugees. I want to do the same for others. I volunteered for the Calling as soon as I could."

Thank you! If only Catrice could hear that. They weren't all monsters. His Crows did more for this country than the Followers ever had. He looked over the young woman in front of him. She couldn't be older than sixteen, and yet she still understood that. Maybe he wouldn't reprimand her after all.

"Is there anything else, High Cro—I mean Blaze." She furrowed her brow at his name, like it was illegal for her to say it.

"My companion and I will be coming through the checkpoint tomorrow morning. I'll need you at the gate to let us through. No papers."

"Undercover, sir?" Her green eyes sparkled with excitement.

"Uh—yes."

"I've always wanted to go undercover. I haven't even been on a real mission yet."

"Well." He placed a fist over his chest. "Next time one comes up, I'll make sure you're first on the list, Crow..."

"Dalon. Nolly Dalon, sir." She beamed and returned the salute.

"Thank you, Crow Dalon." He dropped his fist and pointed to the checkpoint. "Make sure you're there bright and early tomorrow."

"Will do, sir."

He smiled and turned to walk back down the street toward the inn. If he was lucky, they would arrive at home by the next night, and his mission would be over within the week. His thoughts would be clear, the Havens would be gone, Catrice would be out of his hair, and he would be back to managing his district as the Onyx Crow. It would be perfect. He couldn't ask for anything more.

The pit in his stomach grew heavier with each step he took on the dusty road.

13

CATRICE

Catrice stared into the metal sheet that served as the room's mirror as she brushed out her hair. The image was distorted and smeared, but she could still make out most of the details. She shifted her gaze from her own reflection to Blaze's.

He was sitting on the windowsill, dagger resting on his knee and eyes on the street below. The thick glass magnified the moonlight streaming through the pane and highlighted the strong features on his face. His jaw was clenched like it usually was when he was focused, and his foot tapped against the floor in no particular rhythm. His brown cloak lay over a chair at his side, his scarf hung around his neck, and his hair was a tousled mess. The stubble on his face had grown into a short beard over the past week, but it suited him well.

He certainly wasn't hard on the eyes.

The brush slipped out of Catrice's hand and clunked loudly on the chair before hitting the floor, despite her best attempt to catch it in the air. She glanced at Blaze as she gingerly picked it up from the floor and set it on the vanity. A small smirk played at his lips; the only sign he had noticed what happened. She frowned and turned back to her reflection.

He had remained oddly quiet since they left Zradit. She had expected him to relax as they approached his home, but he seemed to grow more and more tense with each passing day. Not that she blamed him. The raid had her on edge too. She had tried to push away any thoughts of it, but every time a memory flashed across her mind or she caught a whiff of smoke, her heart pounded, and hot anger brewed in her gut. It did no good to dwell on it. The best thing she could do was move forward and alert the Havens about Mother and the attack. If raids like that were occurring across the country, something had changed, and they needed to be prepared.

But maybe the attack had affected Blaze more than she thought. He had been Called by force, after all. She never asked him what he had gone through as a Crow, but she couldn't imagine that living through a raid would bring back any happy memories. He had said Izaak had died a few years earlier. Was that when they were Crows? Is that what made Blaze leave? What had happened? Did he blame himself for it? The chair creaked in protest as she turned around. She studied him again as her mind swirled with questions.

"What?" he asked, voice dry and eyes still on the street below.

"What was it like?"

He turned with his brows brought together in a quizzical look. "What?"

Catrice paused and bowed her head as she struggled to voice her next words. "Being a Crow."

"Boring. Everyone wears black."

She rolled her eyes. "I mean it."

He took a deep breath and repositioned on the windowsill. "I know it's hard to believe it, but we did good work too. Everything they taught us was meant to help the country. We were designed to protect the people and keep the districts united under the throne." He paused, eyes downcast. "The Crows aren't perfect. But they try to do what's right. If they don't, who will?"

Catrice turned his words over in her head. He spoke about the Crows almost like he missed being part of them. Like there was a sense of honor to be one. Anger rose inside her again, and she pushed it back down. There was nothing honorable about the Crows.

She lowered her voice. "Did you *want* to become one?"

"I told you. I didn't have a choice. I was Called after Ontiach."

That wasn't an answer. "I thought less than a

third of the Called make it through their training. The rest are sent back home to serve in their district army."

"That's right."

"So... if you didn't want to, why didn't you just drop out? Fail the training?"

"It's not that simple." Blaze stared at the blade in his hand. "They had Izaak too. And he was good. Really good. They wouldn't have let him go."

Catrice raised her eyebrows. "You felt responsible for him, just like when we were children."

Blaze tossed the dagger up and snatched it from the air. He turned back to the window, ignoring her statement. His entire body went rigid, as if every muscle was flexed and expecting an attack at any moment.

She stood from her seat slowly, weighing her next words. "What happened to him?"

"I told you. He died."

"But what *happened*?"

He sucked in a sharp breath, his azure eyes shifting to her. "Since we're asking so many questions, why didn't you and Vivian leave Whittam when you had the chance? You clearly had the means to escape if you were able to stay hidden for so long."

"I, uh..." Catrice blinked, taken aback by the accusatory tone in his voice. Where was this coming from? "I already told you. Whittam is our home. That's why so many Followers have decided to stay. We had a responsibility to our people. We couldn't have left them behind."

"You wanted to when we left Deln, and you didn't seem to have any problem with it at Ontiach."

She frowned and crossed her arms. Heat flushed her cheeks. "What is that supposed to mean?"

Blaze shook his head and waved his hand in the air as if to dismiss his comment. "Forget it."

She stepped forward. "If we hadn't fled Ontiach, the king would have killed us like he did my father. And I wasn't thinking straight in Deln. My mother had just been *murdered*. The Followers count on my family. They look to us for direction. You know that."

"Yeah, well, we counted on you too," Blaze snapped, eyes hard and brows lowered. Catrice froze, and his expression softened. "You were my family."

The heat faded from Catrice's face as Blaze's words faded into the air. She hadn't considered that before—how the people they left behind in Ontiach might have felt. How many turned away from the Creator because of her family's actions?

Blaze looked away and rested his head against the cold glass, his shoulders slumped in a defeated posture. Catrice relaxed her arms at her sides. She had a sudden urge to sit by him and take his hands into her own, but she resisted it.

"You were my family too." The quiet words slipped through her lips before she could think about what she was saying. They were true.

Blaze dropped his gaze and tapped the dagger against his knee. He nodded slightly, but the hurt behind his eyes remained.

An awkward moment passed in the silence of the room, and Catrice bit her lip. "Well, I'm going to get some rest before the morning comes. Please try to do so as well."

Blaze forced a small smile. The dagger at his side seemed to take on a life of its own as he twirled the blade between his fingers.

Catrice pulled her hair up with a strip of cloth and crawled under the covers. When she turned to the window, Blaze was watching her, shadows obscuring his expression. He flitted his eyes back to the street below, and she tilted her head as curiosity swelled in her chest. What was he thinking? She brushed the thought away before blowing out the candle on the nightstand and sending the room into darkness.

Catrice woke to the bright rays of the morning sun shining on her face. She propped herself up on an elbow and rubbed her eyes, brushing any stray curls that had escaped from her bun during the night.

Labored breaths filled the quiet space; Blaze was in the middle of the room between the beds and vanity, completing his exercise routine. His own bed looked untouched from the night before. She rolled her eyes and tossed the covers from her lap.

"Do you ever sleep?" she asked.

Blaze launched himself to his feet from a completed set of push-ups and shrugged. His shirt stuck to his chest and his sleeves were rolled back to his elbows. He whipped his head back and forth, sending beads of sweat flying from his dark hair. He was relaxed. The tension from last night had dissipated. He smiled at her, setting her at ease in the small room.

"I'll take that as a no." She yawned and stretched her arms over her head. Keeping her arms raised, she rotated her wrists. "That's as much as you'll see me moving in the morning."

Blaze chuckled. "Did you sleep well?"

She slipped out of bed and walked to the water basin on top of the vanity. "Well enough. Did you?"

He grunted something she didn't quite catch in response. So, he wasn't sleeping. Something *was* bothering him, but he wasn't sharing it with her.

He stood. "I'll go get us something to eat. Meet you at the wagon in an hour?"

Catrice nodded and sat at the vanity as he left. She took down her hair, brushing her fingers through the locks as best as she could. She splashed cool water from the basin and scrubbed her face and neck, hoping to finally rid herself of the smell of smoke. She had done her best to wash her clothes and bathe in a creek they had stopped at the day before, but the acidic stench still clung to her skin and hair, reminding her with every stray breeze of Gleena's cries.

She sighed and swallowed the lump rising in her throat. If she could keep such an attack from happening to the other Havens, she would. Pulling her curls into a long braid, she glanced at herself in the mirror.

"I will protect them," she whispered to her reflection. "I will. No matter what."

THE MORNING FLEW by after they smoothly passed through the checkpoint like Blaze had promised they would. After making it to the countryside, Catrice had started working on a list of the Havens across the Seven Districts. She only had a few pieces of clean parchment left and one unbroken quill from what she had scavenged in Deln, but it would have to do until they reached Blaze's house. She sketched lines dividing the parchment into seven sections—one for each district—and jotted down the towns she knew Havens to be located in under their respective districts. She would reconfirm the locations when she got her hands on a map and had a few days to rest and think.

Then would come the point where she would have to send out letters to warn them all. Some of the Haven Elders would probably have to go into hiding for a while, which meant the Followers in that area wouldn't be able to meet for Fellowship. The thought sent a wave of sadness over her. Her people didn't deserve to have to hide. They deserved to worship freely together. But they couldn't do that scattered in random groups throughout the country. Mother had chosen to keep them disconnected for their own safety. But was that really the right decision?

She leaned down to add another Haven under the Onyx District list. The Galian Haven was one Mother had only mentioned a few times. They were a larger group, but had rarely requested extra portions of the Testimonies. She vaguely remembered Blaze mentioning Galian as one of the towns close to his home. If they had time, she wanted to stop and check it out on their way.

The wagon stopped suddenly, and she lurched forward, causing the quill to skid across the parchment in a long, jagged line before the tip snapped. She groaned and straightened before looking around at the clearing Blaze had pulled the wagon into. He jumped from the bench and grabbed a few bags from the bed of the wagon. Catrice rolled up the list and shoved it in the bag with the other materials between her feet.

"Where are we?"

The clearing was a small gap in the trees lining the right side of the path. On the other side of the path were rolling, open hills as far as she could see. Flowers in full bloom dotted the landscape, shifting and flowing in the light breeze like sunset waves undulating across the earth. In the distance, the hills reached up to the sky in a mountainous pattern. A strong wind shook the woods behind them and lifted the hem of Catrice's dress, followed by the rich floral scent of thousands of blooms as they spread across the land.

"The Onyx Hills. Or the start of them, at least." Blaze dropped the bags in the grass and pulled a blanket from one of the packs. "They cover the northern half of the district, including where I live, before stretching past the border into Rewon. We should arrive at my home by dark."

Catrice stepped down from the wagon and stared at the colorful view in awe. "I've never been to the Onyx District before."

"Well,"—Blaze spread the blanket on the ground —"there's a first time for everything." He smoothed the edges of the fabric and walked over to the wagon. "We'll let Ace graze for a bit. There are some fruit trees nearby I'm sure he'll enjoy." He unhooked Ace from the wagon and patted his horse on the neck.

The horse wandered off the worn path to graze underneath a row of trees as Blaze pulled their last crate of food from the wagon. He arranged their meal and sat back on the blanket. Catrice settled across from him.

A high-pitched buzzing flew by her ear, and she swatted at the air. Blaze grimaced and slapped the back of his neck, pulling his hand away to reveal a dead mosquito squished against his palm.

"Maybe we should eat on the wagon," Blaze suggested as he wiped the bug guts onto his pants.

Catrice scanned the small clearing and spotted a patch of wild daisies lining the forest's edge. She stood and marched over to pick some. After she'd gathered a handful, she returned and laid them out on the blanket.

"What are the flowers for?" Blaze asked.

"Here." Catrice grabbed a stem and rubbed the flower between her hands, breaking it up into bits. She leaned across the blanket and grabbed his hand, dumping the crumbled plant into his palm. "They keep the bugs away."

Blaze stared at it skeptically. "Really?"

Catrice crumbled another flower and rubbed the powder onto her neck and arms. "My mother and I used them during the rainy season when we'd travel at night. The mosquitoes don't like the smell."

"Seriously?"

"Yes, *seriously*." She dropped her voice to match his and gave him a look she hoped mirrored his own deadpan expression.

Blaze shrugged and dumped the contents of his

hand onto the back of his neck. Bits of petals and pollen stuck to his hair and sweaty skin, but the majority of it tumbled off his shirt.

Catrice sighed. For a former Crow, he could be rather clueless at times.

"Not like that. You have to rub it onto your skin."

She grabbed another stem and crushed a flower again. Crawling across the blanket, she reached up to his shoulder and rubbed the plant against his skin. He bowed his head, giving her access to the back of his neck and part of his other shoulder. She paused at the wide, bumpy scar running from the base of his skull down his spine to beneath his shirt.

"*We counted on you too.*" His words rang in her ears.

Would he have been forced to be a Crow if her family had saved them? Would Izaak still be alive if she had taken them with her? How many other people's blood did her family have on their hands?

"Everything all right?" Blaze's voice interrupted her musings, and she shook her head.

"Yes, of course." She swiped the rest of the daisies from the blanket and grabbed his wrist, pulling his arm out with one hand while rubbing the plant on his exposed forearm with the other.

His arm relaxed under her touch, and she sat back on her knees to continue her work. He turned his arm over, gently cupping her hand in his own, and warmth spread across her skin from the light contact. Her fingers traced the veins near his wrist as they disappeared behind his feather tattoo. She frowned. How would things be different if they hadn't lost ten years?

She looked up at him, only to see his eyes already on her. The azure orbs held her brown ones as he plucked a broken daisy from the ground and tucked it behind her ear.

Catrice's lips parted, and Blaze smiled—a crooked, soft, warm expression that turned up the corner of his mouth and crinkled the edges of his eyes. She jerked back and brushed the excess flower dust from her dress as her face flushed.

"I think you can get your other arm." She cleared her throat and crawled back to the other side of the blanket, absently touching the flower in her hair.

"Thanks." Blaze did so, seemingly unfazed by the interaction.

Catrice snagged a roll from the blanket and bit into it, crumbs flying from her mouth as she nodded in response. He stared at her as she chewed, as if he was waiting for something else. She swallowed the chunk of bread and grimaced as the dry food slid down her throat.

"What?" she asked.

"What were you working on this morning?" He gestured to the wagon where her bag sat under the bench.

Catrice glanced at the bag. "I was making a list of

all the Havens I know of and which districts they're in."

"You can do that all from memory?"

"Sort of. It's a rough draft, really. I'll need to do some more research when we get to your home. A map, for example, would be helpful."

"I have updated maps of every district in my study."

"Oh, that would be perfect."

"So, what's your plan? With the list of Havens, I mean."

Catrice grabbed a piece of dried fruit and broke it apart in her hands. "Well, first, I need to update them all about my mother and the Zradit Haven. We've never had a Haven raided like that before, and they need to be ready in case the same thing happens to them."

"And after that?"

She paused, staring at Blaze's curious expression. This was the most engaged she had seen him since they'd left Zradit. A part of her didn't want to tell him. A part of her seeded dark, baseless doubts in her mind. What if something happened? What if he turned on her? He had been a Crow, after all. But that hadn't stopped her from trusting him before. He was her friend. There was no reason to stop trusting him now.

Mother hadn't trusted anyone, and look what happened to her.

She inhaled and squared her shoulders. "I'm thinking about uniting the Havens."

Blaze raised his eyebrows. "What do you mean?"

"Well, if they're able to communicate freely with one another, think about how much stronger we would be. They could send resources to each other, help others running from Crows, warn each other about potential raids... even fight back if they needed to."

Blaze frowned, looked down, and picked at his roll. "That sounds a lot like the rebels, Catrice."

"Yeah, so?" She popped a piece of fruit in her mouth. Her jaw tightened as she chewed. "At least they do something."

He remained quiet, but his eyes flickered back up to her. Any remnant of his earlier smile was gone, replaced by a mask of concern and... was that anger? What did he have to be angry about?

She steeled herself and stood, tucking the daisy further behind her ear. "I think I'm going to take a walk and get some exercise before we start traveling again."

"Of course." His tone was cold, detached. He tore off a piece of dried meat and put it in his mouth. "I'll clean up, and we'll head out when you get back."

Catrice forced a smile. "Sounds good."

She wandered to the tree line where the daisies grew in abundance along the outside of the forest. She needed some air.

Well, *different* air.

Air that Blaze wasn't also breathing.

As she strode further into the woods, yellow and white pops of color lit up the dark forest floor, and other flowers of various colors sprang up among the trees, reaching heavenwards for the thin rays of sunlight peeking through the canopy above them. Normally, such a beautiful view would have brought her a sense of joy or peace, but now her chest grew tighter every second, and she felt hotter with every breath. She stopped next to a wide oak tree and sat down in the brush.

How could he be upset with her? She was right. The rebels did do something, and under the White Owl, their numbers were growing every day. Tay had been right to want to join them. She just didn't know it at the time. At least the White Owl didn't want to run at the first hint of danger. At least he didn't let his people get killed or captured on his watch, which was more than she could say about herself.

Leaves and twigs crunched on the forest floor behind her. She huffed and wrapped her arms around her knees. "Blaze, I just need some space right now."

A rough hand covered her mouth, muffling her scream as a thick arm encircled her torso and yanked her to her feet. Two armed men stepped out of the trees in front of her. One of them pulled a flyer from his pocket and stared at it as a smile broke onto his ruddy face. He turned the paper to the man immobilizing Catrice to reveal a crude sketch of her face on the parchment along with the words: WANTED: CATRICE AETOS OF ONTIACH.

A deep voice chuckled in her ear. "Look what we have here, boys. The White Owl will be mighty pleased."

14

BLAZE

"THE BLACK CROWS CARRY THE THRONE'S AUTHORITY. THEY HAVE THE RIGHT TO PASS JUDGMENTS, AND IF NECESSARY TO SAVE LIVES AND PRESERVE THE WAYS OF WHITTAM, EXACT HEAVY SACRIFICES TO DO SO." - THE ROYAL ARCHIVES OF WHITTAM

Blaze flicked the blanket over the grass, shaking any loose crumbs from the cloth, and rolled it up under his arm. He braced the crate between his other arm and hip and carried both to the wagon. The crate landed with a *thunk* inside the bed of the wagon, and he tossed the blanket on top of it. Bringing two fingers up to his mouth, he released a shrill whistle across the clearing and into the forest. Ace would hear it and come to him, they would be ready to go as soon as Catrice returned from her walk or whatever she was doing.

Not that he cared.

He wandered to the middle of the clearing and focused on a broken daisy in the grass, trying to ignore the pit in his stomach. He hoped his letter had made it to the Commander. Maybe he would send another when he got home. The Followers were delusional, but maybe they weren't as dangerous as he had initially predicted—but the raids could change that. Especially if all of the attacks were as violent as Nikita's. There was a fine balance between keeping people in line and driving them to insurrection. Catrice's newfound fascination for the rebels proved that.

The crumpled flower faced the heavens, and he grunted as he picked it from the ground. He twirled the stem in his fingers, and the image of Catrice blushing as he had placed the other one behind her ear filled his mind. How could she be so blind? The rebels did nothing but destroy what his father had worked so hard to build. And the Followers knew the consequences of following the teachings of the Aetos prophets. It was their own fault they had to meet in secret and were scattered throughout the country. He shook his head and frowned before shoving the flower into his pocket and strutting back to the wagon.

The bag under Catrice's seat caught his eye, and he paused. He glanced around the clearing. She probably wouldn't be back for a while anyway. He walked to the bench and pulled the top piece of parchment from the bag. Spreading it out on the seat, he studied the scribbled list of Havens. He focused on a note under the Onyx District.

"Galian," he whispered.

He traveled through Galian several times a month whenever he left or returned home. It was the closest town to the Onyx Nest. There weren't any Havens there. But he hadn't thought there would've been any in Zradit either.

Hoofbeats sounded from the clearing behind him. Ace exited the forest slowly, his heavy hoofs matting the grass where he stepped. Blaze returned the list to the bag and shoved it back under the seat. The horse stopped and raised his head, ears twitching.

Blaze stepped away from the wagon. "You hear something, boy?"

Ace arched his neck to the side and looked back at the forest. Blaze narrowed his eyes and advanced closer to the trees, listening carefully. Faint, muffled voices carried lightly on the wind as it blew through the clearing.

"Catrice?"

The hairs on the back of his neck stood on end, and his hand hovered above the dagger at his side. Something wasn't right.

"Blaze!" A strangled, panicked scream echoed from somewhere deep in the woods.

He launched into a sprint.

"Catrice!"

Darting across the clearing, he broke into the forest, jumping across fallen branches and bushes.

"Catrice!" His heart raced in his chest as he called out again, but no answer reached his ears.

He spun around. Blurs of green and brown flew past his eyes as he scanned the trees for any sign of her. Figures in the distance caught his eye. He squatted low, dropping behind a line of bushes and creeping forward as he watched a small group move through the woods a dozen yards away.

Two burly men struggled to restrain a gagged Catrice as she kicked and flailed relentlessly with her hands tied behind her back. They wore cut-off leather vests with worn trousers, and each had a sword secured at their side. A massive third man stood a few more feet away, watching her struggle with a smug smile. His long, matted hair was pulled away from his face, exposing a deep red scar across his left cheek. He wore a lengthy brown coat across his bare chest, and the hilt of a sword peeked out at his side.

"Hurry up and get her on a horse. I want to make it to the camp by sundown," the man shouted at the other two. Blaze set his jaw and kept a growl from escaping his mouth.

Rebels.

He pulled the dagger from his belt and gripped it in his fingers with his thumb over the hilt and the point at his forearm, wishing he had his two short-swords instead. Another blade pressed against his shin as he pulled it out of his boot. His two daggers and the handful of throwing knives that lined a second belt under his shirt versus three men with swords and unknown skill sets.

It wasn't much, but it would have to do.

Catrice wrenched herself loose from the cloth tied across her mouth and screamed again. "Blaze!"

"Shut up!" the third man shouted at her. He grabbed her chin, shoving the gag back into her mouth and forcing her to look up at him. Blaze's blood boiled. "You're a pretty one, aren't you? That poster don't do you justice."

Catrice lifted a knee into his groin. He cursed and doubled over as the two other men pulled her back. Their leader straightened and slapped her across the face, knocking her to the ground.

Blaze's heart tightened, and his knuckles whitened as his fingernails pricked his palms. He ground his teeth together, waiting for the right moment. If they saw him coming, Catrice could be dead in seconds.

"You wretch! You'll pay for that!" The rebel grabbed her braid, pulling her towards the horses as she continued to scream.

The other two rebels dragged behind, turning their backs to Blaze. He took a deep breath, slowing his heart rate and focusing on the fight in front of him. The crunch of leaves beneath his opponents' feet. The musky scent of moss and dirt as Catrice dug her heels into the ground beneath her. The coolness of the dagger in his palm. It all came into focus as he vaulted from the bushes and dashed toward the rebels.

He cleared the distance between himself and the first two rebels in a matter of seconds.

"What the—" The man on the right jumped at the sound of Blaze darting across the forest floor, turning just in time to meet the dagger thrust into the side of his neck, cutting off his sentence.

The second rebel shouted and reached for his sword. Blaze released his weapon, and the first man crumpled to the ground in a mess of gurgling blood. He tackled the other brute, pushing him to the ground and pinning his arms under his knees in a series of memorized, nearly instinctual moves. His hand moved on its own, effortlessly, as the blade sliced through the man's throat. He wiped a sleeve across his face, clearing his vision.

Scarlet dripped from Blaze's hand as he shifted the slick handle and turned to the leader. The last rebel was running toward the horses and dragging Catrice with him, not even attempting to help his comrades. Catrice continued to fight, despite him being twice her size.

Blaze pushed himself to his feet and pulled a throwing knife from his belt, launching it at one of the geldings. The blunt end of the weapon smacked into the horse's hindquarters, causing it to buck and take off into the forest, followed by the other two animals.

The lone rebel stumbled back from the horses and spun around, pulling Catrice flush against him and glaring at Blaze.

"You must be Blaze. She belongs to you, then?"

Blaze growled and took a step toward them.

"Eh, eh, eh." The rebel tsked and drew his sword,

pointing it at Blaze and pulling his other arm tight against Catrice's neck. Blaze froze.

"Let. Her. Go." He spoke through gritted teeth.

Catrice gasped behind the gag as the man's arm flexed against her throat. Blaze's fingers twitched on the hilt of his weapon.

The rebel examined him, taking in his lowered stance and single, short blade. He laughed. "Fine." He tossed Catrice to the ground beside him. "She won't get very far after I gut you."

She fell to her knees and struggled to get back on her feet. Blaze gestured behind him without taking his eyes off the brute. "Get to the wagon."

She stumbled forward, shaking the gag from her mouth and stopping a few yards from Blaze. Fear shone through her soft, umber eyes as they darted between the two dead bodies at his feet. Whether her fear stemmed from the men who held her captive or his bloodstained hands, he did not know. She hesitated and opened her mouth to speak. Blaze held up a hand to stop her.

"Go, Catrice. It's fine. I'll be right behind you."

She took off toward the clearing, leaving Blaze and the rebel alone, weapons drawn. Blaze rotated his grip on the dagger, turning the blade in his hand so the point faced forward and his thumb sat under the crossguard. The rebel's sword was long, too long for Blaze to get close enough to strike. He rotated it through the air and sneered at Blaze, egging him to step within range of the steel.

They danced throughout the trees, each daring the other to move first. The rebel lunged forward, bringing his sword down in a wide arc set on Blaze's neck. Blaze moved back, dodging the attack by a hair. He swung again. Blaze sidestepped. He thrust. Blaze jumped away. Back and forth. Blaze was too fast for the rebel, but not fast enough to step into the short openings left between swings.

Finally, the brute's footing slipped as he brought the sword down for another attack. Blaze raised his dagger, catching the steel in the crossguard and walking into the gap. He grabbed the rebel's sword hand and twisted the hilt out of his grip. The weapon tumbled to the ground as Blaze moved closer and stabbed with his blade, aiming for the heart, only to be met with thick muscle and hard bone as the rebel raised his arm to block the thrust. The dagger sank deep into the man's forearm, but he hardly reacted. He headbutted Blaze, driving his broad shoulder into his chest.

Blaze fell to the ground, but his weapon remained embedded in his opponent's arm. The world spun as his blade was torn away and tossed to the side. The brute knelt over Blaze's torso and brought his over-sized fists down on him. Instinctively, Blaze raised his arms over his face and bucked his hips to throw the man off balance, but his sheer size and weight kept Blaze pinned to the ground.

One of the punches broke through Blaze's guard and connected with his cheek, throwing his head to the side and burying half his face in damp leaves. A shiny glimmer of steel marred with red sparkled beside Blaze's head, and he dropped an arm to grope for the weapon. His fingers wrapped around the hilt of the dagger lodged in the dead man's neck, and he yanked it out. He shoved the six-inch blade between the rebel's ribs and twisted.

The barrage of fists stopped as his attacker grunted and fell to the side. Blaze kept a firm grip on the dagger's hilt and flipped the man over. He stared at the squirming fallen figure, let out a deep breath, and raised his arm to expose the bloodied feather tattoo on his wrist.

"Now would be the time you beg for the mercy of your king."

The man glared up at him, eyes widening as they landed on the feather, and he spewed blood across the ground. "Tenaris is no king of mine, dirty Crow."

Blaze gripped the rebel's leather coat and yanked him upright. The man responded by coughing up more blood. Parchment crinkled in the rebel's pocket, and Blaze pulled a poster of Catrice out of the coat. He shoved it in the brute's face.

"Where did you get this?"

The rebel smiled, revealing broken, bloody teeth. "Long live the White Owl."

He fell into another coughing fit and went limp in Blaze's arms. Blaze froze, releasing the now-lifeless body, as dread settled in his chest.

The White Owl?

That was impossible. The White Owl had no presence in the Onyx District. Not for the last two years. Not since Izaak had died. Setting his jaw, he shoved the poster into his own cloak.

He kicked the dirt as he marched around the battlefield to retrieve his weapons. With a grunt, he rolled one of the dead men over and searched through his pockets. Rough pieces of leather met his fingertips, and he pulled them out to reveal two patches. The first was an image of a dagger impaling a crown—the symbol of the DaggerThorn rebels. Blaze grimaced. They should have been wiped out two seasons ago. The last thing his district needed was to deal with this rebel group again. He would have to dispatch a unit to clean up this mess and find their new camp when he arrived home.

He shifted his gaze to the second leather seal, and his heart dropped. An outline of an owl with its talons extended forward was embroidered on the patch. The White Owl. Blaze dug into his cloak and retrieved the wanted flyer of Catrice. It was similar to the one he received from the king, except the pressed outline of the owl was in the corner replacing the royal seal of a crowned crow.

Impossible.

The DaggerThorns, he knew, were disjointed and reckless, which was why he had been able to wipe them out so easily. But now they were in league with the White Owl? The Commander had been right. This new threat was growing too powerful. For the first time, rebel groups were uniting across the districts. They couldn't afford the White Owl gaining any more support.

He crumpled up the poster and patches and stuffed them into his pocket. He didn't know how the White Owl had managed to get his hands on this information, but it didn't bode well if there was a leak in the Crows. He glanced at the dead rebel again. The country was unstable enough already.

A light breeze dried the mud and blood on his skin into a crusty paste by the time he approached the clearing again. Bits of the dark, clay-like substance crumbled from his hands as he wiped them on his pants in an attempt to clean them off. Catrice stood by the corner of the wagon, rubbing her wrists against the edge of the bed in an attempt to saw through the rope. She spun around at the sound of him exiting the trees, wide eyes darting back and forth. Blaze held up his arms.

"Everything's fine. They're gone."

She nodded sharply, and her chest rose and fell

rapidly. He pulled out one of his daggers again, and she lifted her arms, exposing her bound wrists. In a swift movement, he cut through the ropes; she stepped away, rubbing her wrists.

"Catrice." He reached out a hand, and she flinched.

"You're covered in... I can't."

Blaze glanced down at his formerly white shirt—it was now a deep crimson. Blood hardly bothered him anymore. His job had demanded too much of it, and while he never enjoyed it, he was desensitized to the metallic scent and dark stains it often left behind. He swallowed and motioned to the wagon.

"I'll get changed. Can you pass me a towel and a new tunic?"

Catrice jumped to the wagon, seemingly glad to do anything other than look at him. She dug through his bag and pulled out another shirt and a rough towel. Holding a hand over her nose, she approached him with the items out in front of her to create distance between the two of them. Blaze took them gently and backed away. Catrice turned her back to him as he slid his soiled shirt over his head and dropped it onto the ground. He wiped his face off, wincing as the cloth dragged across a tender spot on his cheek, and shoved his arms through the fresh clothing. He adjusted his necklace, making sure his ring was hidden under his shirt.

Catrice peeked over her shoulder timidly. "Are you done?"

"Yeah." Blaze scrubbed what dirt and blood he could off his arms with the towel. "I'll finish cleaning up tonight."

The coarse cloth scraped against the inside of his forearm, and he sucked in a breath as a stinging sensation rippled up his arm. He jerked the towel away to reveal a long, shallow cut across his feather marking. It wasn't deep, but a steady flow of blood pooled in the gash and ran down his wrist. He sighed and wrapped the towel tight around it.

"Are you all right?" Catrice asked.

He glanced up to see her shuffling toward him. The fear plastered across her face a moment earlier had been overtaken by a deep look of concern as she stared at his arm.

"I'm fine. Just a cut."

She took his hand in her own and turned his forearm over, pulling back the towel to examine the wound. The light touch sent an electrifying warmth up his arm.

"We'll have to dress it properly tonight. Don't want to risk running an infection." She focused on his cheek and touched the swollen skin gingerly. Blaze grimaced. "You have a cut on your cheek too. It's not as deep, though." She pulled her sleeve down over her palm and dabbed the abrasion lightly.

Blaze caught her wrist, holding it gently in his hand. All his training screamed at him to step away and create a distance between them again, but he didn't want to move from her touch. He had almost lost her. Those brutes had tried to take her, and he had almost been too late.

He brushed a thumb over her reddened face where the rebel had struck her. "I should have gotten to you sooner."

Catrice took a deep breath and stepped out of his reach. His heart sank. Tucking a stray curl into her braid, she cleared her throat. "Please. I was doing perfectly fine kicking and screaming all on my own."

Blaze raised his eyebrows. "Really?"

"Absolutely. Five more minutes and those men would have been deaf in both ears and curled up on the ground, hugging their bruised shins. You did them a mercy coming when you did."

"Oh, did I?" He grinned. "Was that all part of your master plan, then?"

She flashed a tired smile and shrugged. "Hasn't failed me yet. I'm just disappointed you didn't get to see it in action."

Blaze chuckled and swiped his bloodied shirt from the grass. Catrice's gaze registered the stains, and the smile dropped from her face. She wrapped her arms across her chest.

"Are they all dead?" she asked, her voice soft.

He wadded the tunic into a ball and moved toward the wagon. "Yes. They were part of a dangerous local rebel group called the DaggerThorns. I encountered a lot of them when I worked as a Crow."

Catrice crawled onto the bench. "Did you kill them then, too?"

Blaze tossed the clothing into the bed and climbed up to join Catrice. "Sometimes. Only if they posed a threat to the district or its people."

Tight wrinkles lined the space between her eyebrows and above her upper lip, but she didn't say anything else. Was she thinking about all the people he could have killed? Was she going to look at him differently? He had done more in his life than Catrice could ever imagine. More than he ever wanted her to know about.

"How are you doing?" he asked.

"I'm fine."

"Are you sure?

"Yes."

"Because that was a lot, and I—"

"Yes, Blaze! I'm sure," she snapped, cutting him off. The sudden change caught him off guard, and he raised his eyebrows. She sighed and shook her head. Her voice softened. "I'm fine, really. I'm just done talking about it right now. We want to get to your home before dark, right?"

Blaze frowned. Turning off your emotions was something they taught in the Crows. It made the job easier. Feelings cloud judgment. Emotions make you freeze when you should move. He had froze once, and it cost Izaak's life. But Catrice was never taught that.

Which also meant she was never taught how to deal with it when the emotions had to come back on.

He turned his gaze to hers as she waited for an answer, her umber eyes holding his own as if he was the only one she could trust. Warmth filled his chest, overpowered swiftly by the growing pit of guilt in his gut.

"Right. We don't have to talk then." He swallowed the guilt down and grabbed the reins. "How about, for now, we just drive?"

15

CATRICE

Catrice's cheek throbbed. She resisted the urge to touch the swollen skin. Instead, she rolled the leather straps from her bag in her hand, focusing on the rugged material against her palm to still the incessant trembling of her fingers. The shaking hadn't stopped since they had left the woods an hour earlier. Every time she allowed her mind to drift, it wandered back to the rebel's scarred face and the rope burns on her wrists. And worse yet, the blood—blood that transported her back to the room in Deln.

Her hands renewed their shaking.

Blaze sat still beside her. His posture was relaxed, but seemingly intentional at the same time, like he was afraid she would snap again at any moment and was trying to make her as comfortable as possible. If anything, it was more uncomfortable. His shirt was clean, but his hands were reddened with stains that matched the smeared streaks across his face: blood from those men.

The tremors rippled up her spine, and she shivered. In an instant, Blaze was reaching to the back of the wagon. The sudden movement sent her heart racing, and she jumped. He slowed, watching her carefully. He pulled a blanket from the wagon and draped it gently over her shoulders. Her heart continued to pound so loud he was sure to hear it, but he resumed his forced lounge against the bench as if nothing was wrong. It wasn't cold, and the blanket felt heavy on her back, but another shiver ran down her spine anyway. She gripped the leather tighter and rolled her shoulders, working up the courage to say something and break the silence between them. Blaze pointed ahead of them before she could.

"That's Galian coming up. It's the last town before my house."

Catrice craned her neck to see above the treetops. In the distance, less than a mile away, thatch rooftops and stone buildings peeked over the forest. She latched onto the thought of the Galian Haven as it passed through her mind—anything to distract her for another moment.

"Can we stop there?" she asked.

Blaze glanced down at the blood on his skin. "Uh, I don't know if that's the best idea right now. We can always come back another time."

Catrice frowned. He was right. The Haven would still be there tomorrow. "Of course."

The path curved around the trees, revealing dozens of buildings stretching across the fields to their left. Men and women dotted the streets as the sun continued to sink behind the rooftops. Galian was considerably smaller than Deln, but it held a comfort Catrice had learned to yearn for. The road smoothed out as they passed the first few buildings, and Blaze leaned over to her.

"Are you going to tell me what you wanted to stop for?" he asked.

She sighed. It's not like there was any point in keeping it a secret from him if she was just going to come back another day. "There's a Haven in town."

"Huh." Blaze raised his eyebrows. "When were you going to tell me about this?"

"What do you mean?"

"We've been traveling all day and you didn't even mention it. It would have been nice to know, is all."

"I told you the next Haven was east of us a few days ago."

"Yeah, I thought you meant east, as in the Black Pines. Or near the Rewon border. Anywhere east of my house, really. Not five miles away from it."

"I told you what you needed to know." Her throat tightened as she traced the stitching on her bag. The leather pricked her fingers as if every nerve was on end, and she drew back, tightening her hand to a fist to still its shaking.

Blaze stared at her. "Are you sure you're all right?"

Catrice opened her mouth to respond but was cut off by shouting down the street. A young man ran down the center of the road yelling panicked warnings she couldn't quite make out. The crimson stains on his hands held her attention as he grew closer, and a small crowd gathered around him.

"Help! They're dead!" he shouted. "They're all dead!"

An elderly shopkeeper grabbed his shoulders, and held him still as the youth continued to squirm. "Whoa, Travis. Calm down, boy. What are you talking about?"

Tears carved a path in the fine layer of dust over the young man's cheeks, and he struggled to catch his breath. "Gad, Hollard, and Perrin..." he hiccupped. "I found them. They're dead. In the woods." He sniffled and drew his hand against his nose, leaving a long streak of red across his face.

The crowd drew back, and a low murmur echoed down the street.

Catrice's stomach dropped. Blaze straightened beside her and brought the wagon to a stop a few yards away from the crowd. She leaned over. "Do you think he's talking about—"

"Shhh," Blaze spoke low. "Not here." He yanked his

sleeve over the makeshift bandage on his wrist and gathered the slack in his hands to pull the wagon around slowly. "Grab my scarf from the sack behind you."

Catrice leaned back and shuffled her hand against the bag in the bed of the cart. She found the opening and shoved her fingers inside. The soft cloth brushed over her skin, and she gripped the green scarf, laying it across her lap. "I got it."

"Wrap it over your face."

"Why?" Catrice fidgeted with it.

"The others had a poster of you. We don't know who else might."

She froze. There were *more*? More men could come after her like the ones in the woods? She pressed her lips together to keep them from trembling and wrapped the scarf over the lower half of her face.

"What do you mean they're dead?" the older man spoke up again.

"I found them in the forest. They were just lying there. I tried to move them... to help... but there was so much blood." The young man started to shake again.

"Did you find anything?" another voice called out.

The boy nodded, reached into his belt, and removed a short, flat blade the size of his hand with a rounded end. Blaze stiffened next to her. Was that one of his weapons? A figure stepped out from the crowd and examined the knife.

"This is fine steel. See the stamp?" He held up the weapon. "It's from the king's army," he spat.

A second murmur rippled through the throng of people.

"A Crow?" someone asked.

"Why would they kill Gad and his boys?" another raised his voice.

The crowd continued to stir and ask more questions as others flocked from the surrounding stores and houses.

Blaze bowed his head. "We have to get out of here."

Catrice nodded. As Blaze continued to turn the wagon, another small group formed on the other side of the street. She narrowed her eyes. A few rugged men huddled by an alleyway, speaking in low voices as they glanced back and forth between the crowd and their wagon. Catrice turned away. Her eyes settled on her shoes and her tongue dried in her mouth.

"Blaze," she whispered. "Those men over there..."

"I see them." He patted her knee gently. "They're probably from the same rebel camp. Just try not to draw any more attention."

Ace was now facing the store in front of them, and the wagon stretched across the road. She whipped her head around, scanning the busy street. They wouldn't dare try anything here... would they? An alley to her right caught her eye and she sucked in a breath. If they did, she could make a break for it. She'd have to be fast, but she could do it. A leap from the bench and dart between the buildings, careful to avoid the uneven ground and puddles dotting the dirt—

"Catrice." Blaze's voice broke through her thoughts. She jumped and gripped the skirt of her dress. He examined her rigid posture with a furrowed brow. "Hey." He placed a hand over her whitened knuckles. "I'll get us out of here, but I need you to take a deep breath in for me. Can you do that?"

Catrice held his eyes for a moment. He had already saved her twice. She nodded and glanced back at the group of men who were now entirely focused on the wagon. Their dark expressions stayed on Blaze as they started crossing the street.

Blaze jerked up on the lines, pulling the horse around completely. "Change of plans."

He flicked the reins and sent the wagon hurtling down the road and away from the crowd. Shouts from the men behind them echoed off the buildings as Catrice latched onto the bench.

"Where's the Haven you were talking about?" he asked.

"Uh..." Catrice scoured the walls on either side of them.

"Where is it, Catrice?" he yelled over the clatter of the wagon.

"I'm not sure!"

"What? What do you mean you're *not sure*?"

"I know it's on Draken Street. At least, I think

that's what it was called. We only ever sent a few letters to them."

"Draken Street. Got it!" The wagon veered to the left and careened around the corner. Catrice gritted her teeth and winced as the wheels bounced on the uneven ground.

She barely caught a faded *Draken* carved into the corner of a building as Blaze made another turn. The wagon dipped and bounced as it rolled through a puddle.

Blaze groaned and shot a look over his shoulder to the road behind them. "Is it marked? Like the last Haven was?"

"It should be. Search for an outline of a dove."

Blaze slowed the wagon and scanned the doors and walls on either side of them. Catrice adjusted the scarf and glanced around.

"Do you think they're still following us?"

Blaze shook his head. "I don't know. The Dagger-Thorn Rebels were supposed to be gone from this area months ago. If they're back and openly in town, they're getting bolder. We should hang tight for a bit if we find the Haven."

Catrice examined the doorways to her right. "Do you think the people here know about the rebels?"

"Maybe. I doubt most of them knew the men who attacked you were DaggerThorns. It's not exactly something you want to advertise in the Onyx District. If you do, you're not going to make it very long."

"The High Crow here is that ruthless, huh?"

Blaze was silent for a moment. Catrice turned and found him staring at a boarded-up, two-story house next to a wide alley. That was strange. It almost looked abandoned.

"He can be." He motioned to the door and a faded symbol of a dove above the frame. "This it?"

"Yes." Catrice threw her bag over her shoulder and lowered herself to the ground. She ran to the door as Blaze directed the wagon into the open alleyway. The wood was rough against her knuckles as she knocked on the door. "I don't know if anyone's here right now, but normally there's a Haven Elder that lives..." her words trailed off as the door creaked open.

Blaze was at her side in an instant. He pulled the dagger from his belt and held a finger up to his lips. Catrice closed her mouth and retreated as he placed his shoulder against the door and pushed it farther open. The house was dark, but sunlight spilling in through the gaps in the boarded windows and front entrance revealed glimpses of a well-kept living space, fresh dirt tracked across the room, and candles still trailing wisps of smoke from their wicks. Blaze held up a hand as he walked further into the house, keeping Catrice behind him at the entrance outside. He passed the door and slowly turned; blade ready at his side.

The door slammed shut, separating the two of them.

Catrice jumped back as the solid wood crashed into the frame. Someone shouted inside the house, then Catrice heard a series of heavy thumps like multiple bodies hitting the floor. She grappled with the knob, but it held steady in its place. They had locked the door.

No. This couldn't be happening. Not another attack. Not again.

"Blaze!" she shouted, pounding her fists against the wood.

More muffled cries and rustling sounded through the walls, and she ran to one of the windows. Splinters pricked her cheeks as she pressed her face against the boards to peer inside. She could see fleeting shadows of various figures flickering through the beams of light piercing the darkness and hear multiple voices overlap as the fight continued.

Catrice stepped back and grabbed one of the planks, ripping its nails free from the house. Broken glass jutted up from the sill as if the window had been shattered. She tore the lower boards from the wall and took the largest in her hand, knocking away the jagged glass as she crawled through the opening.

Light streamed in behind her enough to brighten the room and reveal the struggle on the floor as Blaze and another man grappled with each other. His dagger lay across the room, and he was pinned under the larger opponent, but he hadn't stopped fighting. Catrice raised the plank to strike the man over the head when a lantern flickered to life at the back of the room, lighting up the large space.

"Jedediah, that's enough!" a woman spoke.

Catrice froze, and the scarf fell from her face as four more figures stepped from the shadows. Blaze's opponent stayed in his position, and an older woman strode toward them holding the lantern.

"Jedediah, get off the poor lad." Her warm voice held a slight tone of annoyance and no room for argument, like she was a mother repeating a common phrase to a small child.

The man gritted his teeth and released Blaze. He glanced at Catrice and the board hovering over his head before standing and stepping back. Blaze launched himself to his feet and placed himself between Catrice and the strangers, pushing her gently against the wall behind him.

"Why do you have a plank?" he whispered.

Catrice lowered the wood to her side. "It's a weapon."

"My dagger's a weapon. That's a stick."

"Yeah, well, a lot of good your dagger did."

"Give me the plank."

"No."

The woman cleared her throat and raised her empty hand in an open gesture. "I apologize for my son. Jedediah is still learning the skill of hospitality." She shot a glare at the man, and he rolled his eyes. "We weren't expecting any visitors. What are your names?"

Catrice glanced at Blaze, and he shook his head. She bit her lip and turned away, scanning the room. A young couple stood in one corner, clasping each other's hands tightly and looking on with fear in their eyes. An elderly man sat on a chair to their left and rested his arms on a cane in front of him. His eyes drooped like he was about to fall asleep at any moment. The man who had pinned Blaze a moment earlier leaned back against the wall to their right with his arms folded and head lowered in submission to the older woman holding the lantern. All the other windows were shattered as well, and pieces of broken chairs and worn cushions were piled up in corners throughout the room. What had happened to the thriving Haven here?

A handful of scrolls lay spread out across the table behind the woman, and fresh ink dripped off the table's edge. Catrice narrowed her eyes at the parchments and familiar handwriting lining the insides.

"What are those?" she asked. The strangers shifted uncomfortably, and the woman moved in front of the table, blocking Catrice's view.

"You haven't answered my question yet. Who are you? And why have you broken into my house?"

Catrice wrinkled her nose. "This isn't your house."

"What makes you say that?"

"It belonged to my people."

"Your people?" The woman raised her eyebrows. She scrutinized Catrice, and her expression softened.

"'My people stretch from sea to sea. Every tribe and tongue. The nations will bow before Me, and all I have created will display My Wonders.'"

Catrice's mouth fell open as the woman spoke the words of the Creator as recorded by the last known Prophet: her father. "You're Followers?"

The woman smiled. "My name is Raina. And you're Catrice Aetos. We have been waiting for you."

16

BLAZE

"TREASON AGAINST THE THRONE IS PUNISHABLE BY DEATH. WHITTAM MUST STAND STRONG AGAINST ANY AND ALL OPPOSITION." - THE ROYAL ARCHIVES OF WHITTAM

Blaze leaned back in the chair and cradled his wrapped arm. He eyed the strangers around him, letting his hard gaze linger a little longer on Jedediah, who was scowling at him from across the room. The sour expression hadn't left the oaf's face since his mother had reprimanded him and banished him to the corner. After a series of awkward and overexcited introductions, the rest of them had settled around the table a little too easily for Blaze's comfort.

Catrice bent forward in her seat as if she was hanging onto every word coming out of Raina's mouth. Her husband, Banner, sat next to his wife, his head nodding in random intervals as he fell in and out of sleep. Tomas and Livia, the young couple at the table opposite Banner, appeared equally as tired, but their rigid postures gave away a wariness the old man lacked. They had mumbled their names a moment earlier in a tone so quiet Blaze could barely catch it, and they hadn't said a word since. Not that he cared. The fact that this Haven even existed here, mere miles from the Onyx Nest, was unnerving. How many others did he not know about?

"I still don't understand." Catrice's voice pulled him from his brooding. She sat back and her hands dropped to her lap. "Where is everyone else? And how did you know I was coming? My mother said this Haven was one of the largest in the Onyx District."

"It was." Raina sighed, brushing her hand across the dusty tablecloth. "My family and I have lived here our whole lives. A few years ago, we had nearly a hundred Followers meeting every week for Fellowship. But then the current High Crow took his position, and Followers started disappearing."

Jedediah's watchful gaze across the room grew hot on Blaze's skin and he looked down, resisting the urge to shield his face. They wouldn't recognize him without his mask. At least, they shouldn't.

Catrice frowned. "What happened?"

"We assume some were imprisoned, but most just got scared or angry. We started losing more when the DaggerThorns came back to town. A lot of our young folk joined their ranks. We did our best to try and convince them otherwise"—she shot a glare at Jedediah—"but I'm afraid we're all that's left, and we just don't have the time or coin to keep up with the place."

Blaze narrowed his eyes at her words. He had been

right. The Followers were being funneled into the rebels. But this was clearly something Raina wasn't happy about. Maybe this was one Follower he wanted Catrice to listen to after all.

"I'm so sorry." Catrice glanced around the room. "But how did you know I was coming?

Banner grunted from his slouched position and tapped his cane on the floor. "The Creator spoke to us."

Blaze fought to keep his jaw from dropping. He leaned forward. This should be interesting.

Raina nodded. "We were praying together three days ago, asking the Creator for direction. We've been thinking about moving to a safer town. That night, three of us"—she motioned to the others—"myself, Banner, and Livia all had the same dream."

Catrice turned to Blaze, wide-eyed. "Three nights ago. That's when the Zradit Haven was attacked." He raised his eyebrows, hoping he looked as engaged and surprised as she did. "What was the dream?"

"We saw your father, Lord Aetos, with your mother holding a baby. The baby grew until she was a young woman, following behind her parents." Raina paused and her eyes fell downcast. "Then a darkness appeared and the parents were gone, leaving the woman alone. The darkness morphed into the shape of a man. The man-shape extended its hand to the woman, but when she touched it, the darkness spread to her too... and she was lost to it."

The silence in the room was deafening. Blaze shifted his jaw, grinding his teeth together. He didn't like how uncomfortable the description of the dream had made him. Were they saying the woman was Catrice and *he* was the darkness? He shook his head. Why was he even bothering with analyzing the story? It didn't matter. It was just a dream—the overactive imagination of people who spent too much time reading mythical stories about an all-knowing Creator. It meant nothing.

He swallowed. Then *why* did it bother him so much?

Raina reached across the table and took Catrice's hands in her own. "Tomas has Insight, and he confirmed you would be coming and that something was wrong."

Blaze resisted the urge to roll his eyes. They got all that from a *dream*? He glanced at Catrice, expecting her to share the same skepticism he felt, but deep lines ran across her forehead and her lips were pressed together as if she was contemplating the strange words. Of course. He should have known by now that she would believe them.

"My mother is dead," she said quietly. "The Crows found her."

Jedediah gave his mother a look like he had been proven right about something. Raina released a breath and bowed her head. "We know."

Blaze jerked upright. That was impossible.

Gideon's men should have removed any false evidence of the Crows' involvement.

"What? How?" Catrice straightened as well, and she appeared as confused as he felt.

Raina nodded toward Jedediah, and he stepped away from the wall. "The rebels. Rumors have been spreading all week that the king tracked down Vivian Aetos and ordered her execution. Got his Crows to do the dirty work for him like they always do."

Blaze gritted his teeth. Jedediah didn't know what he was talking about, and someone was spreading false information.

The oaf continued. "People are angry. Word is that recruits for rebel groups in the Amber and Onyx Districts have doubled. I heard the numbers are even higher in the western districts as more and more people find out."

Blaze stifled a groan. That's why someone had planted the crow pin in that bakery. They wanted the people to think the king had murdered the last of a beloved noble family in cold blood. What better way to pull more support for the rebels than to paint the throne as bloodthirsty and corrupt?

This was big. Bigger than anything the rebels had tried to pull off before. And they had done it the same night dozens of Crows had raided a rebel gathering, where hundreds of potential recruits were sure to see them. This had been meticulously planned. His thoughts wandered to the wanted poster and the patches in his pocket.

The White Owl.

"You know,"—Jed stepped closer to Catrice—"you're the daughter of Marcus Aetos. You could do something."

The hair on the back of Blaze's neck stood on end as the tension in the room thickened. He stood and moved to Catrice's side, his hand resting on the dagger tucked in his belt. Jedediah froze and scowled at him.

Raina patted Catrice's hand and shot her son a glare. "Not now, Jed."

"What does he mean?" Catrice asked.

Raina opened her mouth to speak as she glanced at Blaze and his rigid pose. She closed her mouth and bowed her head. "Nothing. My son is a little too zealous for his own good."

Jedediah squared his shoulders. "She deserves to know."

"Jed—"

Catrice pulled her hand from Raina's grasp. "Know what?"

"The people are angry." He raised his voice. "They're rallying behind the image of the Aetoses and what Marcus stood for. They want to act. Think about what it would mean for the country if an Aetos finally decided to stand up again."

Blaze's fingers twitched against his weapon as he mapped out the best spot on the oaf's torso to strike.

Jed dropped to one knee in front of Catrice and grabbed her hand. Blaze had the sudden urge to break the man's fingers. "Catrice, think about what you could do. With someone like the White Owl, you could turn the tide for the rebels. You would have the support of all the Followers. We might actually stand a chance against the king."

That was enough. Blaze pushed himself between Catrice and Jedediah, forcing the oaf back and itching for an excuse to stab him. "The rebels do far more harm than good."

Jed launched himself to his feet, towering over Blaze. "And what would you, a petty merchant, know about that? Aren't you tired of the taxes Lord Grener raises every year to throw more fancy parties while the king sits idly by?"

"Jedediah, that's enough," Raina spoke again, but her son wasn't stopping

"You think that will get better when one of those High Crows is named heir? They only care about themselves and their kind." He shoved Blaze's shoulder.

Catrice inserted herself between them, stopping Jed in his tracks. Blaze rested his hand on his dagger.

"This is too much. I'm just trying to help our people," she said, raising her chin. "And the rebels hurt people too."

Jedediah widened his eyes, but lowered his gaze as if she was the sun itself. "Well, not all rebels are bad."

Blaze sneered. "And perhaps not all Crows are either."

The room fell silent again. Blaze neutralized his expression. He had said too much.

Catrice closed her eyes and faltered. "I don't think either side is a solution or safe for our people." She sighed and brushed a loose strand of hair behind her ear, skimming her cheek as she did, and winced.

Raina stood and reached out to Catrice, studying the bruise developing on her cheek. "What happened to your face?"

Jedediah shifted his hot gaze to Blaze and scowled as the fire returned to his eyes. "Did you hurt her?"

"No!" Catrice huffed. "We were attacked on the road, but I'm fine. Blaze took the brunt of the fight." She gestured toward his wrapped arm and Raina turned to examine it.

Blaze retreated and pulled his arm away. "It's nothing." He cradled the arm against his chest, and Raina gave him a rather motherly look as she took hold of his wrist.

"Nonsense." She pulled at the towel, unraveling it from his arm. "You're clearly injured and we can get you cleaned up before..." her voice faded away as the towel fell from his wrist to reveal the sliced feather on his skin. "Oh, my."

Raina covered her mouth as Livia and Tomas gasped across the room, retreating further into their corner. Jedediah's face reddened.

"You're a *Crow*." Jed spat the word as if it was a curse.

"Was." Blaze retracted his arm and pulled his sleeve down, covering the mark. "I *was* a Crow."

"No such thing." Jed's lip curled in disgust. "Once a Crow, always a Crow. Isn't that what your kind say?"

Blaze opened his mouth to speak again, but was cut short as a pounding knock resounded from the door. Catrice jumped, and he whipped the dagger from his belt, positioning himself between her and the entrance.

They stood, frozen, for what felt like hours as Blaze waited for someone to act. Raina stepped forward and stared at them as if weighing her options. Her expression remained guarded when she focused on Blaze. He adjusted the weapon in his hand.

These strangers could turn on them. They owed him nothing. He scanned the room, mentally mapping out an escape route. There had to be a back entrance. He could take out Jedediah first if he attacked and anyone else would be easy enough as long as—

Another knock rang through the room and interrupted his thoughts. Catrice threaded her hand through Blaze's arm, wrapping her fingers around his bicep and refocusing his attention on the unknown threat outside the door and the family staring at them.

"Please," she whispered to the group.

Raina startled as if snapped out of a trance and shoved the towel into Blaze's arms. She held a finger up to her mouth while pointing to a closet at the back of the building.

Livia raced forward and gathered the scrolls from the table. She took Catrice's arm with her free hand, avoiding Blaze's gaze, and guided them silently to the square nook. Blaze returned the dagger to his belt and stepped into the closet, moving between two large vases with enough room for Catrice to squeeze in next to him. She hesitated at the tiny space, but when a third round of knocks shook dirt loose from the ceiling, she jumped forward next to Blaze.

The tight quarters forced the two to face each other with their shoulders pressed against the wall. Livia dropped the scrolls into one of the vases and pulled the curtain across the opening, veiling their hiding space from the rest of the room. The thin material only allowed them to see fleeting shadows and shapes as Raina made her way toward the door.

Catrice's warm breath drifted across his collarbone as they waited. The cool intervals between exhales shortened and grew more rapid as she stiffened in front of him. Her eyes fixed on the light of the windows next to the door. He glanced down at her locked jaw and the fists at her sides. Gently, he reached for her hand, allowing his fingers to brush against her whitened knuckles. She jerked at the sudden touch, and her wide eyes darted to his face.

"*It's all right,*" he mouthed. "*Just breathe.*"

She released a shaky breath and nodded. Her hand

relaxed against his own, and he grasped it, rubbing his thumb over her knuckles in a reassuring gesture. Her breathing slowed as Raina opened the door.

Blaze craned his neck to peek through an opening between the curtain and the closet wall. A band of rugged men stood outside, scrutinizing the building. His stomach dropped at their familiar appearance: it was the group who had chased them.

Catrice kicked his boot, and he turned to her.

"*Who is it?*" she mouthed.

He shook his head and turned back to the opening.

Raina stood relaxed at the entrance. "May I help you?" she asked.

The lead man grunted. "We're looking for two strangers who would have come this way. A man and a woman. Have you seen them?"

Raina shifted her weight. "Why do you want to know?"

Catrice gripped his hand and pulled down, but he remained focused on the conversation. She couldn't see, but he couldn't risk drawing any attention.

"Gad and his boys were found dead in the woods this evening."

Raina gripped the door, and Jedediah went rigid at the table with his father. Blaze held his breath.

The man narrowed his eyes. "We think they might've had something to do with it." He paused. "There's a wagon and horse next to your building that's an awful lot like one we saw in the square."

"Yes, well, Tomas and his wife just returned from their travels."

A sharp pain radiated up Blaze's leg as Catrice's boot connected with his shin. He lifted his leg and stifled a groan. Catrice nodded to the front of the house and raised her brow as if she was waiting for him to give her a play-by-play. He held a finger up to his lips, mimicking Raina's earlier gesture. Catrice rolled her eyes. He returned her expression and leaned back to the opening.

"Ah," the man inspected the shattered window on the front of the house. "What happened here?"

"We've had a few break-ins recently. Jed's been working on boarding them up."

"Hmm. You know, we could use Jed at the camp. Always searching for good men to join the cause." The man smiled and stepped forward, scanning the room. "Mind if we come in and take a look?"

"I do, actually." Raina widened her stance, blocking his access. "This is my home."

"Now, Raina." The man crossed his arms, showing off his large forearms and sword secured to his hip. "We don't mean any harm. Just want to make sure everything's good. I'm sure you ain't got nothing to hide."

The rest of the men moved closer to the door, but Raina held her ground. Blaze swallowed. If the men decided to come in, there was nothing Raina would be able to do about it. He and Catrice would have to fight their way out. Jedediah walked behind his mother and rested a hand on the frame.

"Don't worry about it, Petar. I'll keep a lookout." He shrugged. "Maybe even see you at the camp tomorrow."

The man broke into a grin. "Aye, that's what I like to hear." He reached past the door and clapped Jedediah on the shoulder. "See you tomorrow, then. And tell your ma to show a little more hospitality next time. Never know when trouble's gonna come your way." His eyes darkened as the words faded and the group backed away from the house.

Raina's hostile stance remained until the men mounted their horses and disappeared from view. She shut the door and whirled around to her son.

"You are *not* going to their camp tomorrow." She wagged a finger in his face and drove him back toward the table. "I won't have any son of mine getting himself killed in some ragtag group of rebels for the sake of getting to fight."

He raised his arms over his head. "I just said that to get them to leave. And at least they *do* something instead of hiding or fleeing the country. Would that really be so bad?"

"Yes!" Raina threw her hands up. Blaze smirked. At least she understood. "Like Catrice said, our fight is for our people. For the Creator. Not against the Crows or the king." She looked to her husband. "Banner, tell him."

Banner nodded from his seated position. "Your mother's right."

"Thank you."

"But our people are disappearing." Jedediah frowned. "How can we stop that unless we fight?"

"We trust the Creator, Jed." Raina sat. "It's not up to us to decide such things or take the lives of others to make it happen."

Blaze pulled back the curtain, and the family turned to him and Catrice as they shuffled out of the hiding space. The group regaled the two with a new caution in their eyes as they made their way across the room.

Raina stood and forced a smile. "Are you both all right?"

"Yes," Catrice answered. "Thank you for protecting us."

"Of course. Anything for the Aetos family." She hesitated, and the tension returned as she turned to Blaze. "I'm assuming those men were searching for you?"

Catrice closed her eyes. Blaze bit his tongue.

"I see." Raina clasped her hands in front of her torso.

"What did you do?" Jedediah growled at Blaze.

Catrice stepped in front of him before he could respond. "They attacked us in the woods. They tried to take me away, and would have succeeded too, if Blaze hadn't intervened when he did."

"The DaggerThorns attacked you?" Jed faltered, the hard expression dropping from his face.

"Yes. They had a wanted poster of me with the White Owl's emblem."

Raina hit her son in the arm with the back of her hand. "See, boy. They're not all the saviors you make them out to be."

Jedediah grumbled under his breath and sat at the table. "Still better than those dirty Crows…"

Blaze set his jaw and eyed the pouting oaf, but his gaze remained downcast. With that kind of attitude and mouth, he was lucky to still be alive. How the family had remained hidden so close to Blaze's home raised more questions in his mind than he had answers for, but he would have to figure that out later. And he didn't want to spend any more time there than he had to. There were enough surprises already. He placed a hand on Catrice's shoulder and forced a smile.

"Thank you again for your hospitality. But we really should be going. I don't want to cause you any more trouble."

Catrice shot Blaze a quizzical look, but didn't object to his statement.

Raina frowned. "Oh, but it's getting late. Do you need somewhere to rest for the night?" she asked.

"No." Blaze raised a hand. "We'll be fine. We're staying a few miles away."

"That's good." Raina smiled. "Catrice can stop by another day, then."

Catrice returned her smile. "Absolutely. I'll come back soon." She moved from Blaze's touch and embraced the older woman. "Thank you again." She released Raina and walked around the table as she offered a hug and goodbye to each member of the Haven.

Raina focused on Blaze and opened her arms. He took a deep breath and stepped into her embrace, willing his body to relax against the unfamiliar affection.

"Thank you for protecting her. May the Creator bless you," she whispered.

His stomach knotted as she squeezed his shoulders and leaned back. He forced another smile as her attention switched to his forearm.

"Please let me dress your wound first. It's the least I can do for someone who saved an Aetos."

Blaze sighed. "Very well."

17

CATRICE

Catrice climbed onto the wagon's bench and rotated her neck, releasing a series of pops and cracks. She groaned and rubbed the space just above her shoulder blades. A hard, tender knot rolled under her fingertips. Red splotches on her elbow caught her eye as she lowered her arm—bruises to match the ones on her shins and knees, and the rope burns on her wrist. The feeling of rough hands on her skin resurfaced, and her throat tightened.

"Those look painful." Blaze nodded to the discolorations muddling her skin.

She yanked her sleeve down as he climbed onto the wagon. Why did he always have to bring up the topics she wanted to avoid? "They're nothing."

"Is your skin naturally the color of undercooked meat, then?"

"Are you naturally this painfully sarcastic?" She

paused at the unfamiliar bite in her own tone and lowered her eyes. As usual, Blaze seemed unaffected.

"It's a learned skill."

"I'm fine. They'll heal in a few days."

Blaze looked unconvinced. "Can I see?" He gently placed his fingers on her elbow, and she winced, cradling it close to her chest.

"No. I'm fine." At least, she would be if he stopped pushing. It would be better to forget the attack ever happened, and she couldn't do that if he kept bringing it up. "It's getting dark. We should get moving."

He leaned back and gathered the lines, frowning. "Very well."

The wagon jerked beneath them as Ace started down the road. Long shadows cast by the setting sun beyond the buildings covered the street. She glanced back at the Haven as it disappeared behind a corner. Blaze had seemed in a hurry to leave, but she longed to stay the evening with her people. Questions about her family and the rebels swirled in her mind.

I'll be back in a few days, she reminded herself.

As soon as they were settled at Blaze's home and she contacted the other Havens, she could come visit again. Perhaps even stay for a Fellowship. A feeling of nostalgia rested in her chest at the idea, and she smiled.

The memory of Gleena's cries as Catrice ran from the Zradit Haven interrupted her thoughts, and her smile faded.

What if the Galian Fellowship was raided as well? There was no evidence the Crows were tracking them, but she would have said the same about Zradit. Truth be told, there was no way she could know. Not unless she saw the Crows with her own eyes. And that was enough to set her nerves on end and cause the hair on the back of her neck to bristle. She couldn't protect her people. Not on her own. She wasn't enough.

"Catrice, think about what you could do." Jedediah's words echoed in her head. *"Think about what it would mean for the country if an Aetos finally decided to stand up again."*

What would it mean? Would it change her people's fate? Allow them to live in peace again?

"With someone like the White Owl, you could turn the tide for the rebels. You would have the support of all the Followers. We might actually stand a chance against the king."

When he had mentioned the White Owl, fear had gripped her heart. The men who had tried to kidnap her were sent from the White Owl. But there was something stronger than fear growing inside of her.

Anger.

Red, hot anger that burned in her chest with every breath. Anger that made the idea of joining the rebels to take down the king more appealing with every passing moment.

Not that she would admit that to Blaze. She had seen the way he reacted whenever she talked about the rebels. He had his own anger to deal with. She couldn't trust him with her own.

Jed had said the people were angry. That they wanted to act. The White Owl certainly did that. He fought for change. What did she fight for?

What *could* she fight for? She couldn't even stab a Crow properly with a fire poker. Blaze could fight. He had killed those rebels without a second thought. Her stomach turned at the memory of their blood staining his features. But he had done it to protect her. Everything he had done was to protect her.

If only she didn't need protecting. If only she could learn how to do what he was able to do. Then maybe she could have saved Mother. Maybe the Zradit Haven would still be free. She turned her head to look at him.

He cast her a side-eye. "What do you want?"

Now was her chance. "Teach me to fight."

"Ha." Blaze laughed. "No."

She punched his shoulder but only succeeded in knocking herself off balance. "Why not? I want to be able to do more than scream if something happens again."

"You did. I saw that low blow to the brute's groin with your knee. Would've made me think twice about kidnapping you."

She scrunched her nose. "It wasn't enough though. If you hadn't shown up, they still would have thrown me on that horse and ran."

"Good thing I was there, then."

"I'm serious."

He sighed and rubbed his neck. "I am too. I also saw how you reacted after you thought you'd killed the Crow in Zradit. What if you actually did kill someone, Catrice? I have, and it's not pretty. I don't want you to have to deal with that."

She had basically killed Mother. What could be worse than that?

Shaking her head, she took off the green scarf he had given her. "Huh. Funny."

"What?"

"That made it sound like you actually care. And here I was starting to believe that whole dark, brooding"—she lowered her voice and handed him the scarf —"I-used-to-be-a-Crow-and-could-kill-you-with-one-look thing you've got going on."

He yanked it from her hands and wrapped it around his neck, straightening his posture. "I don't sound like that."

"Uh-huh."

"And who says I can't?"

"Can't what?"

"Kill with one look."

She rolled her eyes. "If you could, you wouldn't need the hundreds of hidden knives you have under your shirt."

"I don't have hundreds. That would be unnecessary and cumbersome."

"Then how many do you have?"

He glanced at her, eyes dark and expression neutral. "Enough."

A shiver ran down her spine and she slouched against the back of the bench. "I still think you should teach me how to fight. What if—"

"Never going to happen, Catrice."

She grumbled under her breath and crossed her arms. One way or another, she would learn to fight. She would need to if she wanted to join the rebels.

She stared at the horizon as the sky painted itself with an array of warm colors. They passed trees on either side as the path angled upward. Massive hills blocked the sunset, casting ominous shadows across the valley. The path before them faded, giving way to thick brush and winding vines slithering from tree to tree like long snakes. Catrice eyed them, half convinced they might come to life at any moment.

Ace maneuvered effortlessly through the dark forest, and Blaze guided the horse between trees as if he had done this all his life. Was this where he lived?

They continued up the hill as the sun set, throwing the world surrounding them into a starlit night, but they never slowed in their ascent. Rays of moonlight pierced through the trees and Catrice thanked the Creator for the light.

Then, like stars from the heavens, the darkness began to light up with small glowing orbs the size of her thumb. They glowed for a few seconds before disappearing, only to light up a few feet away again, floating higher each time. Her eyes followed them around the wagon as they continued to climb, and she smiled.

"They're fire lantern lilies," Blaze's voice filled the silence of the forest. He leaned close to her side. "They're like the lantern lilies you had in your garden in Ontiach, only they bloom at night under a full moon and then float away to root somewhere new."

"How do you remember I had lantern lilies in Ontiach?" Catrice asked, staring in awe at the lights. He still remembered that? They had been so young.

"They were your favorite when you were little. I don't forget things like that easily," he whispered into her ear.

Goosebumps spread across her shoulders and neck where his breath had settled. She turned to him. Uneven shadows cast by the glowing lilies fell on his unshaven face. His gaze was set straight ahead, but a mischievous grin played at his lips.

"Now you can keep staring at me, or you can turn and see your new home." Blaze nodded towards whatever was behind her.

Catrice jerked her head forward and looked down as her cheeks heated. She mentally scolded herself for being so brazen about staring at him. If she wasn't careful, he would start to think she found him attractive. The goosebumps returned at the thought.

The rest of Blaze's words registered in her head as

they reached the top of the hill. Peering across the top of the trees, she gasped.

A castle sat in the next valley between four hills. The white stone walls reflected in the surface of the moonlit lake set in front of the large wooden front doors. Two towers rose out of the east side of the castle, while a smaller third tower rose out above the west. Wide windows speckled the stone walls that looked like they would hold against any intruder, except for the thick ivy winding its way up and over the fortress. She squinted, focusing on a courtyard in the middle of the castle and the stable behind it.

"This is your home?"

"It was my father's."

His father's? Curiosity swelled within her. He never talked about his father. Before she could respond, he flicked the reins and they began making their way back down the hill.

The trees covered Catrice's view of the castle, but it didn't stop her from growing more anxious with every passing minute. *This* was going to be her home? Occasionally, she could catch a glimpse of the white walls through the branches and vines. Joy bubbled up inside of her at the thought of exploring the vast corridors and surrounding forests.

Then, as soon as the excitement came, shame overwhelmed her. She didn't have time for that. Havens were being attacked. Mother would have never allowed herself to be distracted when it came to their people. Catrice couldn't afford to either.

As they reached the bottom of the hill, the ground leveled to a point where the wagon rolled smoothly, and the tree line broke. Blaze directed Ace toward the stable at the back of the grounds. Catrice craned her neck one way and then the other, trying to see as much of the castle and grounds as she could. At this distance, the walls towered above her, fading against the dark sky above.

Blaze pulled the wagon to a stop and leapt from the bench before making his way to her side. Stepping down from the bench, she stumbled as her feet adjusted to the uneven ground, and she latched onto Blaze's arm for support. He winced and his forearm tightened under her grip, but he didn't pull away. She had grabbed his bandaged wound.

"I'm so sorry! I—" Her words faded as she looked up.

Blaze's eyes held her own. Amusement danced within the azure twins, and he gently took her hand from his arm. He tucked a loose strand of hair behind her ear. Her breath hitched in her throat, and his fingers grazed her cheek, trailing her jawline until they rested just below her lips.

What was he doing? And why—heavens, *why*—didn't she want him to stop? She swallowed, her eyes remaining on him and her body painfully aware of the mere few inches remaining between them.

A stablehand rushed to their side, and Blaze's smile dropped. He stepped back stiffly, placing himself a full arm's length away, and said something to the boy Catrice didn't quite catch before moving to the back of the wagon.

She watched in silence, struggling to find words as her heart continued to pound. Her skin tingled where his hand had brushed against her skin, and an unfamiliar desire for him to do it again urged her to step closer. Confusion quickly overcame the new feeling, and she steeled herself, choosing instead to clear her throat and tap the edge of the wagon to get his attention.

"So, this was your father's?"

Blaze nodded, hardly glancing up from the supplies. "He acquired it during his service in the military. When I completed a term, the king granted it to me."

"I knew the Crows paid well... but I had no idea it was like this."

"The Commander values loyalty, and he's not afraid to do what it takes to earn and keep it."

"I see." Catrice furrowed her brow. "If this belonged to your father, why didn't it just pass onto you when he died?"

Blaze hesitated. "Land passes on through family name." He lifted a pack from the bed over his shoulder. "I took my mother's."

"Laskaris isn't your real surname?"

He shook his head. "My aunt made sure Izaak and I were registered under my mother's name to avoid association with my father after he left."

"What is it then?"

"What is what?"

"Your father's surname." Catrice retrieved her bag. When she refocused on Blaze, he stood rigid at the end of the wagon. "Blaze?"

He jumped as if startled by her voice and swung another sack across his body. "We should get inside. The stableboy will take care of the rest of this and stow the horse."

He avoided her gaze and strutted toward the castle. She vaguely noticed the boy leading Ace into the stable behind her and another servant appearing to gather the rest of the supplies from the wagon. Her focus was on the dark-haired man walking away from her. What had happened? One moment, he had been caressing her face, and the next, he was running away like she had the plague.

She adjusted the pack on her shoulder, picked up her dress, and jogged after him. A doorman opened the large wooden door from the inside and bowed as they passed. She nodded to him and turned to Blaze's back, only to immediately be distracted by the wide halls and tall ceilings around her.

Iron sconces lined the walls, lighting the carved white stone and arched doorways. Wool rugs with intricate black designs woven through the fabric lined the smooth, cobblestone floors that were so clean they shone. Even as she moved, the doorman behind her swept away the trail of dirt left from her boots. Servants shuffled in and out of the rooms in front of her, shooting curious glances her way. One older servant walked toward her, arms piled high with linens. Catrice smiled and nodded, but the woman continued without acknowledging her. She frowned, her head following the servant as she passed. When she looked forward again, she nearly ran into Blaze's chest.

"Catrice," Blaze started, his eyes set above her as if he was addressing someone in the distance. "This is Jillian." He gestured to a golden-haired servant at his side. "She will show you to your room and make sure your things are taken care of."

"Thank you. I—"

"I'll see you in the morning," Blaze cut her off and turned on his heel, continuing into the castle and away from her.

Catrice closed her mouth and raised a hand to reach for him, but he was already gone. "Well, that was strange." She turned to Jillian. "Is he always that way here?"

The servant snapped to attention. "I'm not supposed to talk about the master's personal life. Follow me. I'll show you to your room." She turned around before Catrice could object.

Blaze's form continued to recede down the hall,

and Catrice crossed her arms, glancing back and forth between the man she had spent the last ten days with and the servant expectantly waiting for her to follow.

"Miss?" Jillian prompted.

Catrice sighed and turned to Jillian, following her in the opposite direction of Blaze, but her mind continued to spin as his odd actions replayed in her memory. What was going on in his head?

18

BLAZE

Blaze tightened his hands into fists as he walked down the elaborate hallway. He kept his pace quick and precise, putting space between him and the girl who, in less than two weeks, had turned his world upside down.

He grimaced at the thought of his actions at the stables earlier. How could he have been so impulsive? He slowed and glared at his hand. A hand that had betrayed him only a few moments earlier. What had come over him? He had simply helped her off of the bench like he did every day. Then she grabbed his arm like she would when they were children.

But they were not children anymore, and she was right there, standing in front of him under the moonlight. Her thick brown hair never wanted to stay captive away from her face. He had only brushed one strand behind her ear, grazing her skin as he did. That soft skin...

Blasts! He groaned. This was the second time he had acted without thinking, without planning out his steps and actions regarding her. By all of Whittam, he had nearly told her about *Father*.

Flirting to gain her trust was one thing, but he couldn't risk forming a real attachment. It was impulsive and stupid, and a servant had nearly witnessed it. The Commander couldn't doubt his intentions or ability to complete this mission. Not when he still had Nikita's report to worry about. It was nothing. It had to be nothing. And it couldn't happen again.

The hallway broke off into a large room as he made a sharp turn. Harold waited inside and Blaze nodded in his direction before walking towards the carved table that stood against one of the white walls. He yanked his scarf off and tossed it onto the mahogany surface. The hood that shadowed his face came off as well, ruffling his hair. He leaned on the table with both hands and looked into his reflection in the large mirror, willing himself to remember his purpose. He was the Onyx Crow—hand-picked by the throne and primed to become the next Commander. And he wouldn't let some *girl* mess that up.

He reached into his pocket and pulled out the crumpled flyer and patches. A single, crushed daisy fell to the ground. He paused, staring at the flower, and resisted the urge to pick it up, even as the image of

Catrice blushing as he placed one behind her ear crossed his mind's eye. Kicking the daisy under the table, he refocused on the flyer. Distractions weren't something he could afford any longer.

Smoothing it out on the table, he studied the paper. He ran his thumb over the wax imprint of the owl with its talons extended out.

How had the White Owl gotten a copy of Catrice's poster? It was only sent to the High Crows of each district. If there was a leak somewhere, it was higher up in the Crows. And what did the White Owl want with Catrice? He had already pinned Vivian's death on the Crows. What advantage would having Catrice give him? Unless Jedediah was right, and the White Owl wanted her influence. The thought made Blaze's stomach turn. He had to report this.

He looked back at his reflection and spotted the metal chain of his necklace peeking out of the neckline of his tunic. He pulled it out, weighing his dark ring and a bronze key slung around the chain in his hand. The ring was a glaring reminder of his mission, and the fact he was dangerously close to falling behind.

He had no comprehensive list of Havens, and the ones he did know of were either already destroyed or had saved his life.

The only things he did have were an increasingly curious and perceptive Catrice unknowingly a prisoner in his own home, and a growing desire to remain in her presence during every waking moment.

Blasts, what was *wrong* with him? He shook his head and switched his attention from the necklace to Harold's reflection.

"The black crow flies," Blaze said.

"And rests in the darkness," the older man replied from behind him.

Blaze turned. "It's done, then?"

He nodded. "We received your letter this morning. All your classified messages have been secured in your quarters. The servants have been instructed to refer to you strictly as 'Master Blaze' and speak nothing of your profession or heritage. Your Crows have been briefed to direct all communication through sealed air notes until further notice. Some messages have already arrived and are in your quarters."

"And my aunt?"

"Diana was reluctant, but agreed."

"Thank you, Harold. I don't know what I would do without you." He clapped him on the shoulder. "Where is she?"

Harold raised his arm toward the hallway. A gasp sounded behind Blaze, and he turned to a familiar face standing in the archway. He snatched the items off the desk and shoved them back into his pockets as she ran to meet him. He opened his arms to welcome her into a hug.

"You're safe," she said as he embraced her.

"I always am, Diana," he chuckled.

She stepped back, observed his grimy clothes and

bloodstained skin, and swatted him on the arm. "Don't lie to me, son. I know the kinds of dangers you encounter on your missions." She shuddered.

"You have no idea," Blaze mumbled under his breath and smiled when his aunt eyed him. He walked past her and sat in one of the velvet chairs adorning the sitting room.

"You were gone longer than planned," she said as she reclined in the seat across from him.

"There were complications. I sent you a note explaining everything."

Diana fanned her flushed cheeks. "Nearly two weeks after you had left! I was worried."

He rolled his eyes. "Why do all the women in my life seem to worry unnecessarily about me?"

Her eyes widened, and Blaze immediately regretted his words. She leaned forward in her seat. "*All* the women? You speak of Catrice, I assume?"

Blaze whipped his attention to the door as if Catrice would walk in at any moment.

"Don't worry." Diana waved her hand. "Harold already briefed me on what exactly I'm allowed or not allowed to say in my own home over the next few weeks."

"*My* home, Diana."

Harold stepped forward. "My apologies, my lady, but Master Blaze has—"

"My aunt knows why we have certain rules in place." Blaze cut him off. "My position demands it."

Diana raised her chin. "And does your position also demand you use childhood friends as a means to imprison your people all across the country?"

"Yes," Blaze answered, his hard voice echoing across the room. Harold stiffened, and Diana sat back in her seat, eyebrows raised. He tightened his jaw. He was in no mood to debate this. "And the Followers aren't my people. They never were."

"Oh, my boy." Diana stood. He propped his feet onto the footrest and slouched against the back of the chair. She crossed the distance between them. "I know how you feel about the Creator, but Catrice is your friend..."

"She's a Follower. And an Aetos. I don't have a choice."

"You always have a choice, Blaze." She sat on the footrest next to his boots and placed a hand on his knee. "Despite what your father may teach."

Blaze snapped his gaze up to hers. He wouldn't allow her to question the Commander. "Enough."

"Does she at least know who he is?"

"She doesn't need to know."

"Well, what *does* she know? Have you been truthful about anything?"

"As much as she needs to know for me to complete my mission."

"So, after everything, you're still going to use her and turn her in?"

"I said enough, Diana!" Blaze threw his hands up

in exasperation and slammed his feet to the ground, pulling away from her touch. "She's Lord Aetos's daughter. Her people have made their choice. I wish there was another way... but there isn't."

Diana dropped her head. "You could let her go. She wouldn't cause any trouble past the border. You could even go with her. Escape this country and the king's grasp."

Blaze scoffed. "Why do you assume I would want that?"

"It's what you wanted for Izaak."

His throat tightened, and tears rushed to the back of his eyes. He swallowed down a wave of anger. Diana knew better than to bring up his brother. "That was different. He deserved better. I'm right where I need to be."

"You don't need to keep punishing yourself for his death, my boy."

Yes, he did. And it would never be enough. "I'm doing what I must, Diana."

She flicked her eyes back up to meet his own, and he could see her anger building. "Your mission is Catrice's death sentence. Why can't you see that?"

He ignored her question and leaned forward, clasping his hands in front of him. "The Commander spared you. Who's to say he won't do the same for Catrice?"

"The only reason Tenaris let me go was because I am your mother's only living family. I'm not even allowed to leave this castle. He won't be as lenient with Catrice."

"He won't kill her. She may be brainwashed, but she is not her father. She will stand trial just like Vivian would have. The Commander is just, and he will see to it that her punishment is fair."

Her eyes welled with tears. "Please, my boy. You will live to regret this. I've already lost your brother to Tenaris's bloodthirsty agenda. I can't lose you too."

He held up a hand to silence her. "He is my king, and I will do what he says."

As Blaze ran up the steps, his heavy footfalls echoed off the winding stone staircase. His bedroom door stood closed at the top of the tower. With an overzealous shove, he pushed it open and marched to the end of his room, where his desk sat next to the smoldering hearth. A neat stack of sealed scrolls the size of his thumb lay on the top of the wooden desk. They must be the ones Harold mentioned had arrived by air note. Breaking the wax seals one by one, he read through the messages.

Most were simple updates from Crows he had positioned across the district. Lord Grener was still pouting about his tax increase. There was a farmer suspected of setting his crops on fire in protest against the upper family who owned the land. Two of his men were retiring next month. Five others were renewing their contract. A new wave of Rewonian refugees was causing trading delays at the border.

A note with an amber seal caught his eye, and he tore it open. Gideon's handwriting dominated the page in red ink:

Update on rebel incident in Deln:

Most of insurrectionists found and arrested. Rogue evaded capture. New rebel pamphlet published claiming the king ordered Vivian Aetos's murder. Uptick in rebel activity and unrest recorded across district. Will report more in following weeks.

- The Amber Crow

Blaze set his jaw. So Jedediah had been right. People were angry. All because the rebels had killed Vivian and blamed it on the Crows. He crumbled the parchment in his fist and rubbed his other hand through his hair.

If only Catrice knew they had both lost loved ones to the White Owl. Then maybe she would stay away from the rebels for good. But for her to know that, he would have to tell her how he knew who had killed her mother, and right now, he didn't trust his own head to keep all his lies straight.

He dropped the crumpled message and picked up the last note. The royal seal adorned the outside of this one, and he swallowed down a lump that bubbled in his throat.

New assignment:

Followers confirmed as rebel group in connection with the White Owl. Seize and eradicate any known Havens. Insurgents to be sent to the High Nest for judgment.

Effective immediately.

This was his doing. He should be proud. Excited, even. It was a move like this that would put him first in line for becoming the next Commander. And as Commander, he could wipe out the rebels for good. Finally, make the country at peace and avenge Izaak's death. This was what he had been working toward during his whole career as a High Crow. This was a good thing. Blaze rolled up the message and chewed on the inside of his cheek.

Then *why* did he feel like he was going to throw up?

Moving to the hearth, he swiped a black, carved wooden box from the mantle. The cool metal of the key hanging around his neck disappeared as he pulled the necklace from under his shirt and unlocked the small chest. Various rolled scrolls matching the ones on his desk, folded parchment, ribbon, a pen, and red and black ink sat snugly on the inside of the box in their own individual compartments. He sorted the new messages into their designated spots.

A sharp cry reached his ears and he turned to his window. In the distance, beyond the open window-pane, a small, black bird approached the castle, nearly indiscernible from the night sky behind it.

Good. Right on time.

Blaze ignored the nausea churning in his gut and walked towards the windowsill. He reached his arm out as a perch for the bird to land on. The familiar sensation of a crow's talons gripping his sleeve made him feel more grounded, and he pulled his arm back inside. The bird eyed him curiously before hopping to the windowsill and ruffling its feathers. Blaze grabbed a small bowl of water and seed from under the window and placed it next to the crow.

He returned to the fireplace and retrieved a blank square of parchment, a wooden pen, and the red ink. Dipping the metal point into the ink, he pressed the pen to the paper.

Update on assignment:

Subject secured at the Onyx Nest. Collecting intel on Havens.

DaggerThorn rebels connected with the White Owl located in the district. Wanted poster of subject compromised. Assigning Crows to investigate and disperse.

Blaze paused, lifting the pen from the note. He should report the Galian Haven, but the Commander had ordered that all Havens be eradicated. If he reported it and the Haven was raided, Catrice would be able to connect the dots and figure out it was him. He couldn't risk blowing his cover, not when he was so close.

But if he didn't report it and somehow word got to

the Commander... Blaze shook his head. The Galian Haven was small, anyway. They wouldn't cause any trouble. He didn't *need* to arrest them. The Commander would understand.

Previously unknown Haven discovered in Galian. Request to delay seizure until intel is complete.

- The Onyx Crow

He stamped his seal in a blot of black wax on the edge of the message. Pulling another blank parchment from the box, he repeated the note in black for his own records. Bits of dry paper crumbled off the edges as he rolled the copied message and tucked it inside the compartment with his last months' worth of assignments. The chest clicked as he closed the lid and placed it back on the mantle.

The crow lifted its head from its feeding as Blaze approached, wrapping a black ribbon around the scroll as he did. He tied the letter to the bird's foot and sent it out the window in the direction of the High Nest.

19

CATRICE

"WHEN ALL WAS LOST, FIRE RAINED DOWN;
THE FIRE THAT BURNS AND CLEANSES,
AND LIGHTS THE HIDDEN CORNERS OF
MAN'S DARKNESS. THEN THERE WAS PEACE
ONCE MORE." - TESTIMONY OF PROPHET
GERIS AETOS

Catrice paused in the doorway, catching her breath. Her room was located at the top of one of the towers, and the stone stairs had taken more of a toll than she expected.

"The linens are freshly pressed and there are extra towels and blankets in the chest at the foot of your bed. I'll draw a bath, and another servant will be bringing up your things shortly." Jillian strolled through the large bedroom.

Catrice scanned the space, taking in the carved furnishings arranged around her. It was immaculate, even surpassing her childhood home in Ontiach. She swallowed.

"Blaze must do well in his travels to afford all this." She gently grazed the smooth surface of a desk with her fingertips.

"Much of it was passed down to him, but Master Blaze works hard to maintain it."

"From his father, right?"

Jillian blinked and gestured to a rope slung through a hoop jutting from the wall and disappearing into a hole in the stone. "Just pull this if you need anything else. It's connected to a bell in the servants' quarters."

Catrice nodded absently, but her thoughts remained focused on Jillian's reaction, or lack thereof, to her question about Blaze's father. Did no one talk about him here? What kind of reason could there be for that?

A new set of footsteps echoed through the open door as an older woman appeared at the top of the staircase. Catrice's heart leapt.

"Diana?" she whispered.

The woman beamed and opened her arms wide as she entered the room. Catrice shrieked and ran forward into the embrace, grinning. Silver hairs tickled her nose and stuck to her skin as tears flowed down her cheeks. She pulled away and sucked in a deep breath, struggling to control her laughter. Diana cupped her face and cocked her head to the side.

"My goodness, dear. Laughing *and* crying. Are you well?"

"Yes." Her vision blurred. "I'm fine." Catrice hiccupped and triggered a fresh round of tears. "I'm just... it's just so good to see you."

Diana wiped the drops from Catrice's skin and stepped back as her own brown eyes filled. "It's good to see you too, my dear. Now, let me get a look at you."

Catrice brushed the loose strands of hairs back from her face and opened her arms as Diana examined her.

"My... you look just like your mother." She turned over Catrice's wrists to reveal the rope burns and bruises dotting her skin. "What happened here?"

Catrice pulled her arms back to rub the wounds. She had been hoping Diana wouldn't notice. She didn't need to relive that again. "We were attacked on the road."

Diana's eyes darkened. "Rebels?"

"Yes... how did you know?"

"That explains why Blaze is so on edge."

"What do you mean?"

Diana shook her head. "I'm afraid our family has a rather sordid history with those groups."

So there was a reason why Blaze hated the rebels so much. "If I may ask, what happened?"

Diana glanced past her, and Catrice turned her head to see Jillian waiting against the wall, watching them carefully. An odd tension filled the space between them. When Catrice returned her gaze to Diana, the woman was frowning.

"It's not my place to say, I'm afraid. You should ask Blaze."

Oh, she was planning on it now.

"Enough about us." Diana sucked in a breath, and a soft smile returned to her expression. "I'm so sorry about Vivian. Blaze told me what happened."

A bitter taste settled in Catrice's mouth, and she swallowed, shaking her head. "It all happened so fast. I'm just trying to do what she would have wanted."

"I'm sure you are doing a wonderful job. She would be proud of you. Both your parents would."

"That's actually something I wanted to talk with you about." Catrice sniffled. "I've been working on comprising a list of Havens and wanted to know if you—"

Diana held up a hand, silencing her, and glanced at Jillian again. Catrice narrowed her eyes. She hadn't stopped to think about whose ears would be safe in the castle. Something was definitely going on. Something that was keeping Diana from speaking freely.

"Jillian, do you know if Blaze is around downstairs?" Catrice asked. "I would like to speak with him before we go to sleep for the night."

The servant pressed her lips into a thin line. "Master Blaze is quite busy and prefers to rest after his travels."

"It would just be a moment." Catrice smiled in what was hopefully a reassuring manner. If she could get Jillian out of the room, then maybe it would give her and Diana enough time to talk.

"Well... I'm sure it wouldn't hurt to check." Jillian

returned her smile and bowed to them. "I'll be back shortly."

Catrice waited until the servant's steps faded from the tower to direct her gaze back to Diana. "Is it not safe to talk freely here?"

"It is better to keep our circle small for now. We can never be too careful. What about the Havens?"

"I've been working on a list. But there're some holes, especially in the districts I've never been to before, including this district. I wanted to check and see if you knew of any or have attended any Fellowships since living here."

"I'm afraid I haven't had the pleasure. It's been... difficult to make it to any Fellowships."

"Because of the High Crow here? I heard he's ruthless."

"He's lost, more than anything." The light in Diana's face faded. She took a deep breath and sat on the edge of the bed. "Catrice... there are some things you should know."

Catrice frowned and settled beside her. "About what?"

Diana opened her mouth to speak, but returning footsteps echoing up the stairs cut her off. A male servant entered the room, carrying Catrice's bags. He set the items down gently on the chest and bowed to the two of them before exiting.

As he left, Jillian entered and curtsied. "Master

Blaze has gone to bed, but he would like you to join him for breakfast tomorrow if you are able."

"Thank you, Jillian." Catrice stood. "I'll be there."

The handmaiden nodded and looked at Diana.

Diana sighed. "I'll be there too, as always. Is there anything else you need, Jillian?"

"Master Blaze requests everyone retire for the night."

"Oh." Diana raised an eyebrow and her tone hardened. "Does he, now?"

"Yes. I'm to stay in the room at the bottom of the tower in case Miss Catrice needs anything."

"I see."

The odd tension returned, and Catrice glanced between the two of them. Jillian remained at the doorway with a relaxed, expectant smile plastered on her face. Diana was the lady of this home, yet it almost sounded as if Jillian was giving her orders. A shiver rippled down Catrice's spine. Diana had been right. She couldn't trust everyone here.

"Well then..." she broke the silence. "I'll see you in the morning, Diana."

"Yes." Diana stood and brushed out her lap. "I'll see you in the morning, my dear. Get some rest." She gave her a brief hug and strolled out of the room, ignoring the maid as she passed.

Jillian turned her doe-eyed, cold gaze to Catrice. "I'll draw your bath."

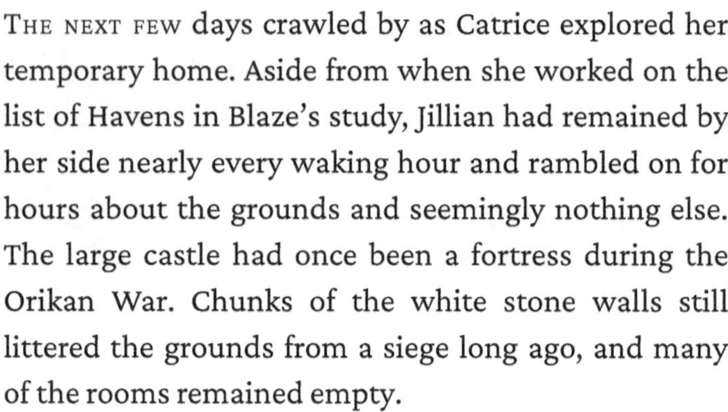

THE NEXT FEW days crawled by as Catrice explored her temporary home. Aside from when she worked on the list of Havens in Blaze's study, Jillian had remained by her side nearly every waking hour and rambled on for hours about the grounds and seemingly nothing else. The large castle had once been a fortress during the Orikan War. Chunks of the white stone walls still littered the grounds from a siege long ago, and many of the rooms remained empty.

Jillian had also provided everything Catrice had asked for, including the parchment and ink she needed to write letters to every Haven. Aside from meals, which they took together in the dining room, she had hardly seen Blaze. It was almost as if he was avoiding her.

So Catrice had started penning letters. *So* many letters.

Her hand ached from gripping a quill for hours on end as she scribbled about Mother's death, warned the Followers about possible raids, and requested updates on the Havens. One of the servants had taken the stack of messages to town that morning and, if everything went well, she would start hearing back by the following week. Then, once she had an updated list of the Haven locations and their Elders, she could start facilitating contacts and routes between them.

She clasped her hands behind her back and

rounded the corner into Blaze's study. She froze—Blaze was sitting on the floor in front of the fireplace, pouring over the maps she had marked up with Haven locations the day before. She hadn't expected to see him until breakfast, and she willed the flush that had filled her cheeks at his presence to fade.

His white linen shirt lay loose around his torso and the sleeves were rolled up to his elbows in a casual fashion, revealing his bandaged forearm. Ink stained his exposed skin and was smeared across his forehead in uneven streaks. Catrice fought the smirk teasing at her mouth at his disheveled appearance. He was certainly more comfortable at home.

"I didn't expect to see you here." She walked toward him.

He raised his head and motioned to the papers. "This doesn't appear complete." He pointed to the map of the Sapphire District and lifted a list she had penned of potential Havens there. "There are discrepancies between the two. You're missing the Jerit Haven on the map."

"That's because it's *not* complete." Catrice settled on the ground across from him. "I've never been to that district, so I'm going off what I remember from my mother's records, but I'll have to wait until we hear back from the Havens to complete the rest. Hopefully, some of the Elders will know the missing details about their neighboring Havens. Thankfully, the Sapphire

District seems to look the other way most of the time with our people."

"Really? I've heard their High Crow was one of the king's original advisors."

"Maybe. I wouldn't know." Catrice shrugged. "I just know we've lost fewer Followers there than anywhere else." She glanced over her shoulder at the open door. She normally closed it when she had the Haven information out. "Are you sure it's safe to have these out here?"

He nodded. "My servants know not to bother me when I'm working. Why? Are you worried?"

"It's just something Diana said the other day. She seemed concerned about letting anyone else in our circle or discussing the Havens openly in your home."

"Well, I would agree with that. But my aunt can be paranoid at times. Don't put too much thought into it." He picked up the map of the Onyx District and set it in front of Catrice. "Why isn't the Galian Haven on here?"

"I'm thinking about moving them. The Haven isn't secure. The building is falling apart, and there's a lot of rebel activity nearby. It's only a matter of time before they're found. The fact there's even Testimonies there right now makes me nervous. If it was raided, they would be able to arrest Raina and her family on the spot."

Blaze shrugged. "I didn't see any Crows in town. I wouldn't be too worried."

"I didn't see any Crows in Zradit either, but then they burned the Haven to the ground with our people inside." She bit her tongue as the familiar heat, like low burning coals catching to a dry log, gathered in her chest.

"Whoa, hold on." Blaze dropped the papers and sat up. "The Crows didn't kill anyone."

"What about when they murdered my mother?"

"You don't know they did that."

"How can you say that?" She reeled back. Was he seriously *defending* them? "Of course, they did."

"Stop and think about it, Catrice." Blaze tapped a quill to his forehead. "Why would they do that? Think about the Zradit Haven. They attacked, yes, but they didn't kill anyone. They were just doing their jobs. Why would they kill your mother?" He returned to his scribbling. "If anything, she would have been brought to the High Nest for judgment."

The coals burst into flames. "They killed my father."

"That was different." He sighed. "It was a battle."

She stood, fists clenching against her thighs. What did it matter? Father was still murdered. "Whose side are you even on?"

"Listen, Catrice." Blaze dropped the quill and lifted himself to his feet. "The Crows may not be that great, but at least they're just. Your people will have fair trials. That's more than they would get from the rebels, especially under the White Owl."

Diana's words about their family history with the rebels flashed to the front of her mind, and she relaxed her hands. "How do you know that?"

He set his jaw, and his eyes darkened, but he didn't respond. That was the line. The unspoken line he wouldn't let her cross.

"Does this have to do with Izaak?" She stepped forward. "Blaze, why won't you tell me what happened?"

"I'll see you at dinner." He marched past her.

He was impossible. She groaned and spun around. "I won't be there. I'm meeting with Raina in town."

He froze mid-step and cast a look over his shoulder, eyes wide. "What?"

"I'm visiting the Galian Haven this afternoon. I told them I'd be back for a Fellowship, and I need to talk to them about potential locations for the move. I was going to ask you to go with me, but—"

"You can't." He turned around, backtracking toward her.

Catrice scoffed. "What do you mean?"

He stopped again and closed his mouth, staring at the floor as if choosing his next words carefully. Something was wrong.

"Blaze, what's going on?"

"Nothing, but you should really stay here today."

"Why?"

"We have lots of work to do." He motioned to the

documents. "Half of these don't even have any Havens on them."

"The maps are fine." He was stalling. No, he was *lying* to her.

"Just, please..." He took her hand. "Stay here. You can go tomorrow."

Her heart pounded in her chest. "What aren't you telling me?" She pulled her hand away. "Blaze, what do you know?"

He shifted his azure eyes, avoiding her gaze. When he finally looked back at her, the orbs were cold and guarded. "I received word from one of my old friends in the Crows. He said to stay out of town."

"Why?"

"They're doing a raid on the DaggerThorn rebels tonight."

20

BLAZE

"Catrice! Catrice, slow down!"

Blaze gripped the reins as Ace galloped down the beaten path. He ducked under a low-hanging tree branch reaching out over the road. Catrice ignored his calls as she rode ahead of him on one of his horses, guiding the steed through the woods as if she had done it all her life. He had pushed Ace to catch up to her when she had taken off from the castle, and he couldn't keep up at this speed.

"Catrice!" he shouted again.

When she didn't slow, he raised two fingers to his lips and released a shrill whistle into the forest. Her horse dug its hoofs into the ground, nearly sending her flying from its back as it stopped. He guided Ace next to her as she tried unsuccessfully to direct her horse forward again.

"What did you do?" she asked, her voice sharp.

"That's my horse." He stared at her, trying to catch his breath without her noticing. "He listens to me."

"Well, tell him to go again."

"No."

She glared at him. "I have to warn the Haven. If Crows are going to be in town, they need to know. What if they connect Jedediah to the rebels? What if they raid the Haven like they did in Zradit?"

"They won't."

"How do you know?"

"Because I know how these things work." And because he had given the Crows explicit commands to stay away from the Haven. "As long as they stay home, they'll be fine. Same goes for you."

"I'm not going back. Not until I warn them."

"Well, good luck doing it without a horse."

"Fine." She tossed the reins and swung herself off the saddle, landing solidly on the ground. Lifting her skirt, she marched toward the field barely visible through the trees a few dozen yards away.

Blaze groaned and leaned over to the buckskin, swiping the reins up and urging Ace into a trot after Catrice. He should never have told her about the rebel raid, but how was he supposed to know she would react this way?

"You won't make it there until after nightfall on foot."

"Then give me my horse back."

"*My* horse. And no. By all of Whittam, Catrice, you don't even have your boots on."

She continued walking, her eyes set on the field ahead and bare feet matting the grass beneath her. He tapped Ace on the hindquarters and pulled him in front of Catrice, cutting off her path.

"Let me through." She stepped to the side, and he guided Ace to follow. "You're really not going to let me go?"

He shook his head. "It's not safe."

"Then it's not safe for the Haven either!"

He held her gaze.

She huffed and rolled her head back. "Fine." She opened her hand.

Blaze raised his brow. "If I give you these reins, you're going back to my home?"

She nodded, her eyes flicking away in annoyance. He offered the reins slowly, watching her body language for any sudden changes. She snagged the reins and pulled herself back onto the buckskin's saddle. Blaze smiled.

"Good. Now, you can always go back tomor— Catrice!" he yelled as she turned the horse and took off into the field.

Butterflies spun in the air around him as he followed her through the grass, trampling wildflowers at a breakneck pace, but still failed to catch up. He could whistle again, but there was no guarantee Catrice wouldn't pull the same antics a second time. If he had known she could ride like this, he would have set a guard at the stable.

Pink and purple hues fading into a dark blue sky painted the horizon above as Galian appeared in the distance. His Crows would be rounding up the rebels in town now. The DaggerThorns never went down without a fight. It would be messy, and Catrice could be caught in the middle if she ran in blind.

He urged Ace forward, nearly reaching Catrice's side as they entered the village. She barreled into the street, hardly slowing down as she steered through the alleyways on her way to the Haven. Blaze fought to keep up.

Dark shadows shifted in his peripheral vision as they flew past buildings; the Crows were getting ready to move. He almost collided with Catrice as she stopped in front of the Haven. She jumped off the horse and pulled him into the alley next to the Haven. Blaze dismounted and led Ace next to his other horse.

"Isn't there something in the Testimonies about lying?" he whispered.

She cast him a narrowed side-eye and finished securing the horse. "You should have told me about the raid."

"I did."

"I mean before. I could have come and warned them earlier."

"I told you. They'll be fine. The Crows are after the DaggerThorns."

"That's what you think, but you don't know. You're not a Crow anymore, Blaze. What if your contact lied to you?"

Blaze pursed his lips. He was the contact. "Since when are you so skeptical?"

"Since the lives of my people may depend on it," she said as she walked around to the front. "I couldn't do anything for my father. I couldn't save my mother. I couldn't save Tali and her family. I won't let the same thing happen to another Haven."

He bit his tongue. She had no control over that. "At least they fixed the boards." He gestured to the window she had broken into before.

When Catrice didn't respond, he turned to see her frozen at the entrance of the house. The hinge creaked as a stiff breeze blew the door ajar, revealing a shattered jamb as if someone had kicked it in.

Blaze stepped in front of Catrice, pushing the door open slowly. Shattered glass and broken chairs littered the floor among bits of charred and torn-up parchment. The curtain over the closet on the other side of the room was ripped, and the vase previously holding the scrolls lay cracked and broken on the ground. He knelt by the burned papers and examined the writing on some of the pieces.

"It's the Testimonies." He held up a fragment toward Catrice.

She scanned the room with wide eyes, ignoring the offered scrap. "This was the Crows. Followers only burn Testimonies if they're at risk of being compromised."

"We don't know that..." Blaze stood and placed a hand on her arm. She jerked away.

"You said they were after the rebels."

"They were." He frowned, crinkling the paper in his hand. This shouldn't have happened. Something was wrong.

Shouts from outside rang through the open door. Catrice ran into the street, leaving Blaze alone in the dark. He sprinted to stay on her heels as the commotion continued deeper into town.

A crowd was gathering in the village square, surrounding Crows as they led a small group down the road. Catrice pressed forward into the swarm of people. Blaze grabbed her arm and pulled her into an alley, away from the mob. She shrugged away from him and stood on her toes, straining to see over the heads of the crowd.

"I can't see anything. What's going on? Do you see Raina and her family?" she asked.

Yes. Blaze's stomach dropped. Yes, he did.

At least a dozen Crows walked through the crowd, guiding Raina, Banner, Tomas, and Livia in chains to a makeshift platform in the town square. The people shifted and grumbled uncomfortably as another group of Crows behind them pushed forward, crowding them closer to the stage. Blaze's heart raced; he had only assigned a handful of Crows to round up the rebels. There was no need for this many unless someone was trying to make a point—like a public execution.

"Blaze." Catrice bumped his shoulder. "What do you see?"

His tongue went dry, and he swallowed, unable to respond. The Crows led the Followers onto the platform, and Catrice gasped. She covered her mouth, muffling a cry as it escaped her lips.

This was wrong. He should do something.

One of the Crows stepped forward to address the crowd. "These men and women have been found guilty of the practice of forbidden religion and conspiracy and treason against King Warren Tenaris, High Commander of Whittam. The penalty for such crimes is death. May this be a reminder for all not to fall back into the dark ways purged from our nation."

He raised his hand, and a Crow stepped behind each Follower, forcing them to their knees. This couldn't be happening.

"No..." Catrice moved forward, and Blaze gripped her arm again, holding her back.

Why wasn't he doing anything? He could stop this.

Screeching metal filled the air as the Crows drew the swords at their sides and placed them against the throats of each person.

"No," Catrice whispered as she pulled against him.

He wrapped his arms around her, pinning her

flailing limbs to her sides and carrying her back into the alley. He couldn't let her be seen.

"No!" She screamed as the platform disappeared from their view.

But her scream was drowned out by the chorus of shouts and gasps and the sickening sound of steel cutting through flesh and bone. Four muted thumps followed, and a handful of people in the throng screamed.

Blaze held fast as Catrice continued to fight against him. The Crows surrounding the town square retreated, allowing the crowd to disperse. He closed his eyes, and his throat tightened. This wasn't supposed to happen.

"No! No, no..." Catrice pounded against his chest and mumbled between the sobs shaking her torso.

"I'm sorry, Catrice. I'm so sorry." He held her head against his shoulder, but his own voice sounded foreign and detached. This couldn't be real. She pushed him away, breaking the embrace. He kept his hands on her shoulders. "Catrice, look at me. Breathe."

She smacked him across the face. Hard.

The shock rippled through his body, and he suddenly found it hard to think straight.

"Why didn't you do anything?" The anger lacing each of her words stung even more than his cheek.

"What?" he breathed, feeling his own anger build.

"I saw what you did with the rebels. You could have stopped them!"

"You think I didn't want to?" He pulled back, chest tight. "There's dozens of them, Catrice! We couldn't have done anything."

He could have. He *should* have.

"I'm supposed to protect them!" Her voice cracked, and the broken sound felt like a punch to his gut. "And you're supposed to help me! You said you would help me."

"I *am* helping you! Do you know what would've happened if you had intervened? They would've taken you to the High Nest." The thought turned his stomach, and he hated it. Why did it matter if they took her? He was going to do the same.

"Do you even care about what happened to them?"

Yes, he did. It burned inside of him, mimicking the pain he had felt when Izaak died. And it didn't make any sense. "I care about you! I care about keeping myself and those around me safe. That's what I've always had to do ever since you and your mother left us in Ontiach!"

"What?" Tears spilled from her eyes, but a scowl still marred her face.

"You just left us. You could have taken us with you, but you left us!" He choked back a cry forming in his throat. Why was this coming up now? Scrambled emotions and memories swirled around in his head like a raging waterfall. "Why didn't you take us with you?"

Catrice scoffed, shaking her head as if he was

spouting nonsense. "You survived! Unlike most of Ontiach. Unlike the people who just gave their lives for what they believe in."

"But Izaak didn't!" Blaze raised his hands to grab her shoulders and shake them, but stopped short and balled them into fists instead. She didn't understand, and he hated that he ever believed she could. "If you hadn't left us, he would never have been Called. He would never have become a Crow, we would never have been on that mission, and your beloved rebels would have never shot him in the face with a crossbow!"

Catrice stepped back, eyes wide and skin pale. "And you're blaming *me* for that?"

"Tell me, Catrice,"—he dropped his hands—"who else should I blame?"

Fury burned in her eyes as her lip quivered. "I thought you were different."

"Different than what?" he spat.

"Them." She motioned to the Crows dragging the limp bodies off stage.

He faltered, her sharp tone and hot gaze forcing him to look away. The heat faded as Catrice turned and disappeared down the alley in the direction of the horses, leaving him alone between the buildings.

Blaze fought to still his racing heart as his fists clenched at his sides. This wasn't supposed to happen. It was all wrong.

He moved toward the town square, now nearly

empty as the crowd continued to scatter. A Crow stood a few feet away, watching the people as they left. Blaze marched up to his side and placed a hard hand on his shoulder, spinning him around.

The Crow's eyes widened above his mask. "High Crow Laskaris." He bowed his head and placed a closed fist over his chest in salute. "The black crow flies."

"What was that?" He gestured to the bloodied road. "This isn't what I instructed."

"My apologies, High Crow. But our instructions were clear."

"What do you mean? We're not authorized to do mass executions. Commander Tenaris will be hearing about this."

The Crow raised an eyebrow. "I would hope so. He was the one who ordered it."

"What?"

"He said it was a gift for you. A 'thank you' for revealing the Followers as the rebellious cult they are, and an encouragement to stay focused."

Blaze froze, and the Crow saluted again. He inclined his head and turned his focus to the street as if he had finished relaying a message. Heat returned to Blaze's face, and he scanned the square, suddenly realizing how many of the Crows were watching him. The Commander did this?

He struggled to keep his expression neutral as he backed into the alley. Once he was out of view, he ran.

Pushing his legs to go faster, he careened around a corner, coming to a stop at a dead-end. He leaned a hand against the wall, bending over and placing his head against the cold stone as his heart pounded in his ears.

The Commander had executed the Haven. He had murdered—*slaughtered*—them without a trial. That wasn't what the Crows did. They were just. The rebels were the savages. They were the ones who killed without thought. Not the Crows. Not *his* Crows. Not his father.

Haunted screams echoed in his head, and he squeezed his eyes shut. Bloodied skin flashed across his mind's eye. Pale blue eyes pleading for help as he ran away. His brother's cry. Blaze slammed his fist into the wall.

"No," he grunted through clenched teeth as he fought the memory. "Not now."

He straightened and rubbed the hot tears welling in his eyes. Scuffling behind him set his nerves on end, and he spun around. Large hands slammed him against the building, knocking the air out of his lungs, and a thick forearm pressed against his collarbone, pinning him to the wall. The tip of a cool blade pricked his side.

Jedediah's face appeared in his blurred vision, and Blaze gasped for air. He reached for the dagger at his hip, only to come up empty. He hadn't had time to grab it before leaving the castle. The only weapon on him rested inside the calf of his boot—far out of his reach.

"Don't even think about it," Jedediah spat as Blaze squirmed. His eyes were red and swollen, and blood marred his hands and face.

"Jed…" Blaze rasped.

"No! Don't talk." He pushed his arm closer to Blaze's throat, cutting off his airflow. "I should have killed you when I had the chance. Two days. *Two days* after you visit my home, my family is arrested. You're a Crow." His face crinkled into a twitching, distorted expression. "Did you do this too?"

Blaze opened his mouth to respond, but stopped as the blade cut into the skin above his ribs.

"Did you kill my family?!" A vein in his forehead bulged.

"*No*," Blaze mouthed.

"But you are a Crow."

Blaze blinked, unable to respond as his lungs spasmed. Jed turned his gaze to Blaze's chest, where his necklace lay. He lifted the chain with the tip of the blade, pulling it out of the shirt and letting the ring hang free between them. His eyes darkened.

"You're the Onyx Crow."

Spots of gray clouded Blaze's vision, and he grabbed at Jedediah's arm, desperate for a breath of air. Jed held fast; eyes set on the ring reflecting the evening light.

He dropped his arm.

Blaze collapsed, gasping as the world spun. His limbs shook as he pushed himself up to his knees, swallowing big gulps of air. The dark spots faded, and he looked up. Jed stared at him.

"My mother wouldn't want this." Jedediah stepped back, his face downcast. He sheathed the blade on his belt. "Because of her, you're alive. Remember that, Crow. But if I ever see you again, I'll kill you."

He backed out of the alley and disappeared from view.

Blaze pressed a hand against his side, wetting his fingertips as the prick on his ribs bled through his shirt. His throat ached and his head pounded as he stood. The cool metal chain settled against his chest again as he adjusted his shirt to cover the ring. Leaning against the wall for support, he stumbled down the street toward the abandoned Haven and his horse.

BLAZE THREW the reins down on Ace's neck and slid off the saddle as his stablehand approached. The sandy-haired boy smiled at Blaze and took the lines in his hand.

"Master Blaze." He bowed.

The memory of arriving with Catrice a few nights earlier and brushing the strand of hair behind her ear flashed through Blaze's mind. Had the stableboy seen that? The boy couldn't be older than fifteen and had worked for Blaze since he became High Crow. He turned away and the scene replayed in his head.

Marching toward the castle, he looked up as Harold opened the door for him. Blaze walked through the entrance and ran his hand through his hair.

"Is Catrice here?" he asked.

Harold nodded. "She arrived shortly before dark. She requested all her materials be sent to her room and hasn't come down for dinner. Is everything all right, Master Blaze?" He glanced at the bloodstain on Blaze's side. "Did something happen in the village?"

Blaze hesitated. The balding butler had been his faithful companion for years, and his dry humor always managed to brighten his day. But as he regaled him now, the only thing he could see were all the times he confided in the man without thought or heed for who he might, in turn, tell the confidences.

"No. Everything's fine." He straightened his shoulders. "Have her stay there. I'll be taking dinner in my room as well."

Harold frowned, but inclined his head in resignation. Blaze continued down the hall, eyeing each servant who passed. This was his home. He was supposed to feel safe here, but with every echoing footstep and open door he passed, the hair on the back of his neck stood on end. The Commander doubted him. For some reason, because of something someone heard or saw, he believed Blaze was distracted. It had been a mistake to request a delay in the seizure of the Galian Haven. Maybe they would still be alive if he had arrested them like his father had commanded.

He took the steps two at a time as he climbed the tower, ignoring the stinging sensation at his side as the cut tore with every stretch. Throwing the door open, he marched to the window, leaning against the frame and sticking his head outside in the cool evening air.

He wanted to scream.

He needed to calm down.

He was going to throw up.

Blaze ground his teeth together and closed his eyes. Hot tears pricked the back of his eyelids. The raging waterfall of emotions continued to spill over and he couldn't breathe in the rapids. This was too much.

He sank to his knees and pressed his head against the cold stone, willing his mind to stop its racing. He needed to rest. Gather his thoughts.

Deep breath in. Deep breath out.

BLAZE BREATHED in as the cool breeze ruffled his hair. His usual dark Crow's garb had been replaced with a simple cotton shirt and trousers, allowing the warm setting sun to beat down on his back. The rich scent of wildflowers filled

the air, and a quiet city sat nestled between two forests on the far side of the field. Ontiach. He breathed out and closed his eyes. He was home.

"Blaze! You can't hide forever!" The high-pitched squeal filled the peaceful meadow.

His eyes flew open. A young Catrice stood among the flowers.

A flock of birds retreated to the nearby trees, and a thousand butterflies took to the air as her small feet ran through the tall grass. Had she been paying attention, she may have stopped to gaze in wonder as the colorful wings filled the sky. But she wasn't paying attention to the sky; she was searching for someone, and it was clear she wasn't planning on giving up any time soon. She stopped for a moment and planted her chubby fingers, all balled up in a fist, on her small hips.

"Blaze, come on. Let me win this time, at least" She pouted and crossed her arms.

Gazing across the wide expanse of the meadow, she searched for some sign her friend had heard her. Blaze followed her gaze to a small mop of black hair visible above the grass a short distance away. Catrice's face lit up in excitement.

"I found you!" she squealed. A boy—young Blaze— stood from the grass and stuck his tongue out at her.

"You may have found me, but you still have to catch me," he said before taking off deeper into the meadow.

Blaze watched the scene play out in front of him as the

two children ran through the field, seemingly oblivious to his presence. He smiled.

"Wasn't it my turn to catch you?" Izaak's voice broke the happy memory, and Blaze spun around. His grown brother stood a few feet away, taking in the serene scene with a forced smile. He clicked his tongue. "But it was always you two, wasn't it?"

Blaze turned back to see his younger self slow, letting Catrice catch him. Her light giggle rang through the field.

Izaak sighed. "I remember when you let me catch you. When you wouldn't have left my side. Not that I blame you, though. She is a beauty."

Blaze frowned and whipped his head around, expecting to see Izaak, but his brother was gone. He returned his gaze to the scene in front of him, and his breath caught in his throat. A grown Catrice stood among the flowers in place of her younger self. The hem of her white dress rippled in the wind, and she smiled. The dark curls that could never be tamed blew over her face, masking her sparkling eyes. She reached a hand out to Blaze.

"I found you." Her quiet, assuring voice settled over his heart, and he smiled.

Instinctively, he walked toward her, taking her hand in his own and brushing her hair away from her face. She blushed and looked down, the small gesture that caused his heart to skip a beat. A tap on his shoulder pulled him away from the moment. He glanced back to see Izaak pointing towards the hill on the far side of the meadow.

"Better watch out, Blaze. They're coming."

His heart sank as a stallion appeared on the horizon. The rider on its back was covered in dark armor and held a sword up in the air. Bells rang from Ontiach in the distance. The dark rider locked his gaze on Catrice as a horde of soldiers stepped up behind him. Terror gripped Blaze's chest.

He took off in the direction of the city, bringing Catrice along behind him. Vivian stood just inside the gates, surrounded by Tali and her girls, Wyatt, Raina's family, and dozens of other Followers. The thundering march of a thousand assassins shook the earth, but Blaze didn't dare turn back. The large, wooden gates of the city started to close and he yelled, pulling Catrice harder.

She fell.

He stopped, frantically lifting her to her feet and turning back to the city. It was gone. The Followers were gone.

He spun around, trying to find the safe haven they called home, but soldiers surrounded them. Blaze grabbed at his sides, searching for his weapons or anything that could protect the woman beside him. Nothing.

The circle of Crows closed in, and Blaze wrapped an arm around Catrice. The dark rider dismounted and walked towards them. Another masked assassin broke from the circle and followed. Blaze shifted Catrice behind him, and she gripped his arm. He stared down the two men approaching them.

"Father, please..." he pleaded to the dark commander.

Disappointment marred his father's features. He

placed his hand on Blaze's shoulder. For a moment, it looked as though he would listen to him, then rage flashed across his face, and he tore him away from Catrice.

Blaze fell to the ground, and the other masked assassin drew a sword and ran it through Catrice's chest. He screamed. Her eyes widened, and her mouth opened in shock. The blade left her body, and she collapsed into the tall grass. Blaze crawled over and cradled her in his arms. Hot tears ran down his cheeks. His blood boiled as the assassin's cold blue eyes stared back at him, blank.

"Why?" he shouted.

The assassin blinked.

Blaze opened his eyes and stared at the heavy sword in his hand. Blood ran down the tip and into a small puddle forming on the ground. Rough cloth rubbed against his face, and he yanked the familiar black mask off. The tears that had soaked his cheeks were gone.

He was standing where the assassin had been.

"Why?" a broken voice shouted at him.

His younger self cradled a young Catrice in his arms. Her small dress was stained a deep red, and her pale body hung limp in the boy's arms. His bloodshot eyes stared up at Blaze, filled with anger and despair.

"Why?!"

Blaze took a step back. The blood pooled at his feet, fueled by other streams flowing from the bodies of Followers —hundreds of them—scattered within the circle of Crows. A hand rested on his shoulder.

"Not fair, Blaze." Izaak sighed. A crossbow bolt

protruded from his face, and blood poured from the wound to join the lake of red, drowning the soldiers around him. "Not fair."

~

Blaze jerked upright at the sound of a crow's caw. His skin was cool where he rested against the stone floor, moonlight bathed the room an eerie blue, and the fireplace crackled beside him. He shook away the odd dream. He didn't remember falling asleep.

Another caw echoed through the room, and he glanced up at the window where a crow sat on the sill, waiting. Its beady eyes stared at Blaze, unblinking. His stomach knotted at the sight of a small piece of parchment tied to the bird's foot with a black ribbon. He pushed himself to his feet and pulled the message off the crow. Unrolling the parchment, he scanned the letter written in red:

For the Onyx Crow only. Do not delegate.

End mission. Bring subject to the High Nest. Effective immediately.

What? No. He flipped the paper over, but there were no further instructions. Only the royal wax seal weighing down the bottom of the message. That couldn't be right. The Commander wanted him to bring Catrice in. Now? He hadn't even sent in a report about the Havens. Did the Commander think he could get that information another way?

Blaze's stomach turned in rebellion, and he paced the length of the room. His father was strategic. He wouldn't compromise the possibility of finally eradicating all Havens, even if he doubted Blaze's ability to complete the mission. Blaze couldn't imagine any reason why the Commander would cut the assignment short.

He froze, reading over the message again. Unless Jedediah was right. Unless Catrice walking around outside of the throne's grasp was too dangerous. Unless the rebels were getting too powerful. Unless the White Owl was about to make his move on her.

Blaze swallowed. If it was too dangerous for Catrice to be in the Onyx Nest—in a High Crow's home—would moving her to the High Nest even make a difference? There was only one true way to neutralize a threat.

"Your mission is Catrice's death sentence." Diana's warning rang true.

No. No, that couldn't be right. He groaned, marching to the foot of his bed and sitting on the mattress. He dropped his head into his hands and bunched his hair in his fists.

His father wouldn't kill Catrice. She wasn't a threat. She was zealous, angry, a tad misguided maybe, but not a threat. He would see that. He would understand. But then, Blaze had thought the same thing about the Galian Haven.

The image from his dream, hundreds of Followers

lying at his feet in a pool of blood, dominated his thoughts. He shook his head. Was his father ordering the execution of Followers across the country? Were hundreds of innocent people dying because of him?

"No, no, no..." He launched to his feet, crumpling the note in his hand and throwing it into the fire. The flames devoured the parchment, leaving nothing but a fading pile of ash and melted wax among the coals.

He had been wrong. The Followers weren't rebels. They weren't plundering and murdering in the name of freedom. There may have been some overlap, but it was because the Crows had driven them to that extremism. The Followers were families. Women, children, immigrants who wanted to worship in peace. Blasts, he couldn't believe he was starting to agree with them. They may have believed in a myth, but they weren't hurting the country. They didn't deserve to die.

But how was he supposed to prove that? What would make the Commander stop? Blaze had tied everything back to the White Owl in a neat little bow. The White Owl was a threat. He couldn't deny that.

A third caw broke through the night. Blaze whirled around to the window and spotted a second crow approaching. The bird landed next to the first one, and the two clucked back and forth as they hopped on the stone sill. He retrieved the note from the new crow's leg.

Intel update:

Suspected DaggerThorn base on Geen River banks at the border of Silver District. Possible sighting of the White Owl.

Request permission to engage.

- Crow Uri Rendal

Blaze lowered the message. This was his chance. This was the answer he was looking for.

He grabbed the items needed to pen a response and scribbled down his answer. Signing it with his seal and tying the message to the crow's leg, he sent the bird back out the window.

The crow disappeared in the distance as he gathered his supplies. His bloodstained shirt and brown slacks came off as he changed into his Crow garb. The rough, black cloth felt good on his skin, reminding him of his purpose. Pulling the necklace from his chest, he removed the ring and slid it over his first finger before putting the necklace back on and tucking the key under his shirt. He tightened his gloves over his hands and the straps on his boots, and tied a black cloth around his face, covering everything below the eyes.

Lastly, he picked up the two shortswords that had taken numerous lives into his hands. The steel edges bit into his gloves as he stared down at the sharpened blades. Gritting his teeth, he secured them to his sides. Throwing his cloak around his shoulders, he turned to the mirror.

Guilt hit his gut as he took in his reflection in all of its dark glory. A deep, unsettling fear crept into his soul at the sight of himself. This was the last image countless people had laid eyes on before drawing their final breath. This was the sight that had struck fear into the hearts of men for years. This was the picture of death.

Catrice's words repeated in his ears: *"I thought you were different."*

Blaze jerked away from his reflection. He was doing this for her. This was the only way to save Catrice and the Followers. The only way his father would back down. If they were a threat because of their connection with the White Owl, then the answer was clear.

He simply had to kill the White Owl.

Avoiding the mirror, he retrieved another piece of parchment to pen a note to Harold with his approximate return date. Once the ink was dry, he walked out the door, pinning the note to the rough wood as he passed.

Silence filled the castle as he ran down the stone stairs and corridors. The sconces hadn't yet been lit for the night, leaving only the moonlight to shine through the windows. He slowed as he approached the staircase that led to Catrice's room. For a moment, he debated on whether or not he should say goodbye, but just for a moment. He would be back soon, and when he was, she would be free. He exited the castle through the back door and made his way to the stable.

Ace raised his head as he approached and stomped

the ground with his hoof. Blaze saddled the horse and secured a few supply packs onto the leather seat before swinging himself up beside them. With one last glance at Catrice's window, he kicked Ace's flank and sent him into a full gallop away from the castle.

21

CATRICE

Catrice was thankful for the moonlight pouring through the windows as she wadded up the last of her clothes and shoved them into the leather bag. Drawing the top shut, she tossed it onto the bed next to the other full sacks.

She shot a nervous glance at her closed door. It was late, but that didn't mean Jillian or another servant wouldn't decide to make a midnight visit. Her absence at dinner would have been noted; a part of her was surprised Blaze hadn't checked in on her himself. Though, most of her was glad he hadn't. She was sure he wouldn't appreciate being slapped across the face... again.

As it turned out, it was lucky for him that he had refused to teach her to fight.

It hadn't taken long to pack her few belongings. The hardest part had been deciding what to do with all the maps and lists of Havens. She couldn't take all of them, but she didn't want to leave them either. So she had resorted to burning any extra copies, and her room was all the warmer because of it.

She pulled her hair back into a low bun and surveyed her supplies. A few changes of clothes. Her leftover dinner of meat, bread, and potatoes. Basic hygienic items she had gathered from the bath. Writing utensils and her documents. It wasn't much, and she wished she had more time to prepare, but hopefully, it would last her long enough to find the rebels.

Any doubts in her mind about leaving to join the White Owl had been decimated when the heads of four of her people were lopped off on stage.

Prayers and waiting weren't enough. Whatever the Creator was doing wasn't enough. They needed to fight back. Otherwise, they would die.

She had hoped she could trust Blaze. She had hoped he would help her unite the Havens. She had *prayed* confiding in him about the Havens wasn't a mistake. But she had been proven wrong. If nothing else, she could no longer trust him to put her people's safety first. He had lied to her. He knew how dangerous the Crows were, yet he had chosen to put Raina and her family in harm's way by not warning them. If only she had found out sooner. Then they might still be alive.

A white corner of fabric sticking out from under a sack on the bed caught her eye. She grabbed the soft square, and a heaviness settled over her chest. Blaze's handkerchief—the one that had belonged to his mother. Despite Catrice's many attempts at washing it, blood still stained the corner where she had cleaned the cut on her head. She had been hurt, and he had given this to her without any hesitation. Oh, how easy it would be to believe she could trust him as much as she had in that alley. As much as she had when they were children.

The ringing of footsteps echoing off the stairwell outside her door filled the room. She stuffed the handkerchief into the top of her chemise and grabbed the bags, shoving them under the bed and smoothing out the covers where they had lain. She dashed to her desk as a series of light knocks sounded on the door.

"Come in," she called, busying herself with random papers.

Diana creaked the door open and stepped into the gap, holding out a steaming cup of tea and a plate of biscuits in front of her. "I saw you missed dinner with us. Thought you might like some company. Harold brewed the tea fresh for you."

"Thank you." She wasn't hungry, and would prefer to be alone, but she could use the extra biscuits for her supplies. Catrice cleared a spot on her desk for Diana to place the refreshments. "I'm surprised you're up this late."

"Couldn't sleep. Blaze left for another trip this evening."

He had? Catrice glanced at where her bags were stashed under her bed. That was good. She could sneak out tonight without him knowing. "I didn't know he was leaving."

Diana pulled up one of the ornate stools that decorated the room and sat next to Catrice. "Neither did I. But such is the nature of his job. He should be back in a few days. I think he just needed to clear his head after today."

"He told you what happened?"

"No." Diana frowned and folded her hands in her lap. "I didn't speak with him, but one of the servants filled me in on the executions."

Catrice picked at a biscuit. She gritted her teeth, and her chest burned like someone was holding a hot coal to her sternum. "It never should have happened."

"No, it shouldn't have." Diana laid a hand over Catrice's. "It's not your fault."

Yes, it was. She should have been there. "I know."

Diana cocked her head, unconvinced. "My dear, you cannot blame yourself for what the king has done."

Catrice stared at the mug. The steam swirled in clear tendrils around her face before disappearing into the air. "The king shouldn't have this much power. What have our people done to deserve this?"

"You know the Testimonies speak of other times our people have been persecuted. This isn't the first time, and it won't be the last. In the meantime, we pray and trust in the Creator. He will guide us."

That wasn't enough. Her people were dying. She gripped the mug and shook her head.

"Catrice." Diana placed a hand over her whitened knuckles. "There was nothing you could have done to stop the execution."

"Blaze should have told me what he knew."

"My dear, you cannot trust Blaze to tell you everything."

Catrice straightened and narrowed her eyes. "What do you mean?"

Diana pulled back, face paling. "Nothing."

"Diana." Catrice stood. "What are you talking about?"

The older woman fiddled with the edge of one of her sleeves. "I know you're probably angry with Blaze, and rightfully so. He has gone through some difficult times since you were children. I'm afraid he didn't have the same upbringing as you after Ontiach was attacked. He was practically raised by the Crows."

"Do you think things would have been different if his father hadn't died?"

"What?"

"He said his father was killed in the war."

"Is that what he told you?"

The fire crackled beside them, sending sparks flying while the flames danced in Diana's eyes.

"Yes." Catrice hesitated. "Is he not dead?"

"He might as well be." Diana sucked in a breath and held her gaze. "I told you. You cannot trust Blaze to tell you everything."

She was trying to tell her something. What did Diana know? Catrice leaned forward and opened her mouth to ask another question, but heard someone else's footsteps approaching the room. Diana stood, straightening her blouse, and Jillian appeared in the doorway. Surprise broke through her usual courteous mask at the sight of Diana, but she quickly recovered.

"Miss Catrice. Miss Diana." She curtsied to the two of them and shifted her attention to Diana. "I didn't expect to see you here. I just came up to check on Catrice before bed."

Catrice held up a hand. "We're in the middle of a conversation. Can you come back later?"

"No, dear. It's fine." Diana avoided her gaze. "I wouldn't want to keep Jillian waiting." She forced a smile. "It was nice talking with you again, Catrice. I'll see you at breakfast." Without another word, she turned and left.

Jillian nodded. "Is there anything you need before bed, Miss Catrice?"

"No." Catrice fought to keep her tone polite. "Thank you, Jillian."

The maidservant flashed a tight smile and curtsied again before following Diana out the door. Their footsteps faded away and Catrice stood, shuffling toward the doorway and peeking her head around the corner. She watched as Diana and Jillian walked further down the stairwell until they were out of view.

Diana's words swirled in her brain, and she bit her lip. *"You cannot trust Blaze to tell you everything."*

Blaze had lied to her about his father and the raid. What else had he lied to her about? Clearly, there was more. If Diana wouldn't—or couldn't—tell her, she would find out for herself.

Catrice exited her room and snuck down the stairs until she reached the hallway where Jillian's quarters resided. The door was shut, but she could hear the servant moving around inside. The rest of the hall was empty, and she tiptoed past the room toward the south tower. Without stopping, she climbed the cold stone steps. Blaze's quarters sat at the top of the tower with a single note tagged to the closed wooden entrance.

Out for work. Return in 2-3 days.

Catrice's heart pounded as she reached for the doorknob. She hesitated, listening for any sounds on the other side of the door or the staircase behind her. After a moment of silence, she turned the knob. It opened smoothly, granting her access.

She stepped inside and scanned the wide, simple area. The only furniture dotting the room was a large, unmade bed, an organized desk, a closed wardrobe, a mirror, and a chest at the foot of his bed. His floor was spotless, aside from the clothes he had been wearing the previous day, which lay crumpled in a pile by the chest. She couldn't imagine he spent much time here at all.

She visited the various furniture pieces around the room as she searched for anything that could give her answers. The large chest at the foot of his bed was locked. Miscellaneous supplies and random documents filled his desk drawers. District maps covered the top of his desk. She frowned, looking closer.

Markings stood out on the papers where she had confirmed Havens. Her blood chilled. Why would he have his own copies of the Haven maps? There was no reason... unless he needed the information for something else.

The coal against her chest burned hotter, burrowing its way deeper into her skin.

Striding to the wardrobe, she flung the doors open. A dozen different weapons lined the inside. Her own reflection in the folded steel glared back at her, distorted by the edges of the blades. Her heart pounded as she took in the various swords, spears, crossbows, and other items she wasn't able to name. Was Blaze trained in each of these? Were they left over from his time as a Crow? Why would he still need them in his room?

The answer loomed over her, creeping from the

recesses of her mind, dark and forbidden, and she refused to voice it. Her insides were boiling, like she was being burned alive from the inside out.

She slammed the doors shut and backed away from the smooth wood as the questions continued to rise. Spinning around, her eyes landed on the fireplace. A single black box sat on the mantle of the smoldering hearth, the only other obvious object in the room. She swallowed and stepped closer.

Her heartbeat thudded in her ears as she reached for the intricate box. The carvings were rough against her skin as she tried to pry the top of the box open. Upon closer inspection, she found a small keyhole that had been placed so it blended in almost seamlessly against the designs. Catrice set the box down, and her heartbeat slowed.

She didn't need to know what was in the box.

She didn't want to know.

A part of her already did.

And what if that part of her was right?

She snagged the box off the mantle and threw it to the ground. It held strong. Running back to the wardrobe, she grabbed a double-sided axe. She raised it above her head as she approached the small chest.

Last chance to turn back. She didn't have to know. She could trust the Creator. She could leave tonight without answers. Nothing would change.

She swung the axe, splintering the box in two.

Scrolls, shattered ink bottles, and blank parchments spilled onto the floor. The axe clattered to the ground as she dropped to her knees and sorted through the contents. She gripped one of the scrolls and unrolled the tiny message written in red ink. A miniature wax seal with a crowned crow was pressed into the blot stuck to the corner of the message.

Potential rebel gathering located in Deln in the Amber District.

Infiltrate, observe, and report. If needed, eliminate.

High Crow Gideon Askin will accompany you.

- King Warren Tenaris, Commander of the Black Crows

She flipped over the small scroll to see a note written in black ink in Blaze's handwriting.

Accepted

Placing the scroll down, she reached for another message. She swallowed. Unrolling it slowly, the paper trembled in her fingertips as tears stung her eyes and the hot coal engulfed her in flames.

Update on assignment:

Subject secured at the Onyx Nest. Collecting intel on Havens.

DaggerThorn rebels connected with the White Owl located in the district. Wanted poster of subject compromised. Assigning Crows to investigate and disperse.

Previously unknown Haven discovered in Galian. Request to delay seizure until intel is complete.

- The Onyx Crow

The message slipped through her fingers and floated to the stone below.

Blaze had lied.

All he had done was lie.

CATRICE RAN THROUGH THE FOREST. The bags slung over her shoulder bounced against her back with every step, as if urging her to go faster. Her feet ached and her lungs burned. How long had she been running? She just had to make it to Galian. From there, she could find the rebels. From there, she would have help.

Her initial plan had been to steal one of Blaze's horses, but when she snuck out to the stable, the stableboy had been waiting outside, almost like he was guarding the horses. So, she had run. Run as if the more distance she put between her and the castle, the clearer her head would be. But with each heavy thud of her boots against the ground, the more gathered in her mind, and the more she wanted to scream.

She was on fire. Every inch of her body burned with a rage she had never felt before. How had she been so stupid? Blaze had lied to her about *everything*, and she had played right into his hands.

Mother was dead because of her.

The Galian Followers were dead because of her.

She hadn't killed them. The king had. Blaze had. But she had let it happen.

The *Creator* had let it happen.

The forest broke open to the rolling, flowered hills outside of Galian, and she stopped, doubling over and resting her hands on her knees. Her eyes burned. Whether from the cold night or hot tears streaming from their edges, she didn't know. She gulped down lungfuls of air and stared at her worn boots. They wouldn't last many more days of traveling through the wilderness.

She had a map in her pack, but she had no idea where the DaggerThorn camp was, or if it still existed. Blaze had ordered a raid on it. They could all be dead by now. But what other option did she have? Blaze was using her. The Havens would give her sanctuary, but it was only a matter of time before the king tracked them down and they were destroyed. They wouldn't fight back. She needed the rebels for that.

"Catrice?" a vaguely familiar voice called out into the night.

She spun around, squinting her eyes to try and make out any shadowy shapes in the darkness. A figure approached her in the meadow. She grappled for one of the daggers she had stolen from Blaze's room and brandished it in front of her.

The stranger raised his arms and continued forward, his broad shoulders casting an ominous silhouette against the moonlight. "It's me, Jedediah."

"Jed?" Catrice gasped and lowered her weapon. "What—how are you alive? I saw your family—"

"I was with the DaggerThorns when my Haven was attacked." He shivered and tightened his cloak over his torso. "The Crows raided our camp at the same time. I barely escaped." He was close enough now that his features became clear. His eyes darkened. "I cornered Blaze after the execution. Catrice, he's been lying to you. He's a High Crow."

"I know."

"What?" Jed gaped. "Is that why you ran?"

She nodded, and a bone-chilling gale whipped across the hills. "Have you been watching me?"

"When I told the remaining DaggerThorns about Blaze, we hatched a plan to rescue you. We were on our way there now when we spotted you in the field."

The rebels were here? She scanned the hills around her, but they were empty. She glanced back to the forest and could just make out a group of mounted horses by the line of trees.

Jed reached out his hand. "They say the White Owl is visiting the DaggerThorn base near the Geen River. I'm to bring you to him. If you want to come, that is."

She stared at his outstretched palm. This was what she was looking for. This was what she needed. Yet her stomach tied itself into knots at the thought of taking Jed's hand.

The White Owl had sent those men after her. He had tried to kidnap her. But at least he hadn't murdered her family. At least he hated the king as much as she did.

She took a deep breath and closed her eyes.

Creator, is this from you?

No response other than the whistling of the wind. But by now, what was she expecting? He had never answered her before.

She opened her eyes and locked them on Jed. Steeling herself, she adjusted the packs on her shoulder and grabbed his hand.

"Let's go."

It took them a full two days on horseback to reach the Geen River. The body of water split Whittam in two, and each of the Seven Districts bordered it at some point. It was no surprise the DaggerThorn Rebels had set up their base near its banks. It was the perfect staging area to move messages and supplies across the country. Yet another reason the rebel's resources would be valuable to the Followers.

Catrice gripped the shirt of the rebel in front of her as their horse dipped down a short incline on the path. She had taken turns riding double with various men in the group as they traveled so the burden wouldn't be on one horse, but outside of Jed, they had hardly spoken to her. Instead, most cast her wary glances from the corners of their eyes or avoided looking at her completely, as if they didn't want to acknowledge her presence.

Did they know what had happened to the last rebels who crossed her path? Were they afraid of *her*? If so, she didn't know why. It had been Blaze who killed those men, not her. But something was keeping them from meeting her gaze.

The roar of nearby rapids had been a constant background noise for the last few miles, so the river had to be just past the woods surrounding them. But now, new sounds were rising above the commotion. Metal grinding. Hammers pounding. People talking. All of it clashed together in an odd chorus as the caravan entered a clearing in the forest.

Dozens of tents dotted the wide expanse between the trees. Men and women of all ages mingled throughout the camp carrying various supplies or working over smoldering fires. Everyone seemed to have a purpose: cooking, sharpening weapons, grooming the horses, or building carts and other tools. Most paused to nod at Catrice and the group as they rode by, some even staring with shocked expressions. Had they been waiting for her? Was this the Dagger-Thorn base?

"Elynn?" a young man's voice broke through the camp.

Catrice's heart leapt. It couldn't be. She jerked her head around, scanning the clearing. A familiar head of sandy blond hair caught her eye.

"Tay?" she called back.

He ran toward her, eyes beaming. "Elynn!"

She slid off the saddle, stumbling as her feet landed on the uneven ground. Tay crashed into her, lifting her into his arms and spinning her around in a tight hug. She laughed, gripping his shoulders tightly. He was here. How was he here?

He set her down and stepped back. "I... How— what are you doing here?"

She shook her head, grinning so much her cheeks hurt. "I was going to ask you the same thing!"

"The rebel meeting in Deln. I looked for you the morning after we got separated, but your home was empty. Completely spotless." His smile faltered. "And I heard Ratton was dead. I didn't know what to do. The Crows were waiting at my home, so I ran off with the rebels. I got assigned to this camp." He opened his arms and gestured to the space around them. "How are you here?"

"I..." Catrice glanced at the rebel caravan that had stopped behind her. Jed dismounted his horse and walked toward them; eyebrows raised in an unspoken question. She turned back to Tay. "It's a really long story. But you should know my name isn't Elynn."

"Oh?" He chuckled and crossed his arms. "Don't tell me you're actually my long-lost cousin from Rewon."

"It's Catrice. Catrice Aetos."

Tay stepped back, mouth agape. Any surrounding

people who hadn't already stopped to watch dropped what they were doing and moved closer. They stared at her with similar awestruck expressions. Like she held all the answers to their problems. She shrunk back as a deep sense of unease settled inside her. What was going on?

Jed stood beside her and whispered in a low voice only she could hear, "I told you. The people will rally behind you. You can do something."

"You're an Aetos?" Tay blew a hard breath from his mouth and ran his hand through his hair. "The White Owl has been looking for you."

"You've met the White Owl?"

"No. Not yet, but I've heard the news. That the Crows killed Vivian—" Tay covered his mouth. "Oh, no. That was Mari. I'm so sorry, Elynn. I should have been there."

"It's fine, Tay. It's not your fault." She glanced at the rebels, who were all still staring at her. It was odd. Creepy even. But there was also a sense of power that swelled in her chest at their sudden attention. She cleared her throat. "Is the White Owl here?"

The rebels looked to each other as if someone else had the answer, but no one responded.

She leaned over and whispered to Jed, "I thought you said he was here."

"I thought he would be."

She frowned and straightened. What was she supposed to do now?

"Catrice Aetos," the voice of someone new boomed through the crowd. The crowd in front of her parted, allowing a tall, bronze-skinned man dressed in black garments lined with red thread to walk through the camp to her. His thick braids and wide smile were oddly familiar, and he stopped in front of her, offering his hand. "We've been waiting for you."

Catrice placed her hand in his, and he brought it to his mouth to kiss the back of her fingers in a low bow. "My name is Tanner. It's a pleasure to make your acquaintance."

His odd decorum triggered a memory of the rebel gathering. She widened her eyes. "You were in Deln. You revealed the Amber Crow in the balcony."

He nodded. "One of my finer moments. Please, follow me." He led her through the crowd as it stepped back to widen their path. Tay and Jed started following, but Tanner stopped and turned to them, raising a finger to his lips. "I'll be speaking with Lady Catrice alone."

Lady? She had never been called that before. Not even when she was a child. Technically, it was true, but the title still sounded foreign.

Tay and Jed stiffened, glancing at each other before relenting, and slinked back. She didn't want them to leave. They were the only two people she knew in this camp. But Tanner was clearly of some importance here, and if he wanted to talk alone, there had to be a reason. She offered them an apologetic smile and followed Tanner to a large tent in the middle of the base.

He pushed the front flap open, and she stepped inside. Her eyes took a moment to adjust to the dim lighting, but when they did, the details of the space came into view. A large desk sat in the middle of the tent, covered with various maps and writing utensils. Lanterns hung from wooden poles supporting the canvas top, and the light reflected off racks of swords and knives of different sizes lining the edges of the tent. At the back, behind the desk, was a massive tapestry with the embroidered symbol of an owl with outstretched talons. She swallowed. Was this the White Owl's command post?

Tanner walked past her and sat down behind the desk. He motioned to a chair opposite him, and she took a seat. A stack of wanted posters was piled on the corner of the desk; her face dominated the pages. Just like what the rebels in Galian had. Her stomach knotted as she reconsidered her decision to come here. She didn't even know what they planned to do with her.

"I can see you're on edge." Tanner interrupted her thoughts. She snapped her gaze up to him. "Let me put your mind at ease. The White Owl is not going to hurt you."

"Tell that to the men who tried to kidnap me."

Tanner grimaced. "An unfortunate misunderstanding. The White Owl would value your full cooperation, but not if it's against your will. He believes we can help each other. I understand you're concerned about the safety of your people."

How did he— Catrice shook her head. It didn't matter. What mattered was that the White Owl would help. That was what she was hoping for. "When can I talk to him?"

"He won't be able to make it today. Prior commitments, I'm afraid. But I can arrange a meeting within the week."

A week? That wasn't good enough. The Crows could be killing her people as they spoke. She lifted her chin. "No. I want to see him tomorrow."

Tanner raised his eyebrows, and a crooked smile crept up his cheek. "You've got spirit. The White Owl will like that. I'll see what I can do. But he will ask for something in return."

"Like what?"

"Your loyalty." His dark eyes held her gaze. "It's rather hard to come by these days. And he will need it for what he has planned."

Catrice sucked in a breath. "And what's that?"

Tanner's grin spread across his face like it was carved with a knife. But his eyes remained wide, unblinking. A chill swept across her body. Whatever it was, it would be worth it for her people. It had to be.

He cocked his head at her. "Do we have a deal?"

She opened her mouth to respond, but was cut short as someone shouted outside the tent. Then she heard a series of gasps and a commotion like something was being dragged across the ground. Tanner stood, his smile dropped, and he marched to the entrance of the tent. He pulled back the flap just enough for Catrice to catch a glimpse of a crowd forming around a dark figure in the dirt outside. What was going on? The flap closed, and Tanner turned back to her.

"Stay here." He stormed through the entrance.

Heavens, there was no chance of that.

She jumped to her feet and rushed to the tent opening, peeking through the gaps in the flap. Tanner approached a group of rebels that had gathered in a circle around something on the ground. He pulled the people back, revealing a man—no, a *Crow*—bound and kneeling on the forest floor. Blood caked parts of his black garb and dark hair, bruises littered what little skin was exposed, and his face was downcast. He was hurt.

Her heart dropped, and she steeled herself. If there was a Crow here, it was his own fault. He deserved whatever was coming.

Tanner glared at one of the men standing behind the bound Crow. "What is this?"

"We found him tracking us in the woods. Gave us quite a fight too. We were going to kill him, but then we saw this." The rebel pulled a black ring from his pocket and held it up to the light. "He's the Onyx Crow."

Blaze. Her breath caught in her throat. No. He couldn't be here. He wasn't supposed to be here.

Tanner grabbed the ring from the man and examined it. The rebel nodded toward the piece of jewelry. "Figured the White Owl would want to see him. I mean, how often do we get the chance to take out a High Crow?"

Tanner dropped the ring in his pocket and began to laugh. He planted one hand on his waist and dragged the other over the short beard protruding from his chin. The rebel faltered, and the crowd seemed to take a collective step back at the Rogue's disconcerting response. The hair on the back of Catrice's neck stood on end.

"What's... what's so funny?" The rebel asked, glancing back and forth between Blaze and Tanner.

"You..." Tanner's laugh faded as he held up a finger to the man's face. "You *idiots*!" He swung at the man, clocking him square in the jaw and knocking him to the ground next to Blaze. "You brought a High Crow here? How do you know he didn't want you to capture him? His men could be on their way here right now!"

Cries of panic rang throughout the camp. Terror gripped Catrice's chest. The Crows were coming? This couldn't be happening. Not now. She had just escaped.

Blaze raised his head, meeting Tanner's gaze. His eyes were cold, hard—and Catrice's heart stopped at the murderous glint in the azure orbs.

"See," he cracked a bloody smile, "the Rogue gets it."

No.

"Trap," she whispered. Bursting out of the tent, she yelled, "It's a trap!"

Her warning was lost in the sea of screams as dozens of Crows fell from the trees behind Blaze.

22

BLAZE

"THERE IS NO GREATER HONOR THAN TO GIVE ONE'S LIFE FOR THE GOOD OF THE THRONE AND FOR THE GOOD OF WHITTAM." - THE ROYAL ARCHIVES OF WHITTAM

Blaze launched to his feet as the crowd descended into chaos. He ducked under the swing of a nearby rebel and drove his shoulder into the assailant's chest, knocking him to the ground.

One of his Crows ran up behind him, slicing through his bonds with one move. The Crow's copper hair stood out against her dark garb, and she handed him his two shortswords.

"Thanks, Nolly." He took the weapons in time for her to disarm a man swinging an axe toward them. "Hope you enjoy your first real mission, Crow."

She slammed the man's head into her knee and flashed Blaze a smile. "Will do, sir!"

A shout sounded behind him, and he spun around, blocking the attack of a charging rebel. The sound of screeching metal pierced the air as his blades crossed and held back the large sword aimed for his head. His arms shook under the raw strength his opponent exerted through the weapon.

Their eyes met. Sweat dripped down the man's wrinkled skin, and his ruddy hair had streaks of gray throughout the frizzy strands. He was older than Blaze expected, his wrinkled eyes reminiscent of Wyatt's, and there was fear written across his face—the same fear Blaze had seen hundreds of times before.

He shifted his foot to solidify his stance and pushed back with his weapons, ripping them apart and throwing the man off balance. He stepped forward and raised one blade to block the man's sword as it came back down and aimed the other at his heart. Blaze's attack was cut short as the rebel grabbed his wrist. Blaze flicked his hand around, twisting out of the man's grip and slicing his arm in the process. He stepped in and plunged the weapon into the rebel's chest. A pained gasp reached his ears, and he returned the swords to his side, releasing the man to fall to the ground.

The scared, lifeless eyes of the rebel mirrored those Blaze had seen in Banner's decapitated head. Guilt tightened his chest. Blasts, he didn't need this. Not now. He needed to find the White Owl. He needed to focu—

Pain.

Searing pain blocked all thought as something burrowed into his back, and he stumbled forward.

Warm liquid dripped from his shoulder blade, and he cursed. Spinning around, he stared as the rebel who had led him to camp lowered his bow. Adrenaline took over as Blaze's grip tightened over his weapons. The rebel smiled as he drew another arrow.

Blaze took a deep breath. The sounds surrounding him and the pain in his body faded away as he focused on his next movements. He locked eyes on the man and ducked behind a tent as he fired the arrow. It whistled by his ear and struck a tree across the clearing. Blaze jumped from his hiding place and rolled behind a different tent as another arrow flew by. The man's chest heaved, and his quiver fell to the ground as he fumbled to load his weapon again. Blaze took the opportunity to attack.

The world faded away as his body moved with a fluidity and precision ingrained from years of training. His swords sliced through air and flesh as he released both raw skill and rage upon his opponent. When it was over, Blaze stood above the mangled, lifeless body of the rebel.

His limbs weakened as the adrenaline ebbed away, and the pain stemming from his wounds was pushed to the forefront of his mind. Streams of blood flowed down his back and soaked his clothes. The arrow was still in his shoulder. He dropped one of his swords and broke off the arrow's shaft, leaving the tip in his muscle.

His Crows were making quick work of the rest of

the camp. Rebel men and women fled for their lives into the trees. Others swung tarnished and dulled weapons at his skilled soldiers. Collapsed tents caught fire as they landed on smoldering coals. Horses bucked and squealed as riders fought to untie them from their posts. This would be over quickly. He *had* to find the White Owl.

He dashed toward the large tent in the middle of the camp. The Rogue had disappeared the moment the fighting had started, but he couldn't have gone far. Barreling into the tent, Blaze raised his weapons.

The chaos of the camp outside faded as the flap closed behind him, and he struggled to focus in the darkness of the tent. A flash of steel gleamed to his right. He turned in time to dodge a broadsword swipe aimed for his neck, and the Rogue stepped from the shadows of the tent. The scarlet mask he now wore covered half his face and set off his bronze skin. His eyes were dark, hardened, and cold, like the blade pointed directly at Blaze.

Knocking the sword away with one blade, Blaze lunged forward to strike the Rogue with the other weapon. The sharpened steel met nothing but air as the Rogue pushed Blaze's arm aside and spun around him again. Their deadly dance left slashes in the canvas surrounding them; uneven beams of light pierced the dim tent. Dark steel sliced through the air and nicked Blaze's arm. He grimaced as the red liquid dripped down his skin.

The Rogue attacked again, forcing Blaze to backpedal out of the tent. He hadn't taken more than a few steps before a half-buried stone caught his boot and he tumbled to the ground.

The rich scent of pine needles filled Blaze's nose as his head smacked against the forest floor. One of his shortswords buried itself into the earth while the other flew into a nearby stack of hay. His vision blurred and he grappled aimlessly for some kind of weapon. He grabbed a handful of brown needles and sand and flung it into the Rogue's unprotected eyes. His opponent stumbled back, clawing his face with his empty hand.

Blaze crawled towards the hay, sending dirt and twigs flying as he searched for the handle of his weapon. His hand brushed cold metal and he gripped the hilt. Rolling over, he narrowly missed being skewered by the dark sword. He sat up, grabbed the Rogue's sword arm, and pulled him off balance.

As the Rogue fell forward, Blaze dug his foot into his opponent's midsection and shoved. The Rogue tumbled over Blaze's head, hitting the ground hard on his back. Blaze scrambled on top of him. He ripped off the scarlet mask, kneeled on the Rogue's chest, and pressed his remaining sword against the man's throat.

"Where is he?!" Blaze spat through gritted teeth.

The Rogue laughed, spraying blood onto Blaze's face. "You think the White Owl would actually show his face here? In *your* district? He's not stupid." He coughed as blood pooled in his mouth. "The day he does decide to come back here will be your last. And believe me, he's looking forward to it."

No. He had to be here. Blaze pressed his knee against the Rogue's sternum, and the man gasped. "You're lying."

"Afraid not. You've been beat, Crow." He grinned at Blaze.

Blaze scoffed. "Look around, *Rogue*." He stood and pulled the Rogue to his feet. "Your camp is destroyed. Your people are dead. I've won."

The Rogue shook his head. "For every rebel you kill, there's ten more ready to avenge the one. You Crows are my best recruiters."

Blaze scowled, ignoring the sense of dread the Rogue's words put in his heart. He scanned the camp and spotted Nolly a few yards away.

"Nolly!" She turned to face him. He nodded his head for her to come closer. "Take him away. I want this one alive."

"Yes, sir!" She jogged toward him and wrenched the Rogue's arms behind his back.

Blaze sheathed his remaining sword and turned to the rest of the camp. There were only a few skirmishes left. Dozens of rebels sat tied up across the clearing, and even more lay dead. He swallowed down the guilt that had fought its way to the surface. What would Catrice think if she saw him now? He was doing this for her. Not that she would believe him. She thought these people were her saviors.

"Don't you want to know what happened to your brother?" The Rogue's cool tone set Blaze's hairs on end. He spun around.

"*What?*"

The Rogue stared back at him. "Don't you want to know how Izaak begged, *pleaded* for mercy after you left him to die?" He laughed, and blood dripped from his chin. Nolly pulled out a length of rope to secure his wrists. "You were both supposed to die that day, but I suppose killing one of the king's sons is better than none. Got to look on the bright side, right?" He closed his eyes and tilted his head as if recalling a cherished memory. "Mmm, I still remember the sweet sound of his skull breaking as we pried the arrow out of his cold face."

Blaze stepped forward as rage swelled in his chest. "You were there?"

His eyes flew open. "Of course, I was there. Who do you think made the shot?"

The world went white.

Blaze didn't remember what happened next. When the white finally faded, all he knew was that the Rogue was on the ground again, nose crooked and bleeding, and mouth missing a tooth.

Nolly stared at Blaze, her face pale as a sheet. Blaze's knuckles stung, and his chest was so tight he couldn't breathe. He couldn't kill the Rogue. He was needed to find the White Owl, but he wouldn't need his arms to talk, and Blaze was already thinking of clever ways to remove them.

"You were a Crow—one of us," he growled. "He was your brother."

The Rogue spit out a tooth and propped himself up on his elbows "I believed that garbage too until the White Owl showed me a better way. Don't tell me Tenaris has never lied to or used you. You're nothing more than a pawn."

Tali. Wyatt. Raina. Banner. He saw their faces everywhere. All of their names were seared into his mind. All of them were jailed or dead because of the Commander. Because he had used Blaze to get to them.

He ground his teeth so hard his jaw ached, then waved a hand at Nolly, gesturing to the Rogue. "Get him out of here."

A woman's scream pierced the clearing.

Blaze turned. He knew that voice. That voice shouldn't be here.

Catrice fought against a Crow near the forest's edge, kicking and punching the soldier like her life depended on it, but the man held fast as he dragged her toward the camp where another group of rebels lay bound together.

No.

"No, no, no..."

He started toward her. This couldn't be happening.

Catrice was supposed to be at his home. She was supposed to be safe. She was supposed to be away from the rebels. Disconnected completely. She was supposed to be free after today. She wasn't supposed to see him like this.

Her eyes met his. Fear and hatred burned from within them.

"No!" he called out to his Crow. "Let her go!"

The Crow holding her looked up in shock, but then he focused on something past Blaze.

Steel cracked through bone. That sickening sound told Blaze what was happening before he turned.

No. She was just a kid.

The Rogue stood behind Nolly. Her eyes were wide —scared—and her mouth was open in a silent cry. Blaze's second shortsword protruded through her chest, and the Rogue was *smiling.*

"NO!" Blaze grappled for his own weapon, but he was too late.

The Rogue withdrew his blade and lunged. Blaze shifted just enough for the shortsword to miss its mark, and the point pierced his shoulder, penetrating the soft tissue between Blaze's arm and collarbone with ease. He screamed as the tendons and cartilage holding his arm in place tore. Another Crow tackled the Rogue, knocking the sword from Blaze's shoulder, and he fell to his knees.

The world spun, and his vision blurred. What was happening? Blood pooled on the ground beneath him.

Was all that his? Nolly's green eyes stared back at him, lifeless. Bodies surrounded him, soaking the ground in red. He did this. Why did he do this? He didn't mean to. He was just trying to do the right thing. He collapsed, his ears ringing as his head hit the ground again.

Catrice continued to fight across the clearing. Was she trying to reach him? The hatred in her expression had softened, but the fear was still there.

"Catrice..." he whispered. "I'm sorry."

I should have protected you. I should have protected them all.

She screamed something, finally ripping away from the Crow. Was she saying his name?

He closed his eyes, and then his eyelids lit up like the midday sun.

23

CATRICE

"THE CREATOR SPEAKS. WHO WILL LISTEN?"
- TESTIMONY OF THE UNKNOWN FIRST
PROPHET

Fire.

Everything was on fire.

Catrice stumbled through the flames. Rebels and Crows ran for cover throughout the camp. Burned bodies littered the clearing, and black smoke rose from the still forms. She struggled to wrap her mind around what had happened.

One moment, she was screaming while Blaze lay bleeding out on the ground. The next, fire had fallen from the sky, consuming whole tents and people, including the Crow she had been fighting, but she remained unsinged.

The ground shook beneath her feet, and the low rumble contrasted with the screams of those surrounding her like a twisted melody. Flames reached for the trees, licking up the dry wood and catching on the dead leaves and pine needles coating the ground.

She shielded her eyes, trying to see past the burning patches of tents and bodies. She needed to get to the river. The river would be safe.

Falling to her knees, she crawled through the maze of flames, coughing as she breathed in lungfuls of smoke. Her nostrils stung with the scent of smoldering flesh.

A rushing wind swept through the clearing, tossing and turning the inferno around her. She scrambled away from one of the growing fires and toward the trees. If she could get to the trees, she could find the river.

As she rounded a collapsed tent, her boot struck something soft. Glancing over her shoulder, she froze. Blaze lay beside her, his eyes closed and shirt soaked with blood. Soot covered his skin, and the flames roared dangerously close to his body.

He wasn't going to make it.

"Catrice!" someone called her name. She raised her head, and past the next patch of fire, she could just make out Jedediah's form through the smoke. Tay stepped up beside him. They waved their hands at her, motioning toward the trees. "Catrice, come on!"

Praise the Creator. They were safe. She pushed herself to her feet, running through the smoke toward the forest. She was going to make it. She was going to be free.

"Stay."

The Voice stopped her in her tracks. Who said that?

"Catrice!" Tay shouted.

She shook her head and sprinted forward again. Only a few more yards.

"Stay."

The Voice shook her body, reverberating through every fiber and stilling her feet where they stood. She spun around. Who was talking to her?

Her eyes landed on Blaze's body. Flames licked at his boots, but she couldn't do anything to help him. She couldn't carry him. They couldn't both make it out. It was him or her, and she didn't even know if he was alive.

"Stay."

This time it was a still, small Voice, sending a wave of reassurance over her.

She needed to stay.

She glanced back at Tay and Jed. A handful of Crows ran toward them.

"I—" she sighed. She couldn't believe she was doing this. "I can't!" she yelled back. "Go! Run!"

She didn't wait to see if they listened or not. She ran back to Blaze's body, stomping out the flames at his heels. Kneeling next to him, she pulled his unin-jured arm over her shoulder. He groaned.

Good. So he was alive. She could kill him herself.

She took a deep breath and pushed herself to

stand. Her legs ached and something popped in her neck, but she was able to get him to his feet.

"All right, Blaze." She adjusted his arm. "I'm going to need you to work with me."

She walked forward, and Blaze stumbled next to her.

"Oh, Creator, give me strength," she whispered under her breath.

Slowly, one step at a time, they made it out of the fire and into the woods.

24

BLAZE

"IF A BLACK CROW ABANDONS THEIR CALL TO SERVE, THERE IS NO GREATER DISHONOR. SUCH GREAT DISHONOR IS ONLY ATONED THROUGH DEATH." - THE ROYAL ARCHIVES OF WHITTAM

Warmth bathed Blaze's body.

Normally, it was cold in his room. Harold must have added a few logs to his hearth before bed.

He shifted, only to find his face smothered against a rough cloth. Was he lying on his stomach? Where were his pillows?

He opened his eyes. It was dark out, and crickets chirped nearby. He was definitely on his stomach. Pain radiated across his torso, and he gasped. What had happened?

Turning his head to the side, he could see a fire burning a few feet away in a stone-encircled firepit. Beyond the fire, he could make out flowing water reflecting the flames and a small dingy on the bank. A warm, orange glow marred by a pillar of smoke lit up the night sky above the trees in the distance. He was outside. By a river. What was he doing by a river?

The memories of raiding the rebel camp and the Rogue stabbing him came flooding back. But how did he get here? The last thing he remembered was lying on the ground while Catrice screamed—

Catrice.

He jerked his head up, ignoring the searing pain that shot through his shoulder, and tried to get a better view of the area around him.

She sat on a log at his feet, watching the flames. His sword rested across her lap, and her eyes were tired, like she had been up for hours.

"Catrice?" His voice was hoarse, and his lungs burned when he breathed. "What... what happened?"

She continued to stare at the fire. "Good. You're awake. For a while, I was worried you wouldn't pull through."

"You were worried about me?"

She picked up a rock and fiddled with it, but didn't look at him. "We're on the banks of the Geen River by the Silver District, or at least that's the best I can figure. I lost my maps at the camp. Along with any information on the Havens."

"I'm sorry, Catrice."

"Don't worry." Her tone was cold, bored even. "I know you have copies. I burned the ones on your desk, but you're bound to have more somewhere else."

He widened his eyes. How did she know that?

She scoffed. "I found your box, too. The one with all your assignments."

Blasts. He closed his eyes. She knew. That's why she had run to the rebels. He worked to get his arms under him and rolled himself into a sitting position. The simple movement left him breathless and in more pain than he would have been able to describe.

"Careful." Catrice tossed the rock into the fire. "I did my best to dress your wounds. I had to tear up your cloak, but I couldn't figure out how to get the arrow out without causing any more damage, so you're not going to want to lay on your back."

"I don't understand." He touched his ribcage, and his hand came back up wet with blood. How many wounds did he have? "I was stabbed. The Rogue stabbed me. I was lying on the ground. How did you—"

"There was a Wonder."

"What?" He laughed, and the pain it caused made him gasp for breath. "You aren't... you aren't serious, right?"

She turned his sword over in her lap. "Fire rained down from the heavens. Just like in the Testimony of Geris Aetos. Burned up half the camp."

"My Crows?"

For the first time since he woke up, she looked at him. Her eyes were as detached as her voice, like she was staring straight through him. "Some are dead. Rebels, too. The flames didn't seem to discriminate."

"You saved me."

"I didn't want to. I was going to walk away. Leave you to die." She traced the edge of his blade. "I didn't even think twice."

He swallowed, eyeing the blade. She could kill him right now. She could kill him, and he wouldn't even blame her. But then why would she have saved him?

"What made you change your mind?"

The flames danced in her umber eyes. "The Creator told me to stay."

His mouth fell open. "*What?*"

"He spoke to me. Didn't tell me anything else. Just that I couldn't leave you."

The Creator told her to save him? He frowned. "You don't seem too happy about it."

"You lied to me about everything."

"I—"

"And you killed my mother."

"What? No, I didn't." He winced. He wanted to move closer, take her hands in his own. "Catrice, that wasn't the Crows. They were set up. It was the White Owl. He orchestrated everything that night in Deln. He wants the country to believe the Crows did it so more people will join his cause. I didn't even know you and Vivian were in Deln."

She shrugged. "I don't know how you expect me to believe you."

That was fair. He wouldn't believe him either. Not after all he had done. He deserved that.

She sighed and set the sword on the ground. "Not that it matters anyway. I won't see you again after tonight."

"What are you talking about?"

"I stayed. I saved your life. I did what the Creator told me to do. Now you're safe. You don't need me anymore, so I'm leaving. I'm sure someone will see the smoke from the camp and find you."

"Where will you go?"

She laughed, but there was no joy in the sound. "Like I'm going to tell you."

"You're not going back to the White Owl, are you?"

"Why do you care?"

"He murdered Izaak, Catrice." Her expression softened at his words, and tears burned the back of his eyes. "He murdered Izaak and I let it happen. You can't trust him."

There. He had finally told her. Now she would have to see reason.

She stood and stirred the fire. Sparks crackled from the sticks and floated up to join the stars above. He waited. Why wasn't she saying anything? When she returned to her seat, her brow was furrowed in deep thought.

"You expect me to trust you, and how many people have you killed, Blaze?"

Daggers to the heart. That's what her words felt like. Even worse than the bleeding wounds on his shoulder. He shifted his jaw.

"I was wrong, Catrice."

She stared at him as if waiting for him to continue. He let out a breath.

"I was wrong about you, about the Followers, even about the Crows. You showed me that. Everything I thought I knew has been flipped upside down. But I'm not wrong about the White Owl. Please"—tears slipped from his eyes, and he groaned—"for my sake, don't find him."

The flames continued to crackle in the silence between them. She held his gaze, and if he could, he would take all the sorrow she stored behind those deep eyes if it meant she would be safe.

"Fine," she finally said. "I'll stay away from him."

The tension in his chest released, and he collapsed back onto his elbows. "Thank you."

She glanced at the eastern sky as the sun crested over the horizon. "But I don't want to see you again." Another dagger. "I'm still going to find a way to save my people. Even if that means fighting the king."

He swallowed. She wouldn't win. No one would. And he couldn't save her, not from his father. For the first time, a part of him hoped the Creator was real. At least then, she would be protected.

She set his sword next to his legs and tossed a fresh log onto the fire. "I'm sure someone will be by soon. There's a small village just a few miles from here that probably fishes along the river, and I'm sure your Crows are looking for you. You won't be here long."

She pulled a bloodstained handkerchief from her bosom and offered it to him. "Thank you for this, but I don't need it anymore."

He stared at his mother's handkerchief as a wave of emotions swept over him, but only one thought came to mind. "Keep it. Consider it your birthday gift."

She tucked it back into her dress and smiled. It was small, faint, but it was the first genuine one he had seen since he woke up. "Thank you."

He smiled back. "Stay safe, Catrice..." He hesitated; his next words felt like treason, but he wanted them to be true. "And may the Creator bless you."

She sucked in a breath, eyes wide, and mouth slightly agape. At least he had managed to surprise her again. She nodded. "You, too, High Crow."

He watched as she turned away and walked down the riverbank with nothing more than the clothes on her back, determined to make a difference. As her figure faded behind the trees, he knew, one way or another, she would.

Leaning back, he rolled over to his good shoulder and let the rays from the rising sun warm his body. Someone would find him soon. And when they did, he had to make a choice, one he never thought he would have to make.

The Rogue had been right. The Commander was using him, and Blaze couldn't kill innocent people anymore. That wasn't what the Crows stood for. That wasn't what *he* stood for. He would destroy the rest of the Haven information he had stored at home. The Followers would remain hidden and safe. He would still go after the White Owl and put these rebels to rest once and for all.

But he couldn't do it as a Crow. Not anymore. He wanted out.

Oddly enough, the thought settled over him peacefully, and the constant gurgle of the nearby river lulled him into a deep sleep.

HOOFBEATS SHOOK the ground beneath him, startling him awake. He grabbed the sword at his side, gripping the leather-wrapped handle in his hand and whipping his head around.

A group of Crows rode toward him, stopping just a few yards from where he lay. The lead Crow dismounted, sauntering toward him as the sunrise reflected off her silver hair.

"Well, well, Blaze." Nikita clicked her tongue at his disheveled state. "Looks like someone finally got the best of you." She smiled and drew her sword, rotating the weapon in her hand. "Don't worry. I'll find the Aetos girl myself."

EPILOGUE
THE WHITE OWL

The White Owl strode down the wide, stone hallway. Heat radiated off the dark walls reflecting the evening sun streaming through the windows. Thick, humid, Rewonian summer heat. He longed for the day he would be back home in Whittam. But for now, he had to bide his time, and what better place to orchestrate the downfall of a country than to live in an already broken one?

He approached a wooden door at the end of the hall. Rapping the back of his knuckles against it, he waited for a response. When none came, he opened the door to a large room with elaborate tapestries and furniture waiting on the other side. A gaunt and dirty woman sat in a chair facing the window, in stark contrast to the elegance of the room, despite trays of fresh food and a warm bath mere feet from where she rested. He rolled his eyes.

Ungrateful, stubborn wretch.

"Lady Aetos," he called out in a polite voice. The woman turned to face him. Fear flashed across her features, replaced nearly instantly by the regal mask he had grown accustomed to. "I see you haven't touched your dinner... again."

"I will eat when you let me go," she responded, her voice unwavering.

He sighed and flashed her a smile. "You know I can't do that."

She turned back to the window. He strolled across the room, glancing in a mirror as he passed. His blond hair was combed back from his face, the sleek style matching his fitted tunic and setting off his azure eyes. He was the picture of royalty. Exactly what he should be.

He placed his hands on the back of her chair. The view overlooked vast, manicured grounds leading to fields of *sapid* plants scattered throughout stone ruins going on for miles. "It's a beautiful day out. You could walk the grounds if you like."

She stood and stepped away from the window.

He dragged his hand down his face, his fingers grazing the bright red scar under his right eye. "I come here every day. I sit with you, ask you the same thing, yet you refuse to answer."

"That is because I do not know."

"*You—*" he stopped, took a deep breath, and lowered his voice. He needed to stay calm. "You are

Vivian Aetos. You know more about the Followers than anyone in Whittam, and you mean to tell me you don't know who the next Prophet is?"

She shook her head. "The Creator has not yet revealed it. I have no control over that."

"You must know *something*."

"Even if I did, why do you think I would tell you? I work to protect my people."

"I don't want to hurt the Prophet."

"Then what *do* you want?"

He sucked in a breath and clasped his hands behind his back. "There was only one man who had the authority and power to stand up to Tenaris. Only one man who had more influence and threatened his rule. Your husband, Marcus Aetos. I want what he had. I want the Creator's Anointing."

Vivian gasped, and, for the first time, her mask broke before him. "You believe in the Creator?"

The White Owl laughed. "It doesn't matter what I believe. Only what the people do. And if they believed Marcus when he refused to anoint Tenaris, then they'll believe the next Prophet when I'm anointed."

She raised her chin, and the mask returned. "I can't give you what you want."

"Fine." He gritted his teeth. "Then *you* could anoint me."

"I'm not a Prophet."

"But you're an Aetos. The country won't know the difference." He sighed deeply. "But if you won't give me what I need, then I'm sure I can find another Aetos who will."

She snapped, anger dominating her expression. Good. She was finally listening.

"You stay away from my daughter!" She marched up to him, winding her hand back for a strike. He grabbed her wrist as it swung toward his face.

"Ah, ah, ah…" He wagged a finger at her and twisted her wrist back. Vivian cried out and fell to her knees as he lowered her hand. "I have been nothing but kind and gentlemanlike. I've given you this space of comfort, food, drink—anything you could ask for. Yet, you continue to resist. Do you think the king would give you this much grace?"

"You stole me from my home."

"Ha!" he laughed. "You call that hole in the wall a home? You could have so much more, Lady Aetos, if only you would give me *what I need*."

He released her wrist and she scampered away from him, holding her hand close to her chest. He was getting nowhere with this. It had been two weeks and she still refused to tell him who the Prophet was or anoint him herself. He was growing impatient. And when he was impatient, things could get messy.

A knock sounded against the door, and he whirled around. The door creaked open, revealing his second-in-command as he stepped through the gap.

The White Owl growled through his teeth. "This better be important, Tanner."

"Oh, you're going to want to hear this." The Rogue smiled, breathless, like he had run to get there. And he was missing a tooth. He walked into the room. "We've found the Prophet."

"Who?"

Tanner shifted his gaze to Vivian. "It would seem she's been lying to you. She knows exactly who the Prophet is. There was a Wonder at the DaggerThorn camp. The next thing you know, our precious secret weapon is running off with a High Crow."

Of course. He had been right. It was always the Aetoses. He turned to the disgraced lady sitting on his floor. "Looks like I'll be meeting your daughter after all."

Acknowledgments

Wow, I don't even know where to start. This has been such an incredible journey. I started writing this book when I was seventeen years old, and although it's quite a bit different than when I started (thank God!), I would love to tell past Lauren that we did it and about all the people who helped us along the way.

To my amazing husband and best friend, David: this book would not have happened without you. From the late night rants to the early morning proofreads, you have supported and encouraged me through every step. If there is any good world-building or political twists in this story, it is thanks to your meddling when my brain was melting from rewrites. I love you.

To my family (my first fans): I apologize for all the spoilers I leaked around the dinner table. I hope you enjoyed Catrice and Blaze's journey, regardless (and I tried to sneak in a few more twists for you). You were there when I bought my first junker laptop that didn't even connect to the internet, and you've stuck by me through it all. Thank you.

To my brilliant editors, Katie, Belle, and Aaron:

THANK YOU! I can't express my gratitude enough for your expertise, suffering through the dumpster fires of my early drafts, pointing out when I used the same word three times in one sentence, and your tough love.

To my early readers who saw the potential in this story and encouraged me to keep going, my wonderful in-laws (Mama and Papa Perdan), Matt, and my beta readers and ARC team: thank you for your support, fan art, and spreading the word about this book.

And, of course, to my Savior and King, Jesus Christ: may this story be for Your glory.

ABOUT THE AUTHOR

Writing, reading, crafting, world-building, character-loving, average twenty-something-year-old: that's L. B. Perdan. In her free time, (when she's not writing) you can find her rock climbing, studying languages, and staring at the clouds while she sits in her freshly tilled garden. She's been writing since she was 12 years old, and holds a BA in Intercultural Studies with double minors in English and Deaf Culture, as well as a MA in Organizational Leadership. She strives to bring diverse and multi-dimensional characters and storylines to every tale she spins. Please join her on the journey as you discover new worlds together.

Also by L.B. Perdan

The Whittam Chronicles

Book 1: The Black Crow Flies

Book 2: Rise of the White Owl (2024)

Book 3: Red Hawk's Reign (2025)

Other Books

Missed Connections: An Airport Romance Novella (2024)

www.ingramcontent.com/pod-product-compliance
Lightning Source LLC
Chambersburg PA
CBHW021415310726
48971CB00005B/1341